DEEP IN THE TOMBS . . .

The door creaked open. There was a crack in the wall, three inches wide, through which light filtered dimly from above. Stacked up, dumped in heaps in the corners, were mummies. Dozens of them, more than a hundred. None of them were wrapped, they were all naked. Children, adolescents. Twisted, mangled, faces contorted. One could almost hear their screams, see their writhing.

Hank stared into the face of one at eye level. "Poor thing. Poor things. What could have happened?"

"The old . . . " I looked around; could not find words. Death, pain. Death, I tried to tell myself, must have been a relief to them. But no; these were children; they wanted life, they deserved life, got this instead. Seeing them all together made me numb.

There were rats, a dozen or more, chewing busily on the bodies . . .

"An impressive first novel! Fast-moving, scary and a lot of fun to read."

—*Charles L. Grant,*
author of For Fear of the Night

CITIES OF THE DEAD

MICHAEL PAINE

CHARTER BOOKS, NEW YORK

CITIES OF THE DEAD

A Charter Book / published by arrangement with
the author

PRINTING HISTORY
Charter edition / October 1988

ISBN: 1-55773-009-1

Charter Books are published by The Berkley Publishing Group,
200 Madison Avenue, New York, New York 10016.
The name "CHARTER" and the "C" logo are
trademarks belonging to Charter Communications, Inc.

PRINTED IN THE UNITED STATES OF AMERICA

10 9 8 7 6 5 4 3 2 1

for
Wayne Stango

CITIES OF THE DEAD

Prologue

THE STONE WAS cold, like ice. The sudden touch of it on the little girl's back sobered her, stopped her crying. The women in black stood around her, held her down to the stone table by her arms and legs. They were frightening to her so she did not struggle much. Not far away the priest chanted, sang in a monotonous voice; she could not understand the words.

It must have been one of the women in black who had caught her. Late one night; it was very dark and she should have been at home. But she stayed out and played, knowing how angry it would make her mother. The village streets were empty and the noises she made echoed. Then the big black figure came up out of nowhere, clutched her, enfolded her in heavy black cloth.

There was nothing else to remember until she awoke here. Crude black stone arches, dozens of them stretching as far as she could see. Bright lights, blindingly bright. A bitter smell on the air. The women in their heavy black robes. The priest singing.

His chant got louder. The little girl watched him. Slowly

he held up a golden knife; stopped singing. Walked over to her side. He leaned down, smiling; laid a hand on her thigh; whispered something in her ear. The words were nonsense to her. He stood back, looked at her, smiled, and bent over to whisper again. This time his lips brushed her ear and she felt his warm breath. He was chanting again, very softly. She turned her head a little to see his face, next to her own. Their cheeks brushed. Even though she did not know the words he was using, he had a deep, pretty voice. She relaxed a little bit. Then she realized that his hand, with the golden knife in it, was extended high above her. She had only begun to scream when the knife went into her left side, just by the heart.

From the Journal of
Howard Carter
November, 1903–January, 1904

Chapter One

THERE IS A full moon hanging low over the Valley, and jackals are howling in the Theban Hills. While I was off in Cairo, being sacked, there was a rainstorm here, and one of those flash floods that so devastate the Valley. Sand, pebbles, even some sizable rocks came down with the torrent, and the landscape is subtly changed. For once there are no tomb robbers. The hills here are honeycombed with the tunnels they have dug from tomb to tomb; my lamp would certainly have attracted them if they were here. It is odd, paradoxical, but the families of grave robbers here are my closest friends in Egypt, and in many ways I hardly know even them. Perhaps the storm frightened them away for a while; perhaps they are simply plundering somewhere else for a change; I don't know. But I am alone this night in the Valley of the Kings.

That the Valley is not now quite familiar seems appropriate. A week ago I was Inspector of Monuments for Upper
Egypt, important and influential if underpaid. Now . . . I
am unemployed; and I have no idea what I will do. Return
to England, perhaps. Join a band of grave robbers, perhaps.
Die, perhaps. I don't know. I would like to remain an
honest man. There are always tourists willing to pay to be
shown the sights; and I can sell my watercolors of the tombs
and the statues. But if I can't live that way . . . There are a
hundred ways for an unscrupulous man to earn a living in
Egypt, and a better living than he could earn honestly, at
that.

My dismissal came upon me so quickly I still can't quite
realize what happened. There was a trinity of Frenchmen
making trouble around Luxor. Drinking, roistering, abus-
ing the natives, stealing. Then rape. I was sent for in my
official capacity by the alarmed Luxorites, who know all
too well what a sacrosanct thing a Frenchman is in Egypt.
Caught them in flagrante delicto; the girl they were after
cannot have been more than twelve. I drove them off with
my revolver. And the next thing I knew I was in Cairo being
sacked.

Monsieur le Directeur was all sympathy. "All they want,"
he explained through his thick French accent, "is an apology
for the affront to their dignity."

I stood stiffly before him. "Is Monsieur Maspero under
the impression there is such a thing as a dignified rapist?"

He smiled at me, his most charming smile. "Howard."
He stood up, walked round to the front of his desk. "Try to
face the political reality. We French run the Antiquities
Service, which means in effect we run Egypt. At least, we
run the Egypt you care about, the ancient, wonderful place,
the place of linen and gold. You want to keep working, don't
you?"

"Of course I do. You know that I do."

"Then apologize. In a month—in a week—no one will remember this. Bend with the political wind, Howard. Apologize."

I watched him as he circled me, like a sorceror weaving a spell. Maspero is the only Frenchman I have ever really liked. His energy, his charm, his abiding love for Egypt make him irresistible to me. He has so bewitched the British governor that the Antiquities Service gets all the money it needs for its excavations and restorations. Poor Lord Cromer tries to cut off part of the money; makes noises about military needs, about mansions for the British officials. Then Maspero shows up and the governor is done. Gold; he talks about gold and the money in the international art market. Prestige; he tells Lord Cromer how all the world covets the treasures that rest in the Nile Valley. He works his spell, and his English master is finished.

And now here he was, finishing me in the same way. Why lose your job over these brutes, he asked me. I need you in Luxor, he told me, you are the best I have. If you are discharged Egypt will suffer. Always with that spritely charm that is his hallmark, always with the wide smile I know so well.

I was tempted to give in, make the apology. But I couldn't bring myself to do it. I spent my youth in England toadying to privilege. I will never go back to that. Here, I am my own man. Even unemployed, I am my own man. I tried to explain this to Maspero.

"Sit down, Howard."

I took a chair.

"Is that what Egypt is to you? Freedom from privilege?"

I could not look directly at him.

"Howard, I need you in the Service. Even kings bow to political pressure now and then. Apologize."

I remained silent. Maspero reached for a sheet of paper on his desk, handed it to me. "It is a simple enough thing. Sign it and go back to work."

The document was an admission that I was completely in the wrong. The Frenchmen had behaved unexceptionably, I was out of line in my unjustified interference in their holiday, etc., etc. I handed it back to Maspero unsigned.

"Will you be leaving Egypt, then?"

"I don't know. I'll have to think."

"I can give you one week to vacate your official residence. I wish I could give you more. I'll appoint someone to replace you as soon as I can."

"A week will be more than enough, I think."

I could see how disappointed he was in me; stood to go. He came over and took my arm, walked me to the door. "Howard, I'm sorry."

There is a breeze picking up off the desert. The flame of my lamp flickers in it. When I got back to Luxor late this afternoon I stopped only to pick up a few supplies—a lamp, some food, my diary—and came straight across the river to the Valley. Of all the places in Egypt—in the world—this one is my own special place. When I need to think or brood, when I need to be alone, this is where I come. One way or another I have been alone for most of my life. Here, tonight . . . Enough. Mustn't let myself slide into self-pity. That breeze is stronger now. It will be cool for sleeping here, among the Egyptian dead.

I was awakened early this morning, before dawn. Some-one scrambling about, out of sight but making enough noise for a Nile hippopotamus. I rolled over in my sleeping bag, tried to ignore the commotion; my first day in Egypt as an unemployed Englishman was not something I was looking forward to. But the noises persisted, moved nearer.

The sky was grey; the sun had not yet risen. I looked around and could see no one. The intruder must have been up one of the side valleys. I did not really want any company, not yet and certainly not company as noisy as this. Looked about for some way to escape; climbed up the steep path to the tomb of Thutmose III so I could see the intruder before he saw me.

It is a difficult climb; as many times as I have made it it still winds me. There was still no one to be seen. To the east, across the river, the sun was halfway across the horizon, a deep somber red. The landscape was coming to life. Long shadows made the far-off monuments easy to spot. The Ramesseum, Medinet Habu, the Colossi of Memnon; on the opposite bank the great temples of Karnak and Luxor. And the Nile, transparent blue in the morning light. I have lived here more than a decade and the vibrant blue of the Nile still astonishes me every time I see it. I remember the Thames, how muddy it always was.

Finally my noisemaker came round into the main part of the Valley. At first I thought it must be an Egyptian woman, terribly fat; swathed in heavy black robes. She was crawling on her hands and knees, God knew why. But there was something peculiar; no Moslem woman would have come out alone. My impulse all morning had been to flee, to avoid contact with any other members of my species; but now my curiosity got the better of me. I scrambled down the hill.

It was a nun. A fat, black-robed, white-wimpled, rosary-toting nun, sniffing about the Valley of the Kings on all fours, her gaze fixed on the valley dust in front of her. A nun, for God's sake. She was so intent on whatever it was she was doing she had not noticed me. I sat down, settled back against a fair-sized boulder, watched her.

The Valley floor is rough, stony, and from the way she inched forward her knees must have been quite tender by now. None the less she crawled purposefully. Chasing something? Her path kept zigzagging; finally she turned in my direction, made straight for me. I kept expecting her to veer off again but she kept coming. In a few moments her nose was directly above the toe of my boot.

She looked up at me in alarm. I smiled as broadly as I could manage without laughing, tipped my pith helmet. "Good morning, Sister."

She stared at me as if I'd just slapped her. Part of her obviously wanted to bolt from me. But she kept staring down at the ground anxiously. Then glancing back over her shoulder to the entrance of the Valley. Then back at the ground. Finally she found her resolve; raised her left hand and shoved it between my legs; blushed shamefacedly. "You are sitting on my scarab." She is German.

"I beg your pardon?" I wanted to laugh in her face.

"I said you're sitting on my scarab."

I could not resist goading her. "Scarabs belong to the sun god."

"Not this one." She looked around me. Apparently the insect had crawled around to my right. My nun clambered after it, made a frantic lunge. "Got you!" She held her captive out between two fleshy fingers, so I could see.

What could I say? "Very nice."

"It's a nice fat one, isn't it?" Her German accent is like something out of a music hall.

I could not help saying it. "Yes, one of the fattest I've ever seen. You're lucky it didn't crawl into a crack in the earth. They usually do, you know."

She stood heavily up, adjusted her wimple. Her black habit was brown with dust. There was a compartment hidden in her crucifix. She placed the beetle in it and carefully snapped shut the cover.

For the first time I noticed the extreme paleness of her skin. "You are new in Egypt?"

"Yes." She brushed off her rosary beads.

The unexpected oddness of the situation and my desire to be alone had made me forget my manners. I stood up, introduced myself.

She bowed stiffly, like a Prussian dragoon. "Sister Marcellinus."

"Welcome to Egypt, Sister."

So far I had not seen her smile; she looked as grave as if she were at a papal audience. The capture of her quarry had brought a triumphant shout but no change in her stern expression. I was doing my best to charm her; found her unyielding gravity quite odd.

"I am a guide. In all modesty I think I know more about the Theban necropolis than anyone else in Egypt. The Valley of the Kings, Deir-el-Bahri, the Valley of the Queens, the Tombs of the Nobles. Dark, mysterious tombs; vibrant, wonderful paintings; astonishing temples; a whole wonderland is waiting here for you. And I'd be glad to give you a tour." My unction has soothed the sternness of even Italians.

But she would have none of it. "I have already seen all of it once before. *Danke schön.*"

"I see. The right bank, then? Karnak?"

"No thank you. Good morning, Herr Carter." She turned to go; lifted the skirt of her habit and waddled off down the Valley. Her legs, below her round body, were spindle-thin.

I had to try once more. "I could give you a clerical discount," I shouted. But she ignored me, kept walking. In a few moments she was gone. I sat down glumly. My first attempt to earn a living as a guide had been less than a brilliant success.

Then something on the ground in front of me caught my eye; a small scrap of papyrus flapping lightly in the breeze. I picked it up; read. An ancient bit of magic. A love elixir; a spell. The principal ingredient called for is a scarab beetle. It

must have fallen out of her robes. I started to call after her.
"Sister Marcellinus! Hey, Sister! You dropped your pre-
scription!" But I caught myself, thought better of it. Started
laughing over it. A nun who practices sorcery.

The sun was high enough now to fill the Valley with its
light. Other tourists—or, more precisely, the day's first
tourists—would be arriving soon. I stowed my camping gear
in an empty tomb, brushed off my clothes, waited for my
employers to arrive.

And arrive they did. I have seldom seen the Valley so
crowded. This morning I found myself a German baron,
traveling with his niece, who for some mysterious reason was
interested only in the tomb of Ramses III—not one of the
Valley's more prepossessing sights. "I saw his mummy in
the Cairo Museum," he explained. My attempts to steer him
into other tombs were in vain. But he paid me generously,
more than the fee I'd asked.

This afternoon I found a group of students from Cam-
bridge who wanted to see the whole of the necropolis. I
showed them what I could before the daylight waned, being
careful to save the tomb of Seti I for last; it is the most
impressive thing in the Valley and always leaves them
wanting more. We were outside the tomb settling my fee
when I realized that one of them was missing.

"Where is your friend?"

They laughed; they had treated the entire Valley of the
Kings as if it were a colossal joke executed for their personal
amusement. I went back into the tomb. From just inside the
entrance I could hear the sound of scratching, of chiseling. I
ran after him, found him defacing one of the loveliest, most
delicate reliefs in the tomb. He was carving his fraternity
letters into the face of the goddess of truth.

"Stop that! Stop it at once."

He did not glance away from his work. "Don't be

tiresome. How else would our fraternity brothers ever know we'd been here?''

I pulled the chisel out of his hand, threw it into a corner.

He finally looked at me. "See here, Carter, I think you're forgetting your place.''

I pulled at his shirt to get him moving, gave him a strong shove to propel him toward the entrance. Even as I spoke I knew how pompous, how absurd it sounded; but there was nothing else to say. "Egypt is my place.''

They all laughed at me, turned and sauntered out of the Valley. Thank heaven they had paid me before all of this happened. They will not be back tomorrow, of course. But there are always more tourists. At least I feel more confident now of my ability to earn a living here outside the Antiquities Service.

This evening I crossed the Nile into Luxor for the first time since my return here. It was time to move my belongings out of my old house and into an inn. The ferry was a while in coming for me; I watched the Nile darken to its night colors.

Luxor was busy this evening; today was a market day. The streets were filled with Egyptians and there were lights burning everywhere. I recruited two boys to help me with my things; it did not take us long to move my worldly goods. Or rather, it would not have taken us long, if I hadn't been interrupted.

"Herr Carter! Herr Carter!"

I looked to see who was calling after me but the crowd was too thick.

"Herr Carter."

It was Baron Lees-Gottorp, the man with the penchant for Ramses III. "Herr Baron," I shouted through the mob, "good evening."

He pushed his way up to me. The baron is a young man, in

his mid-thirties, and quite handsome in his blond Prussian way. He seemed rather intimidated by the crowd, the noise, the lights; strangers always find it a bit overpowering.

"And where is your niece this evening?"

"Brigit is asleep back at the hotel."

"You are staying at the Winter Palace?"

"Yes, we are."

We walked together through the narrow, convoluted streets. The baron had seemed anxious at first; now he was calm and direct, as he had been this morning. "Herr Carter, I have been offered the chance to purchase some antiquities. I know something about Egyptian artifacts but not nearly enough. Could I impose upon you to give an opinion . . .?"

"You must be careful, Herr Baron. There are shops in the hills where they turn out high-quality forgeries by the score. You could easily be taken." He must already have known this, but it seemed a good idea to make certain he understood how valuable my services would be.

"I will pay you a handsome consultant's fee."

I kept my eyes on the crowd. "Twenty percent of the sale price is usual. Or if there is no sale, twenty percent of what you were saved from spending." This was a lie; the usual commission is ten percent.

The baron stopped walking. "I believe the customary rate is ten." When I looked back at him he was smiling at me. "I will pay you twelve and one-half."

"Fine, Herr Baron." I smiled back at him, shook his hand. "I'll be only too glad to assist you. When can I see the objects?"

"The seller will be outside my hotel at midnight. Can you be there?"

"Yes, of course." The late hour did not surprise me. Antiquities forgers take enormous pains to create the illusion that their goods are legitimate and their operations therefore highly illegal. The sense of clandestine peril seems to fool tourists into believing that anything, quite literally anything, is a legitimate antiquity. And since their purchases are tinged with vice, the tourists are willing to pay more for them. "We will have to be careful," I told the baron, only partly to play him along. "Some of the dealers can be dangerous, especially if their goods are genuine."

It was eleven P.M. when I got the last of my things moved into a small inn just south of the town. Not the most convenient location, but the price is eminently affordable and Mahomet the proprietor is an old friend of mine. He supervised a digging crew for me a few seasons back. And the inn sits on the Nile bank; my room has a wonderful view of the river.

There was still a bit of time before I had to meet the baron. I packed my revolver and walked out to the Nile.

The gibbous moon was rising behind me; the ripples cast its glow back to me. There were frogs croaking loudly all along the bank, and now and again one could hear the heavy splashes they made when they jumped in. Not far from the inn is a little native tavern; there were lights and music and a surprising number of people. I thought about having some wine there but I hesitated; didn't feel like company. I sat down and watched the moonbeams, listened to the frogs.

Around midnight I walked up the bank along Bahr Street to the Winter Palace. The moon was fairly high now; the flowers in the hotel garden showed ghostly colors. The croaking of the frogs carried up from the river. I found Baron Lees-Gottorp and his niece waiting on the hotel veranda. The baron stepped forward, shook my hand.

"You are bringing the girl?"

"I want her to learn about art."

"If things get difficult she may learn about more than that. Blond Western girls are prize items in Moslem harems."

"Don't be ridiculous. We can take care of ourselves. Brigit is a star athlete at the gymnasium."

"The seller may not like it. Women don't mix much in business here."

"If they wish to do business, it will be on my terms."

"Of course, Herr Baron." How German of him.

There was still no sign of the baron's mysterious seller. We made idle chat until nearly 12:20. How did I like living in Egypt? The natives aren't very friendly, are they? And on and on. The stock replies, the banal questions seemed endless. I think we were both on edge. Commercial interests and anxieties aside, I had not exaggerated the possible danger of a midnight sortie into an Arab quarter. The weight of my revolver in my pocket was reassuring. The baron was also nervous; understandably, since he could have no real idea what to expect tonight. Only his niece, of the three of us, seemed unaffected by the night's possibilities. The girl had a distracted air, lethargic, detached, as if she were trying to impress one with her aloof calm. I found her irritating, which did not help my mood.

Finally the seller arrived. Or rather his son did, a slender thirteen-year-old with huge brown eyes. He carried an enormous lamp.

The baron snapped at him. "Why are you late?"

The boy glanced at each of us in turn. "There are three of you?"

"Yes." The baron's face turned red. I half expected him to cancel our expedition. "Who are you?"

The boy raised his lamp so that its light fell full on his face; smiled. "Which of you is the baron?"

"I am." He was becoming angrier with the boy by the second. Apparently cool detachment is something he tolerates only in nieces.

I decided to intervene, in the interest of my commission. "This is Baron Rolf Lees-Gottorp." The baron clicked his heels, bowed. I found myself thinking of Sister What's-her-name. "His niece, Brigit Lees-Gottorp."

Brigit looked at me as if, in her slow way, she were afraid I might be mad. "Brigit Schmenkling," she said offhand-edly.

"Oh. I beg your pardon."

"You are bringing her to my father's house?" The boy seemed incredulous.

Before I could answer the baron snapped, "Yes."

The Arab boy smiled, made no attempt to hide his amusement at this. He had made the obvious inference about this Western woman's virtue. "My father will be pleased to meet her."

I introduced myself, and for the first time the boy's coolness showed signs of heating up.

"Mr. Howard Carter of the Antiquities Service?"

"Not anymore." I smiled as broadly as I could. "I am self-employed now."

He obviously did not believe me. "Why are you here?"

I continued smiling. "I am a friend of the baron's. He wants my opinion of the objects for sale."

The boy looked to the baron, who looked back imperi-ously.

"My father . . . We did not know that you would bring Mr. Carter."

"And who," I asked, "is your father?" I knew the boy would never answer so direct a question, but I wanted to keep myself between him and the baron, who was still clearly angry. Besides, I was genuinely curious. I know all of the legitimate dealers in Luxor, and nearly all of the good forgers. But this boy was unknown to me.

The boy looked back at me. "You are the Antiquities Service." It was an accusation.

"No. Not anymore. Ask anyone. It must be all over Luxor by now. Ask anyone you like."

The boy glanced from one of us to the other, plainly uncertain what to do. There was a long silence. Finally, "I will tell my father. He will know what to do. I will come back tomorrow at the same time." He walked quickly away from us. As he rounded the corner of the hotel he extinguished his lamp, vanished quickly into the park between the hotel and the Luxor temple. In the moonlight, for just an instant, his white-robed figure looked like a distant ghost.

Baron Lees-Gottorp seemed uncertain how to react to this. "I thought the man would come himself."

"It would have been unlikely. That's what boys are for. Did you get the father's name?"

In the moonlight I could see him blushing. "No."

"Well, all we can do is meet here tomorrow night. That is, assuming you still want to go through with this . . .?"

"You actually think he will come?"

"It's difficult to know." I leaned against a porch railing. I was going to continue, to explain the situation as I saw it; but I decided to let it hang there. Arab indirectness obviously gives one an edge over the baron.

He pressed me. "Well, what did you make of the whole thing?"

I smiled, but the moon was behind me so he could not see it. "Well, I think there are two explanations that make sense. The 'objects' may be such obvious frauds that I could spot them in a second. Or they may be quite genuine, in which case the dealer would hardly want the Antiquities Service looking in on things. You are aware, aren't you, that it is highly illegal to take antiquities out of the country without the government's permission?"

The baron glanced at me, looked suspicious; perhaps I should have remained evasive and mysterious. But I went on. "If the objects are genuine, they are the property of the

Egyptian state. You could be fined—quite heavily—and your dealer friend imprisoned.''

For the first time all night Brigit became conversational. ''I don't understand something.''

I turned to her. ''Yes?''

''If these pieces are forgeries, is not selling them also illegal?''

The standard tourist question. I smiled again; it had been a night of patient smiles. ''Technically, of course, it is fraud. But look at it from the government's viewpoint. If all of the tourists are kept busy buying forged antiquities, the real ones will stay here in Egypt, where they belong.''

The baron was incredulous. ''You mean art forgers are never punished?''

''Only when a formal complaint is filed with the local police. That doesn't happen often. Buyers are embarrassed or simply never catch on. And even then the sentences are light.'' I never stop marveling at the gullibility of tourists. I have seen them buy objects with fresh chisel marks clearly visible, in the complete certainty that what they have purchased came from the tomb of a Ramses.

''This is a nest of thieves!'' Brigit was now quite animated. Adolescence.

''No,'' I said quietly. ''This is simply Egypt.''

''But such behavior isn't Christian!''

''Precisely.'' I turned back to her uncle. ''If the pieces are forgeries, the dealer—or one of his relatives—will approach me tomorrow and offer me a bribe to lie to you.''

''And will you accept it?'' He assumed an air of exaggerated casualness.

So did I. I glanced back at the girl. ''This is Egypt. But as guides go, I'm fairly trustworthy. Ask around Luxor yourself.''

''You will be here tomorrow night, then?'' Despite his

studied easiness, I could see in his eyes, even in the
moonlight, concern for all the deutschmarks he stood to
lose or, worse yet, waste foolishly.

"You can count on it. Good evening, Herr Baron." I
touched the brim of my pith helmet. "And to you, Brigit."

And walked back here to the inn, hoping tomorrow night
will be more profitable.

It seemed a good idea to make myself prominent in the
souk this morning. Since I needed some things for my room
at the inn, this was doubly convenient.

Maspero does not seem to have appointed anyone to
replace me. Or at any rate, the inspector's residence is still
unoccupied. It is already looking out-at-elbow, thanks to
the unsupervised servants. I had hardly passed by the door
when one of them ran out and approached me, complaining
that his wages were overdue. "Good morning, Carter
Pasha."

"Good morning, Magit."

"And how is Carter Pasha this fine day?"

"Carter Pasha wishes to be alone."

"I see. May I walk with you?"

I said nothing, kept walking. I had reached the souk.
Magit would not leave me until he was ready to. I walked
among the shops and stands, browsing, trying to ignore
him.

"Carter Pasha, my wife and children are hungry."

"Magit, so am I."

"My sister from the Delta has come to live with me. Her
children disappeared and she thinks her husband murdered
them, so she came here to me. She eats like a camel to cover
her fear."

This was the first thing he said that caught my interest.
"From the Delta? Where in the Delta?"

But he would not be shaken from his purpose. "My wages, Carter Pasha."

"You work for the Antiquities Service. I do not. What can I do?" I looked heavenward, as if to suggest that a surrender to the will of Allah might be the wisest course.

But Magit was persistent. "You have money."

"From tourists. Why don't you find a few of your own?"

This went on for quite a while as I wandered through the souk. I found a lovely red earthenware pitcher, and a copper washbasin. I was shopping for linens when Magit finally went away. There were some beautiful woven blankets from Esna. I bought two.

Everywhere I made myself as visible as possible. Greeted loudly everyone I knew; haggled energetically even over things I had no intention of purchasing. Had lunch at the busiest café in the souk. Friends, acquaintances said hello, offered condolences on the loss of my job. "I'll be all right. There are tourists." Everyone understood this; in Luxor, everyone but the farmers lives off of tourists. Hotel employees, the people at the railroad station, guides, artists, craftsmen, whores, forgers, pickpockets . . .

The day became increasingly hot. November 29, and it was like July. The baron's mysterious dealer had not shown his hand. Like nearly everyone else I decided to siesta. As I was leaving the souk I passed a pair of Italians who were obviously lost in its maze of streets; led them back to the Winter Palace, got a generous little fee. My room at the inn was waiting for me, dark and cool like a tomb. I fell asleep almost at once. And slept much longer than I would have liked. It is now after nine P.M. There will just be time to have a good dinner and meet the baron.

It is an unusually cool night, cooler than I've ever known Luxor, cool as the day was hot, cool as Cairo in midwinter.

I think the temperature must actually be in the forties. The streets were already deserted when I left the inn, the frogs silent. Half a block from the inn I realized how chilly I was; returned for a jacket. There was a slight mist in the air; the stars looked smeared, and there was a wide halo around the moon.

The baron stood on the veranda, as he had last night. Brigit was off in a shadow at the porch's corner. And the Arab boy, the dealer's son, was already with them, lamp in hand. I glanced at my watch. It was ten minutes to midnight.

"Good evening, Herr Baron. Brigit." I looked at the Egyptian boy, smiled.

He ignored me, addressed the baron. "Are you ready to go?"

"Yes. Of course."

Without a word he set off, leaving us to follow him. To my surprise he did not head into the souk but led us north along the bank of the Nile. Baron Lees-Gottorp looked at me, puzzled. I shrugged. The boy, wearing as near as I could tell only a galabea and sandals, set a quick pace, acting as if there were nothing unusual about the night, the cold. The baron turned up his collar against the chill air, looked irritably at our guide. "The temperature doesn't seem to touch him."

"You expect him to show his discomfort to a European?"

The baron tucked his hands in his pockets. Brigit was shivering quite visibly. So much for Prussian discipline. To give her her due, though, she kept up well with our brisk pace.

We quickly passed the Luxor temple, glowing queerly in the moonlight; continued north. Soon we were at Karnak; the colossal pylon that is its gateway towered above us. I could feel the chill from its stones; could not resist pausing for a moment, pressing my hand against them. After all these years Egypt still seems a dream to me. One day it will vanish, I am certain, and I will find myself stranded in the English countryside, forced like my father to earn my living by watercolors of the prize livestock of the prize landowners. It is too awful to contemplate. But while the dream lasts I embrace it. I am here, in this magical place, in this strange and beautiful land, where the earth holds the secrets of man's nature. It is like—

"Look!" Brigit interrupted my reverie. She was pointing to an open field on our right. For a moment I was disoriented; we had left Karnak far behind, continued on north. "Look, frost! There is actually frost!"

"No, Brigit," the baron explained. "Only the moonlight on the soil."

The area to the north and east of Luxor—almost five miles upriver and as far east as the edge of the desert—is dotted with small freehold farms. Our guide led us east now, away from the river, through field after field. There were mudbrick huts, some with lamps burning, most dark. The cultivation is not wide here. Either our goal was one of these farmers' huts or we were being led into the desert. In either case, I had never known an antiquities dealer, legitimate or otherwise, to operate this way.

Because of the chill, the night was eerily quiet. On a normal November night there would be insect sounds, ibises squawking, the frogs of course, and human sounds; and these noises carry. But tonight . . . I found it unnerving; found myself rather often touching my revolver in my pocket, for reassurance. There was nothing, nothing at all to be heard but the weak crunching our boots made in the earth. Our guide moved in complete silence. We walked for miles, and soon the moonlight, the lamplight, the steady, plodding pace became hypnotic, numbing. We could have been anywhere, we could have been nowhere in the world.

I could not tell what the Germans made of all this. They were quiet enough. I suppose they must not have realized how out of the ordinary everything was. So they simply fixed their attention on the one thing in the landscape that kept drawing one's eye, the light from our guide's lamp.

Ahead of us I could see the edge of the desert. There was only one more farmer's hut; lamps burned in four of its windows. I looked at my watch; it seemed impossible, but it was after one o'clock. This had gone on far too long. I was frozen to the bone, and I was surprised the Germans hadn't complained yet. "Stop!"

The Germans stopped walking; the Arab boy kept on.

"Stop!" This time in Arabic.

The boy hesitated uncertainly, turned to face me.

"We have been following you through the dark for more than an hour."

He stared at me. "Yes, Carter Pasha."

"Where are you taking us?"

"To see the objects my father is selling."

"And where exactly are they?"

"Ahead."

I pointed to the last farm dwelling. "There? Is that where you are leading us?"

The boy looked at the lighted hut, back at me, then at the hut again. It was obviously our destination; he obviously didn't want to say so. After a moment of nervous indecision he said, "The weather is inside out. There must be sorcerers at work. We should hurry. You will see soon."

"No, that isn't good enough. We will go no further. If that hut is our destination, say so. If not, we will go back now. Your father can bring his objects to Luxor, to the baron's suite at the Winter Palace, if he still wants to deal."

The boy looked anxiously back at the hut. "Please, Carter Pasha. It will only be another short time."

"Excuse us for a moment. We need to discuss this."

I took Brigit and the baron thirty yards off, where I was reasonably certain the boy could not hear us; explained to them how far out of the ordinary it was for an antiquities dealer, even a forger, to be operating this far out of Luxor. "It's wrong. It's out of place. It's like finding a plow salesman in the heart of Berlin. I think we should refuse to go any further."

Brigit looked past me, at the hut. "It looks warm there."

"Warmer than here, yes. But if that isn't our destination . . .? The desert will be colder yet."

The baron had been thinking; spoke firmly now. "We are here. If it is the farm, let us look."

"I'm not certain you understand what I'm suggesting, Herr Baron. Out here they could do anything, anything without fear of detection."

"We are Germans."

It was exasperating. "You are infidels. Blond-haired, blue-eyed infidels. Infidels with money."

"Oh. I see." Finally his naive self-assurance was wavering. "I have a revolver."

I decided not to show him my own. "You want to go on?"

He nodded; for once he looked almost worried.

"Wait here a moment." I walked over to our guide who, in our absence, had begun to shiver quite badly. Now he tried to stop, to get control of himself, with not much success. "That hut is our destination, isn't it?"

"Yes, Carter Pasha." His teeth were chattering. He looked at the hut as if the only thing he wanted in the world was to be inside.

"Why didn't you say so?"

"My father is waiting."

"Your father and who else?"

"No one else, Carter Pasha." This had to be a lie.

"What is your name?"

"Azzi."

"If there is anyone in the house besides your father, we will leave without looking at the objects. You understand that?"

The boy must have been freezing. "Dukh is there."

"Who is Dukh?"

"My brother."

"And who else?"

"No one else, Carter Pasha. No one."

I stared at him a long moment to emphasize my skepticism. He stuck to his claim. So I waved to the Germans, and as soon as they joined us we crossed the field to the farmhouse. Just as we neared the door, Azzi turned to gesture us in. "This way." And in the light from the hut I noticed something that had escaped me before. Around his neck, hanging on a black cord, the boy wore a silver crucifix.

We were ushered in. Inside, lamps blazed everywhere. The interior was golden with lamplight. The hut was simple. A squarish room, and a second one beyond it through a low doorway. Both rooms were immaculate; both were lit brilliantly. There was an elaborately carved table and four plushly upholstered chairs to match it; hardly farm furniture. Azzi warmed his hands over a lamp. I leaned close to the baron. "Oil is expensive. These people are well off for farmers."

"If that's what they are." He was looking around cautiously.

There was no sign of anyone else. Azzi's father was out of sight in the second room; we could hear him moving about. There was also no sign of the objects we had come to see. Brigit had been standing close to the door; came over to me. "I don't like this."

I decided to be obtuse. "It is a mudbrick hut. What is there to like?"

''The situation, I mean.''

''Oh. Well, for what it's worth I don't think there are more than one or two people in the next room.''

She glanced at me as if she thought me mad.

I smiled. ''The forty thieves must be off somewhere else tonight. Would you feel safer outside?''

She wrapped her arms around herself. ''Alone? No, I think I'll stay here with you.''

''Thank you.'' I found the omission of her uncle's name odd.

Suddenly a man appeared from the second room, tall, slender, with enormous brown eyes. One of the handsomest Egyptian men I have ever seen. ''Good evening. I am Ahmed Abd-er-Rasul.'' He bowed low before us. Behind him a boy stepped into the room, a year or so older than our guide, and an image of his father. ''My eldest son, Dukh.'' Dukh bowed politely. ''Azzi you know.''

The baron took a step toward Ahmed Abd-er-Rasul, hand extended. Ahmed quickly bowed to him again. The baron halted, rather uncertainly, turned a wonderful shade of red, then bowed himself. He looked as if he'd just had his manners corrected in front of the kaiser. Without realizing it he had lost the first round of bargaining to his opponent.

Abd-er-Rasul smiled. ''May I offer you some mint tea?''

Baron Lees-Gottorp was about to refuse; I could see it in his face. Before he could commit another faux pas I interrupted. ''We would be quite honored.''

The baron frowned at me; obviously thought I was wasting time. I was half-tempted to let him handle things himself, only speak when I was spoken to, permit him to make as many mistakes as he wanted to.

Dukh scurried into the second room to make our tea. The baron watched him go, with rather a speculative look in his eye, I thought. There was a break in the conversation. I had a brief moment to think over our situation.

The Abd-er-Rasuls are the most prominent family of
tomb robbers in Egypt. Their pedigree, if that is the word,
stretches back to the Middle Ages and beyond. When the
Crusaders marched for Jerusalem, when Columbus sailed
for the New World, when William conquered England,
there were Abd-er-Rasuls plundering the Egyptian dead.
All those centuries of experience, of perfecting techniques,
of learning infallibly where to look for treasure . . . They
are without doubt the best in the business. Some of the most
important archaeological finds on record were made by
their family and came to light only when the family got too
greedy, flooded the market too quickly with finds from
their tombs. They discovered the Deir-el-Bahri cache, the
most important assemblage of royal mummies in the history
of Egypt.

But the Abd-er-Rasuls have always been, quite emphatically, a family. Operating for their common, familial
interest. Renegades who struck out on their own have been
dealt with unpleasantly, to say the least. If our host tonight
was actually an Abd-er-Rasul, it would explain the remote
location, the late hour. If on the other hand he was an
imposter, he would certainly want to avoid the family's
anger and, most likely, vengeance at his appropriation of
their name.

Dukh returned with four glasses of tea on a small silver
tray. Ahmed served us himself, then took the last glass.
"Please sit down."

We arranged ourselves around the table. There were a few
minutes of small talk—"How do you like Egypt?" "Will
you be here long?"—during which the baron looked
increasingly uncomfortable. I wished he would do something to cloak his impatience; there is nothing worse than
trying to rush an Egyptian.

We finished our tea after what seemed an eon. Finally the

moment was here. Ahmed stood up, assumed as mysterious an air as he could manage. "I have some precious objects I would like you to see." The pretense was perfect: he announced it as if it were a casual coincidence, as if our sole purpose there was to enjoy his hospitality.

For once Baron Lees-Gottorp said the right thing. "We would be very honored to see them."

"Please follow me."

The second room was slightly smaller than the first. Its sole furniture was a massive cedar table, delicately carved with geometric patterns and inlaid with ivory. Six oil lamps burned along its back side. There were three windows in the room, each of which held two more lamps. Beneath the table was a large oblong bundle wrapped in white linen. On the table itself were the objects.

They were an odd mixture of fakes and real pieces. Four ushabtis, from the late period, poorly preserved. A bright green heart scarab that had obviously been finished last week. A pair of shredded, fragmentary Coptic papyri. An assortment of small amulets and charms in various materials, most of them patent frauds. A badly decayed wooden headrest, which was quite genuine, quite ordinary; at that, it was the most interesting piece in the collection, and certainly the oldest. There was a gilded cartonnage mummy mask; it took me only a moment to see that the "gilding" was paint.

Lees-Gottorp's face lit up. I could almost hear him saying to himself, this is what I came to Egypt to buy. He turned to Ahmed. "May I handle them?"

"All but the papyri, if you please. They are very delicate."

Predictably, he picked up the heart scarab. The principal factor working in favor of an antiquities forger is the fact that tourists always want to buy attractive objects, to impress their friends with. Genuine pieces are only rarely as attractive as modern forgeries.

The baron was examining the heart scarab with what he must have thought a careful eye. I pointed to the chisel marks around its rim. He quietly replaced it on the table, whispered to me, "Are they all fakes?"

"No, there are some good pieces. But they are not very spectacular, I'm afraid." I pointed to the headrest; the baron looked disappointed. I picked it up for him, showed him some faint hieroglyphs running around the base. "It dates from the Twentieth Dynasty, from the reign of Ramses III. It would be like having a souvenir of him."

"It belonged to the king?"

"No, only to a minor noble. Still . . ."

He turned to the pile of amulets. "Are any of these real?"

I sifted through them. Three were real: a faience *djed*-column and two "eyes of Horus," one in carnelian, the other in faience. "These are lovely pieces."

"When do they date from?"

"The carnelian eye is Twenty-first Dynasty, the other two are Ptolemaic."

Again he looked disappointed. Tourists always expect to purchase the crown of Ramses the Great or the brass bra of Cleopatra. Anything less spectacular makes them glum. He pointed hopefully to the mummy mask. I shook my head. So he turned to Ahmed. "This is all you have?"

Ahmed shrugged, spread his hands to indicate that it was Allah's will that he possess these objects, and who were we to question it. He paused hesitantly, dramatically. "Unless . . ."

"Yes?" The baron became eager.

"Would Your Grace be interested in the purchase of a mummy?"

"A mummy," he said doubtfully. "Well . . . if it were well preserved, I might consider it."

The bundle under the table. Dukh and Azzi quickly cleared away the other things while Ahmed unwrapped it, lifted it gently up. It was small, the mummy of a girl around Azzi's age. The linen was unmistakably ancient, and the bandaging was most intricately, most elaborately done. The head was wrapped with special attention, the bandages layered in a beautiful geometric pattern over the face. I leaned close to examine it.

"Well?" Baron Lees-Gottorp was impatient.

"I'm a bit puzzled. There are marks on the bandages that date them from the Twenty-second Dynasty. From the reign of Osorkon I."

"Yes?"

"But the style of the wrapping is much later. From Greek times, or even Roman."

He frowned. "There are no earlier examples of such wrappings?"

"None like this, no."

"Similar ones, then?"

"Well, yes. But—"

"Excellent. Then we have here a rare and important find." He beamed.

Ahmed beamed back at him. "I knew it would please a man of your fine taste. It will cost you only five hundred pounds. English pounds, not Egyptian."

This alarmed me. This was twice what the thing was worth, even if it was genuine and untouched. If—and it is what I suspected—Ahmed had unwrapped it, removed the funerary objects, then rewrapped it himself in this elaborate style, then the price was outright exorbitant.

But before I could say any of this the baron piped up. "I'll buy it! Excellent!"

And that was that. No haggling—he could surely have gotten a better price, if not actually a fair one; haggling is a way of life in Egypt. No hesitation. He saw a pretty thing and he bought it. I found myself wondering why he had brought me along at all. Ahmed smiled an ironic smile for me; he knew he had gotten the drop on me.

There was a momentary lull. I was too irritated to speak, everyone else too excited. I became aware that everyone else in the room was staring at Brigit. She stood off in a corner. Her face was garishly lit from below by two lamps; she looked horrible. Slowly she walked across to the table, placed her hand gently on the shoulder of the mummy. She looked around the room, at each of us in turn. Finally her eyes rested on me. "She died so young," she said to me. "Can't you find any sorrow for her?"

I was abashed. It is so easy, so downright simple, to forget that a mummy is the mortal shell of a fellow human being. I have never really felt comfortable working with them, but they are, nonetheless, tools of one's trade; and even hasty reverence takes time. I looked away from Brigit; there was not much I could say to her.

I turned my gaze to Ahmed, who was obviously startled at this public outburst of emotion from this Western woman. For him, even more than for myself, the mummy was merely a commodity.

Brigit turned to him also. In a very soft voice she asked, "Where did you find her? What does her grave look like?"

For an instant Ahmed's eyes widened. This is the last question one ought to ask a tomb robber. Then his composure returned. "It is a great distance from here."

"I want to see it." Brigit's face was red. "I want to see her sepulcher."

"That is not possible, young woman. It is too distant."

Brigit's voice was becoming louder, and it was beginning

to shake. "She is dead. You understand that? She is dead."
She addressed all of us.

"Brigit." I interrupted her as gently as I could. "Surely
you realize that isn't so. Surely you know that her soul is still
alive."

She had been facing Ahmed; turned, rather shakily, to
me. "What?"

I repeated what I had said.

"Her . . ." Brigit looked as if *soul* were a new word to
her.

"The ancients—this girl and her family—believed in the
soul, too. What they did to her body, they did merely in case
her soul—her *ka*, they would have called it—should want to
use it again."

Ahmed had had enough of this. "Baron Lees-Gottorp."

"Yes?" The baron had, I think, been somewhat nonplussed by my exchange with his niece. He had been staring,
rather pointedly I thought, at Dukh.

"There is the price of the mummy to be covered."

"Yes. Yes, of course. And I want these also." He
indicated the three amulets. "Will fifty pounds be enough
for them?"

Ahmed grinned at me again. "Quite enough, Your
Grace."

A few moments later we stepped out of the house into the
cold, moonlit field. Brigit and I carried the mummy between
us; the baron, who seemed annoyed with us, walked a few
paces ahead. He conversed quietly with Dukh, who had
replaced his brother as our guide. Ahmed stood in the
doorway and watched us go, clutching his money in his hand.
He said good night to the baron and me; ignored Brigit.

We must have made a grotesque little procession; a mock
cortege. There were wisps of mist rising out of the earth,
coiling about us, creeping into the sky. Among them,

obscured by them, the moon was a pearl. Our breaths added to the mist. After a while the baron dropped back to walk beside his new possession; beamed at it with obvious pride of ownership. The air was like ice.

"She has beautiful breasts, hasn't she?"

For a moment I was uncertain whether he meant the mummy or Brigit. But his eyes were fixed on the mummy. I decided to deflate him. "Her breasts are likely padded with linen."

"Oh." He looked glum for an instant, then perked up again. "Do you suppose the young men in her time were so attractive?"

"I couldn't say."

He stalked off ahead of us, resumed his conversation with Dukh.

I have never liked working with mummies, touching them, handling them. And I have never been able to decide exactly why. Death, disintegration; the leathery feel of the skin. Most of all I dislike unwrapping them. I have never made an issue of it; it is part of my job, and most of my colleagues take it in their stride. I avoid doing it when I can.

There is a mummy kept in the basement of the Egyptian Museum in Cairo, kept far from public view. It was found in the cache of royal mummies at Deir-el-Bahri, wrapped in wool in a plain white coffin. The sheep was an unclean animal; the wool wrapping was intended purposely to blight the corpse. The absence of carvings or inscriptions on the coffin would ensure his spirit's anonymity in the underworld. The face of this mummy is contorted with pain; I have never seen a human countenance so badly disfigured with pain. The man whose body it is was mummified before he died. Cut open, wrapped with linen, sealed in his coffin before he died. His body is wrenched into a horrible shape by his suffering, by his empty attempt to free himself from the bandages, from the coffin. The mummified muscles are knotted with struggle. The mouth gapes open and the dry tongue protrudes. The neck is twisted. There are theories about who he was, why he was killed in this awful way; but no one knows; no inscriptions. There are records of a prince rebelling against his father Ramses III and it is thought that this may be his body; but that is only a guess. The people who sought to obliterate his identity did so all too well. I have only seen this mummy once, briefly. It haunted me for many nights. Haunts me still. It represents to me the extreme of human suffering, the limit of what we have always done to one another. It was on display for a short while but the people who came to see it found it too awful. So it was put in a black corner of the basement, where such things belong.

Every time I unwrap a mummy I think of that "unmummified" one in Cairo. I am terrified that that is what I will find under the bandages, another horror like that. I can never free myself from that fear.

"Herr Carter." Baron Lees-Gottorp broke our long silence.

"Yes, Herr Baron?"

"I should like to thank you for your services tonight."

I found this more than a little ironic. "My fee will be more than sufficient thanks. I reckon it to be sixty-nine pounds."

"We shall make it seventy." He was the soul of generosity.

"Thank you, Herr Baron. Will you require assistance in unwrapping the mummy?"

"I think I'll wait till we're home to do that."

Good. He won't realize he's been swindled until then, and I'll be out of blame's way. "In getting it out of the country, then?"

He had been walking a pace ahead of me. He stopped,

caught hold of my arm. Brigit stumbled, nearly fell on the mummy. I helped her back to her feet.

"Herr Carter," the baron said in unfriendly tones, "I am not at all happy with your behavior tonight." He was glaring at me.

I was appalled. If he dared complain that I hadn't protected his interests . . . "I beg your pardon?"

"I do not approve," he said heavily, "of filling the heads of girls Brigit's age with superstition and mumbo jumbo."

I stared at him blankly; he could not have caught me more off guard.

"The mummy's *ka*. What rot."

I looked from the Baron to Brigit and back again. "Do you not profess Christianity, Herr Baron?"

"It is not simply a matter of professing it, Herr Carter. I *am* a Christian."

The mummy had been slipping in my grip. I took a firmer hold on it; focused my attention on it. "Well, surely the Christian church also preaches the preservation of the body. And for essentially the same reason. Only the time frame is different."

"In Germany we know how to deal with irreligion." It was a challenge.

But I had had enough of it. I looked around. "Our guide seems to have vanished in the mist."

We were quite alone; no sign of Dukh or of his lantern. There were no lighted buildings in sight.

The baron was instantly deflated. "We are lost."

"No. We can find the river easily enough." I was pleased that it had been so simple to take charge of the situation. I guided by the moon, headed west to the Nile. In twenty minutes or so we could hear it. Another twenty and we were walking south along its bank toward Luxor. The mummy grew heavier, more awkward the longer we carried it; our pace slowed. The baron walked ahead of us once again, sometimes by a good distance. Once he disappeared in the thickening mist.

"Mr. Carter." Brigit sounded fatigued.

"Yes?"

"You don't strike me as the kind of man to believe in the soul. Do you really?"

I was shocked at her rudeness in asking. I became a Moslem. "We will be back in town soon. Are you all right?"

"My back is hurting. It seemed so light when we first picked it up."

"It won't be far now."

I felt her shift her grip on the mummy. "Do you, then?" Brigit is like a Moslem too, if only in her persistence.

"Look. I can see the lamps in the minarets. We're nearly there."

In a short time we were back at the Winter Palace. To my surprise Dukh was waiting for us there, on the veranda. My fee was settled; good nights were said; that was that.

This morning I went to the souk to spend some of Baron Lees-Gottorp's pounds. There was not much of a crowd; the air was still chilly and a heavy mist, like none I have seen since I left London, hung over Luxor; still hangs there. Only a few of the merchants had opened their shops. What conversation I could overhear centered exclusively on the weather.

First to a tailor's shop to have some new shirts made. As I was being measured there was a loud commotion in the souk, not far from the shop. We went to the door to see. There was a fair-sized mob, from the look and sound of them quite angry. In the center of it all were two nuns; one of them was the nun I encountered in the Valley a few days ago, Sister Marcellinus. Her companion was taller, and thankfully, less fat. Whatever offense they had committed seemed not to faze them. They stood their ground and took on every Egyptian who confronted them. Finally things quieted down and the crowd dispersed.

Salid, my tailor, was more agitated by the incident than I would have expected. "They come from the Delta. They ought to stay there," he complained. "But they come and found their missions in Upper Egypt. They are witches. They're probably the ones who caused this foul weather."

"From the Delta? Where in the Delta?"

"The Delta." Salid is a perfect Moslem. "Every time they visit Luxor they make trouble. They have a place in Esna; now they come here."

I told him about the one I had met in the Valley of the Kings, chasing "her" scarab.

"You see? They are evil women." He said this with surprising bitterness. "Filthy."

I was amused by his intensity. "Because they collect scarabs?"

"Because they go in public without veils. They are whores."

I laughed. "Well, if it's any comfort, you're not the first person to think so."

A few minutes later out in the souk I learned what had happened. It was shockingly simple. A small boy, a beggar, approached the two nuns and asked them for a piaster or two. This is common; this is expected. To make baksheesh confers a blessing upon the giver as well as gladdening the receiver. But the two nuns chose not to be blessed. One of them struck the boy, rather fiercely. His face was cut deeply, close to the eye; he was rushed off to a doctor. The nuns insisted with graceless vigor that the boy had been the offender, not they. I presume that they are in Egypt doing missionary work. They will not win many converts if they act like this all the time.

To my surprise, Brigit was in the souk, alone. "Brigit. Good morning."

She smiled at me.

"You really shouldn't be here unescorted, you know. Where is your uncle?"

"He told me I'd be all right. He said that the supposed danger in the souk was just a line you feed tourists."

"Your uncle has a brash way about him, hasn't he?"

She had witnessed the incident with the nuns; gave me her account. "It was quite frightful. They swore like pigs. I was rather shocked."

"Invective is an essential part of an Arab's vocabulary."

"Not the Egyptians. The nuns. They swore like German officers. Like Uncle Rolf, in fact, when he unwrapped that mummy last night."

"He unwrapped it?"

Brigit nodded. "He was like an excited child. He was sure it would be full of gold and jewels. But when the last bandage came off there was nothing. One small amulet, shaped like a falcon. He was so angry he destroyed the mummy. The mummy was deformed, by the way. The muscles were all knotted or twisted. I'm not sure how to describe it."

This was not a thing I wanted to hear. "I could have told him there wouldn't be anything on it."

"Then why didn't you?"

"He never gave me the chance. You saw how quickly he agreed to Ahmed's price. He almost jumped at it."

Brigit smiled. "He's a little bit crazy. All the German nobles are. I'll be mad, too, when I'm his age." She smiled more widely.

Her attitude annoyed me. "Do you have to be so cheerful in your fatalism?"

This time she laughed out loud. "You should meet the Kaiser. His court is like something out of Lewis Carroll. Uncle Rolf finds Egypt very strange. He hates it."

"And you?"

"I enjoy it. I think I even love it a bit."

"You don't find it strange?" This was surprising.

"Yes, of course I do. But its strangeness is beautiful, not ugly. The Nile, the painted tombs, the calls of the muezzins in their towers. Compared to Berlin . . ." She made a face.

I decided I like Brigit; smiled and waited for her to go on.

"I have seen the kaiser's senior military advisors, dressed as women, dancing before him for his amusement."

I could not resist asking. "Baron Lees-Gottorp?"

Brigit nodded, blushed. "It's not the sex that upsets me. It's the bad taste."

"If I told you what goes on in some of the back streets of Luxor, or worse yet Cairo . . ."

"I think I know." She was suddenly cold, distant.

The muezzins called the noon prayer. Brigit listened to them, rapt. The luxuriant sadness of their chant transfixed her. I remember when they affected me the same way; now I seldom notice them.

"Brigit, is there anything else in Luxor you'd like to see? With or without your uncle?"

She was eager. "More tombs. Please. I'd love to see more tombs. And the colossus of Ramses, the one Shelley wrote about."

"When can you meet me?"

"It will have to be now. We are leaving Luxor first thing tomorrow morning. Uncle Rolf wants me to see Abu Simbel, then we return to Cairo."

"You'll like Abu Simbel."

Brigit paused awkwardly. "Can you show me those things now?"

One never goes to the Valley in the midday sun. But today was so cool . . . "Yes, of course. We can get a ferry right away."

"I can't pay you."

"I don't want your money, Brigit. Only your company."

She is quite a young woman. Most Europeans regard Egypt as a freak show put here for their diversion. To find one who loves it, however tentatively, is a rare thing. I took her everywhere she wanted to go, showed her all the tombs and statues. I even gave her a few simple lessons in reading hieroglyphs. Tonight when I returned her to the Winter Palace she hugged me impulsively as she said good-bye. I must confess it embarrassed me. One simply does not act that way with a woman. Not in public. Two Luxorites who had seen the hug smiled at me as if to say, "You see. You are still not one of us, and you never will be."

I decided to treat myself to roast beef at the Winter Palace tonight. Off in a corner of the restaurant sat the two nuns, Sister Marcellinus and her friend. Dined noisily, complained about everything. Midway through their meal they were joined by a priest; blond, handsome, quite German. It seemed to me that Sister Marcellinus doted on him quite heavily. Is he the object of her little love spell, then? She could hardly have chosen a more attractive man.

The three of them were the talk of the restaurant. Half a dozen acquaintances stopped at my table, made remarks about them. No one seems to know what to make of them. One of my friends mentioned an odd coincidence: the boy one of them struck in the souk has disappeared. I think he must have run away. He will have been scarred; the shame for him would be terrible.

The weather is frigid again tonight. There is actually frost.

Chapter Two

"YOU SPEAK ENGLISH?"

This is always the first question Americans ask. Not, "How do you do?", not even "What is your name?" It is as if they haven't the time to be polite, or as if they think themselves too important to bother. I have had several well-paying clients over the last few weeks; was not in the mood to be bothered by an American.

And at any rate I did not want to be disturbed from my midday siesta. The Valley was unusually peaceful today, no breeze, no noisy tourists. I was sleeping happily in a tomb.

"I said good morning. Do you speak English?"

I lifted the edge of my pith helmet; glanced at my nemesis. A young man, not more than twenty-five or so, with piercing green eyes, white freckled skin, and shockingly red hair. If his cheekbones had been a bit higher he would have been handsome, to the extent that redheads ever are.

"You speak English?" he repeated.

For some reason the deep green of his eyes and his oafish smile disarmed me; I found myself smiling back at him, despite my annoyance; propped myself up on an elbow. "I *am* English."

"Well that's great!" He beamed; extended a hand to help me up. "You are Mr. Carter, aren't you?"

I brushed the Valley dust off my clothes. "Yes, I am. And you . . . ?"

"I sure am glad to find you. I must have looked in a dozen tombs."

"I'm happy to be of service to you, Mr. . . . ?"

"They tell me you're the best guide in Luxor."

I stopped smiling. "They are correct. Mr. . . . ?"

"Even M. Maspero, down in Cairo. He twisted that funny little froggy mustache of his and put his arm around me and said, 'Eef you are een need of a guide, or of advice on antiquities, while you are een Luke-sore, you could do no bettair than to luke up M'syoo 'Oward Cartaire.'"

I found myself smiling again. Whatever else this nameless American was, he was a gifted mimic. His impersonation of *Monsieur le Directeur* was perfect. "That was quite generous of my old friend. And how exactly can I assist you, Mr. . . . ?"

He grinned again. I was beginning to wonder about his sanity. "I need both."

"Both?"

"Guiding and advice." He showed his teeth.

And I showed mine back. Dollars, good, sound, American dollars. "My fees are expensive, Mr. . . . ?"

"I can afford you."

This was ridiculous; it was time to be blunt. "Among the ancient Egyptians," I told him in mock-serious tones; put my arm around him, like Maspero, "if a man's name was not known, it was the same as if he did not exist."

He looked astonished. "Yes, I've read enough to—" Then it dawned on him. "Oh. Oh, I see. I'm awfully sorry.

Rude of me. I'm Henry Larrimer. Of the Pittsburgh Larrimers.''

He said this in tones suggesting it should mean something to me, which of course it did not. "And exactly what can I do for you, Mr. Larrimer?''

He walked around the tomb chamber, inspecting the walls; seemed disappointed they were blank. "Hank.''

"I beg your pardon?''

"Call me Hank.''

I did not want to call him "Hank.'' I do not want to call anyone "Hank.'' "What precisely can I do for you?''

"Well . . .'' He smiled again. "How well do you know the rest of Egypt?''

"Reasonably well, I suppose. Luxor has nearly always been my home here, but I've dug all over. Are you planning a tour of the entire country?''

"I'd need your services for the whole season.''

I said nothing, waited for him to go on.

"Through March, at least.''

I stayed quiet.

"The fee I had in mind was ten thousand dollars. Would that be enough?''

Good God, for ten thousand dollars I would not only show him all of Egypt, I'd let him ride on my shoulders. I did not let my excitement show. "Ten thousand . . .'' I tried to sound speculative. "Plus traveling expenses, plus the usual . . . ah, twenty percent fee on any antiquities I advise you about . . .'' I watched him from the corner of my eye, pretended to be lost in my computations. How far would he let me go?

No further, it turned out. "Surely the consultant's commissions should be part of the fee. I mean, ten thousand . . . I'll certainly pay your traveling expenses, but, I mean, ten thousand dollars . . .'' He had finally stopped smiling. He looked as if he might be having second thoughts about the entire enterprise. "Ten thousand . . ."

"Well . . ." I couldn't let him get away, but I couldn't sound too anxious, either. "As long as we have a clear understanding you're to cover my traveling costs."

He smiled again. "Yes, of course." And we shook hands on it.

"Would you like to start immediately? I can begin showing you the tombs here this afternoon."

He was looking around again. The bare rock walls seemed to fascinate him. He laughed. "I've already looked at half of them."

"The good ones? The really beautiful ones?"

Larrimer shook his head. "No, most of them were like this. I expected wonderful paintings, colors; rare stones beautifully carved . . ."

"This tomb was never completed, never used. There are a number like it in the Valley. Let me show you the finer ones."

"No, not today. As anxious as I am to get started, I don't have any of my equipment with me."

I looked at him blankly. "Equipment."

He grinned. "Cameras, lenses, photographic emulsions of various kinds, flash devices, lights . . . I'm attempting a photographic survey of Egypt."

"All of it? That's a fairly large project."

"Yes." He seemed quite pleased with himself.

"I'm not certain you could do it in just one season. It could easily take three."

For a moment Larrimer was deflated. But he perked up again almost at once. "Fine. Three seasons then, if that's what it takes."

I found myself wondering whether he had bothered to learn anything at all about Egypt before coming here. About the magnitude of his project.

He obviously wanted to say something more; hesitated. "I will also conduct experiments from time to time."

"May I inquire as to their nature?"

He ignored this. "I want to see every tomb in the Valley, or at least all of the ones that were used."

"There are quite a few."

"I know it."

I wondered if he did. "Shall we begin first thing tomorrow morning?"

He ignored this also. "And pyramids. I want to see the pyramids."

I walked to the door of the tomb. "I'm surprised you didn't visit Giza while you were in Cairo. Everyone does. Still—"

"I did; I want to go there again. But you don't understand. I want to see *all* of the pyramids."

"*All* of them?" I could not believe it. "But there are dozens. There are more than seventy."

"I'm quite aware of that. That's why I'll need you for the entire season. And Abu Simbel, and Aswan, and . . ." He was pressing his fingers against a spot on the rear wall of the chamber, running them in small circles. "Egypt." He pressed his hand flat on the wall. "I've dreamed of this all my life, Mr. Carter. I can't quite believe I'm here finally."

He is certainly an odd young man, but then a high percentage of the tourists we see are on the eccentric side. I certainly find it difficult to dislike him. Two or three seasons with some of them would be intolerable at any price. With Larrimer I may actually enjoy it. And there is the money, of course. Bless Maspero's Gallic heart.

"Do you know much about photography, Mr. Carter?" He had finished examining the chamber.

"Some, yes."

"Will you be able to assist me?"

"Certainly." I could not resist asking. "And will you need help with the experiments you mentioned?"

Larrimer glanced around the tomb; looked speculatively down an unfinished corridor. "It's stifling in here. I'm heading back to my hotel. Will you join me for dinner tonight?"

"Yes, certainly. I'll be glad to. The food at the Winter Palace is always excellent."

"Shall we make it eight P.M.?"

"Fine, Mr. Larrimer."

I called at the Winter Palace at precisely eight P.M. The aroma of their famous roast beef filled the lobby. My mouth watered as I approached the desk. Only to be told by the clerk that no Henry Larrimer is registered there. I had him recheck. No; no Henry Larrimer. Just as I was leaving, wondering what sort of joke had been played on me, hungry from the smells in the air, I saw Larrimer rushing up Bahr Street from the south. "Mr. Carter! Mr. Carter!"

I walked out to greet him. "Good evening, sir. I was afraid there had been some kind of mix-up."

"There was." He was out of breath; he had been running. "I forgot to tell you where I'm staying. Damned stupid. I'm sorry. It only just occurred to me that you'd assume I'm stopping here."

In the fading sunlight Larrimer's hair shone like copper. His eyes were as green as the fields around Luxor. The dim light in the tomb this afternoon did not do him justice. Henry Larrimer is quite a striking young man. But then all Americans are supposed to be beautiful.

"You are at one of the smaller hotels?"

"No." He had caught his breath. "M. Maspero recommended a little Egyptian guest house."

This surprised and pleased me. "Which one?"

"It is kept by a widow named Nora Ali."

"Well, then we're neighbors. You're just next door to the inn where I live."

He laughed. "I wish I'd known. Is there a good Egyptian restaurant anywhere near?"

I said good-bye to my roast beef dinner. "Raki's—the one just over there by the river—is the best in town."

"Shall we?"

We were seated too near the musicians for my taste, but the place was crowded. We attracted a good bit of attention; or rather, Larrimer did. People kept glancing at him, at the red of his hair; he seemed unaware of it.

The restaurant delighted him. "Electric Christmas tree lights! Look at them, they're all over the room. Where on earth did they get them?"

"Imported specially from New York City, I gather at considerable expense. But this is now Luxor's leading restaurant."

At Larrimer's insistence I ordered for both of us. "It will be a while. Service is slow, to allow plenty of time for conversation."

"That's fine with me. I like to talk." He told me this as if I might not have noticed. "Tell me about the tomb we were in today."

There was a break in the music. The sound of the electric generator filled the room. I shouted. "Progress. I don't hold out much hope for the twentieth century, Mr. Larrimer."

"Is there some way I can persuade you to call me Hank?"

"While you're referring to me as Mr. Carter?"

He laughed again. "All right. Howard." He said the name as if it had an alien sound to it. "Tell me about the tomb."

"Well, there isn't really a great deal to be said about it. It is designated Number Four. Started for Ramses XII, the last of the Ramseses. It was never finished, never decorated, never used.''

''That's sad. Where did they bury him?''

''That isn't known. The final kings of dynasties tend not to have happy fates. Ramses XII was the last ruler of the Twentieth Dynasty.''

''Yes, I know.'' He must have seen the surprise on my face. ''I've been reading about Egypt since I was a boy. I know more about the pharaohs than I do about the presidents. Finally being here, touching the stones in the Valley . . . it's quite wonderful.''

I was amused at his enthusiasm. ''Do you find even modern Egypt wonderful?''

He looked around the restaurant. ''It's Christmas a month early. How could that not make me happy?''

The waiter brought us a bottle of wine. I tasted it, poured a glass for Larrimer. ''Alexandrian table wine. Easily the worst in the world. Taste it and tell me again how you like Egypt.''

He laughed, sipped his wine, made a sour face. ''It's dreadful.''

We both burst out laughing and I filled our glasses all the way to the top. ''Will the food be as bad?''

''No, there you're in for a real treat.''

Larrimer sipped his wine, looked about the room. ''Modern Egypt,'' he said. ''It's strange. It occurred to me in Cairo, and I feel it again here. There is the old Egypt; the temples, the pyramids. And the medieval Egypt, mosques, bazaars. And then there is the latest, up-to-date Egypt.'' He gestured to a string of lights above our heads. ''And there is nothing in between. Everything that isn't spanking new is hundreds of years old. I can't tell you how weird I find that.''

I drank my wine, listened to the music.

''Which do the Moslems prefer, Mr. Carter? Howard.''

I looked at him. "I'm not certain they see any difference. The Moslem mind is nowhere near as fond of labels and categories as the European mind."

The aroma of smoke came drifting to us. Larrimer's face lit up. "Hashish! I haven't smelled that since I left school."

"You'll find rather a lot of it here, if you keep to the Egyptian establishments. Tourists tend to be shocked."

He laughed. "Not me."

"Where exactly did you go to school?"

"The University of Pittsburgh."

I had forgotten he was a "Pittsburgh Larrimer." "I wouldn't have thought fin-de-siècle decadence had penetrated so far into the American hinterland."

"Pittsburgh isn't exactly the Ozarks."

I smiled at this. "I'd be careful. Egyptian hashish is likely to be more potent than the kind you had in school. Here is our dinner."

The waiter brought the dish I had ordered, a thick, spicy meat stew. Larrimer dug in with zest. "This is delicious. What kind of meat is it?"

"*Gemousa.*"

He stopped eating. "I don't suppose you'd care to translate that."

"Water buffalo. It's a favorite of mine."

He took another mouthful. "I like it, too. Is it hard to come by?"

"Everyone eats it who can afford to."

"It tastes like a strong, succulent beef."

We ate without talking much more. Larrimer ordered a second bottle of wine, drank most of it himself. I also had the impression the smoke was affecting him rather more than it was myself. At any rate he seemed to be savoring the food, the music, the lights, the people more than is common for a newcomer to Egypt. I thought he would want to stay all night. But late in the evening when everyone in the place had eaten, belly dancers appeared. The music became feverish as they danced among the audience. Suddenly Larrimer reached across the table and caught me by the shoulder. "This is too much for me. Let's get out of here."

It was nearly midnight; the streets were empty. The Nile frogs croaked, the river splashed quietly. Larrimer had obviously had too much to drink; kept stumbling, brushing against walls. Laughing softly about something private.

"Mr. Carter. Howard."

"Yes?"

It took him a moment to go on. "I want . . . Do you have any plans for the rest of the night?"

"Only to sleep."

"I want to see the desert. Will you take me there?"

"It is late. If we're going to get an early start in the Valley tomorrow we should both get to bed."

"The train from Cairo ran along the edge of the desert. What I saw of it I found quite beautiful. I'd like to see it at night."

"There will be plenty of opportunity for that."

He stopped walking, turned to face me full on. "Can we talk for a few minutes?"

I wanted to get home and to bed, but there was obviously something on his mind. "Of course, if you like."

He sat down on the steep edge of the riverbank, facing away from the river. "There is something about the sky over the desert. There is something about it."

I waited for him to go on.

"On the train coming down here, I could not stop looking at the sky, the sand. The sky is such a deep blue; transparent; open. Inviting. When we moved away from the desert's edge, into the cultivated land, I became impatient to get back there."

I listened.

"Is that common? Do many people feel that?"

I had no idea what he wanted me to say. "I'm not certain just what it was you were feeling."

He looked up at me. "You will take me there?"

"When I can, certainly."

I helped him to his feet, headed him toward his guest house. When we finally reached the door he took hold of my arm. "Come in for a minute."

"I really don't think I—"

"Please. I bought a mummy today. In the souk. I'd like you to look at it."

"In the souk?"

"The dealer took me through dozens of back streets. To confuse me, I imagine. But the mummy is beautiful."

A single oil lamp burned in his room. Heaps of luggage, camping equipment showed faintly. On the floor just in front of the lamp lay the linen bundle containing the mummy. I knelt, lifted the linen carefully. It was the mummy of a young girl. It was almost identical to the one Ahmed Abd-er-Rasul had sold to Baron Lees-Gottorp. The wrappings over the face were layered to form a delicate rhomboidal pattern.

I was about to tell Larrimer the same thing I had told the baron, that the mummy must be from a very late period. But the coincidence struck me. I took the lamp in my hand, moved it close to the mummy's bandages; found a mark.

"There." Larrimer pointed to it just as the light fell on it. "Am I mistaken, or is that the cartouche of Ramses III?" His fingers touched the hieroglyphs one at a time as he recited the name of the pharaoh: User-maat-Ra-meri-Amen.

Within one month I had found two mummies wrapped in a Ptolemaic style, in bandages dating a thousand years earlier. It seemed impossible. Someone was taking unusual pains to fox the tourists. Someone must have found a cache of them somewhere in the Theban Hills; there are certainly more mummies waiting to be found there. I held the lamp up to Larrimer's face. "Who sold you this?"

"I didn't ask his name."

"Was he an Abd-er-Rasul?"

He was shamefaced. "I don't know."

I described Ahmed. "Was that the man? Was he like that?"

"No. This one was older, average height, a bit plump."

I had been tense, on edge. This might be the start of an important discovery. But there was nothing more to be learned tonight. I rested my back against the wall. "How much did you pay for it?"

"One hundred fifty dollars."

I remembered the baron. "You got a good price."

Henry smiled, pleased with himself. "I know. Can we unwrap it?"

"Now?"

"Why not?"

"Because it's after midnight and we both need our sleep."

"I'm not tired. I like the night."

"Even so. Unwrapping the dead is better done by daylight. If only for the light."

"A lot of my work—a lot of what I'll need your help for—will be done by night."

"Henry, this is Egypt. There are scorpions and cobras."

"Even so. We will be working late at night."

Splendid. This employer-employee relationship is not shaping up at all as I'd expected. I tucked my patron into his bed, came back here to make these notes. Now to sleep.

Just before dawn this morning I woke to find Henry Larrimer of the Pittsburgh Larrimers standing over my bed. I had expected him to sleep late and waken with a hangover, but he looked as fresh and rosy as if he'd rested for days. The darker side of him, which the drink and the smoke last night had brought near the surface, was completely submerged again. He grinned at me like the little boy I suspect him to be. "Good morning, Howard."

I rolled over, tried to ignore him and sleep.

"It's time for that early start you promised me."

"Rot." I muttered it to my pillow.

He sat on the edge of my bed, tapped my shoulder. "We have work to do."

I rolled over again, to look at him. "Why aren't you asleep?"

"Get up, Howard. I'm anxious to start."

"I'm not dressed."

"I'm not shy. Get up."

I sat up in the bed, leaned against the wall, sighed. "All right." Yawned. "Excuse me. We'll be working in the Valley today?"

"For a few hours at least. I'd like to get an idea of its general layout. Where the interesting tombs are, what I can safely ignore . . ."

I yawned again. "Fine."

"And I'd like to get that mummy unwrapped today."

"Fine. How much of your equipment will go to the Valley with us today?"

"Just a notebook for starts."

I sent him off to the ferry landing to arrange our crossing and to book two donkeys on the other side. By the time he got back I was washed and dressed.

There was a fairly brisk north wind; the Nile was choppy. The crossing to the West Bank, which normally takes ten minutes or so, took nearly twenty-five this morning. The ferryman had trouble holding his boat on course. Henry seemed to be enjoying it all.

We mounted our donkeys, set off for the Theban Hills. We took the usual route; Henry must have come the same way yesterday when he came to find me, but he smiled, watched everything as if it were brand new to him. And he talked; he obviously did know Egypt, ancient Egypt at least. Pointed out the distant ruins of the Ramesseum and Medinet Habu, "from all the descriptions I've read. I'd like to visit them one morning." When the Colossi of Memnon loomed up before us he was especially impressed. "It's such a pity they repaired the Northern Colossus." He stared up at it with genuine awe in his face. "Its singing must have been a wonderful thing."

The hills drew nearer. He asked more and more questions. "How do we reach the Valley of the Queens?" "How far are the Tombs of the Nobles?" "Whereabouts is Hatshepsut's temple?"

We went first to the tomb of Seti I; after the bare rock of yesterday, Larrimer was suitably impressed. I don't think he was prepared for the imposing size of the tomb; once we had left the daylight far enough behind, our lamps did not cast enough light to reach the sides of the hall. The darkness seemed to put him on edge. He moved next to the wall, where his lamp made a reassuring circle of light; I went to the opposite wall and we moved forward together. The air in the tomb is quite still; our footsteps, even our breathing, echoed around us. A sedate procession of figures in the *Litany of the Sun God* cover the left wall of the long entry corridor; sad, stately pages from the *Book of That Which Is in the Underworld*, row upon row of them, fill the right-hand wall. Walking among these figures, in a small circle of light surrounded by Stygian darkness, watching the line of gods and monsters move into view, shine, then fade again into the blackness, an eerie sense of timelessness envelops one. And Larrimer was affected the same way as everyone else who sees them. For the first time since I'd met him Larrimer was silent.

In Chamber X of the tomb is the famous ceiling that bears the figures of the constellations as the ancients knew them.

Larrimer finally broke his silence. "The sky, Howard. Remember what I said about the sky over the desert." He brightened his lamp, to cast more light on the stars above. "They felt it, too. Seti must have wanted that emotion to be with him through eternity."

I was doubtful; there were perfectly sound religious reasons for every relief in the tomb. "Not too bright," I called out. "The smoke from the lamp will damage the reliefs." My shout reverberated through the chamber.

He lowered the flame again; the constellations flickered dimly above us. "You know how they pictured the sky."

"Yes. Of course."

He told me anyway. "A slender, beautiful goddess, her body arched over the earth below. As if she were protecting it, sheltering it from the outer chaos, from the void. Only a desert race could have conceived of the sky in those terms."

"Are you sure you know the desert well enough to know that?"

He had been staring at the stars on the ceiling; turned abruptly to look at me as if I'd just asked the rudest question in the world. "Seti's body didn't rest here for long, did it?"

Something in the atmosphere of the tombs makes one whisper. "No. It was moved for safekeeping by the priests. It was found, twenty-two years ago, among a huge cache of royal mummies in a cave in the hills above Deir-el-Bahri. There were dozens of them, some of the greatest men of the ancient world, dumped there unceremoniously together. They were finally unearthed by a family of local tomb robbers, the Abd-er-Rasuls."

Henry had gone back to examining the reliefs. He had found a depiction of the sky goddess in one of the registers of gods; stared at her fixedly. "Yes, I remember reading about that once. I was young, ten or twelve. The idea of all those mummies, together in that black cave, gave me quite a chill. Can we visit there?"

How did I know he would ask? "It isn't easy to reach."

"Even so."

"It's your time and money. If that's where you want to go . . ."

"Yes, I want to go there." His finger traced the goddess's outline; then he looked over his shoulder at me. "I think it might be quite suitable for my purpose."

I knew he would refuse to answer, but I had to ask. "And what exactly is your purpose, Henry?"

He turned to face me; lowered his lamp away from his face. His eyes caught its light and glinted in the darkness. "In time, Howard. There will be plenty of time." For whatever reason, he sounded very sad. "Will you do something for me?"

I think I was slightly afraid of his mood. "Yes, of course. What do you want?"

"Leave me alone here for a while."

I suddenly felt cautious. I am beginning to think Larrimer must be a secret mystic. What might he want to do alone in an ancient tomb? "I'm not sure that would be wise. You don't know the way out."

"It's all in a straight line, Howard. How could I get lost?"

"There are bends in the corridor. And steps. And side chambers. You could easily—"

"Please. I'll be all right."

It was against my better judgment but there was not much I could do. "All right. But don't be long. And don't go any farther into the tomb. There is a deep shaft just beyond here. You could break your neck."

But I decided not to leave him completely. I waited at the top of the staircase between the fifth and seventh chambers; the corridor canters here, it would be easy for him to get lost. When I left him he was staring spellbound at the goddess of truth. I walked down the corridor to the head of the stairs, making as little noise as I could; lowered the flame of my lamp; sat down with my back against the wall. The stone walls reflected, magnified the sound of my breathing. Other than that, all was silence. Then I heard it. Very soft, almost imperceptible. The sound of his voice. Larrimer was talking to himself, alone in the tomb. There was a rhythm, a cadence, as if he were reciting or chanting. The low, soft drone continued for a moment or two; stopped. I heard his footsteps moving slowly toward me; stood up, brightened my lamp. His own lamp had gone out, or he had blown it out. He appeared up out of the blackness, stared at me. "Howard. Are you all right? I thought you'd be waiting outside. I forgot to bring matches."

"It's a good thing I waited here. Without light you'd never have found your way out."

The sunlight in the Valley is blinding when one emerges from one of the tombs. We took a few minutes to let our eyes adjust. Larrimer was his usual chipper self. "Where now?"

We spent the morning visiting tomb after tomb. The Amenhoteps, Thutmose III, Ramses VI, and on and on. Larrimer's energy seemed inexhaustible. He did not ask again to be left alone in any of them. But each time, when we had penetrated as far into the tomb as we could, that same mood came over him. Tense, silent, as if he were watching and listening for something.

Just after noon we decided to break for a siesta; made for my favorite unfinished tomb. "We'll be revisiting all of these tombs once you bring all your equipment over?"

"Most of them, yes. I'll want pictures of all the decorated ones for the survey. Possibly some of the others, too."

I decided to settle the mystery, or try to, before we went to sleep. "Tell me about your survey. Has a publisher commissioned it?"

"Not exactly, no." He yawned; the vigorous morning had

gotten to him after all. "Several of them have expressed interest in it, though. Good travel books always sell. With superior photographs—I'm a very good photographer. If no one else wants to publish it, I can do it myself. I'm sure it'd be profitable."

It was time to confront the issue. "Tombs and monuments and reliefs aren't all you want to photograph, are they Henry?"

He had been lying on his back, staring at the ceiling; propped himself up on an elbow. Smiled. "What on earth do you mean?"

I stared straight at him. "I've never heard an Egyptian ghost story from anyone reliable. The spirits that have supposedly been seen in the pyramids and so on—that's stuff for the tourists. It gives them an added thrill." He avoided my gaze. "For which they're willing to pay."

"Then shouldn't you be humoring me?" He laughed at me.

It was exasperating. "Tell me what you expect to find."

"Expect? Nothing."

"Hope, then."

"Really, Howard, I'm open to whatever happens. Either way, the sales of the picture book will more than repay me."

I slept for over three hours. When I awoke, Larrimer was up and about.

"Have some salt pork, Howard."

I ate. "Don't you ever sleep?"

"Not if I can help it. What are we going to see now?"

"I am entirely at your disposal."

"Something small, then. The graves here are too large, too . . . I could never cover them the way I want to."

"The tombs in the Valley of the Queens are smaller." I drank some water. "Would you like to go there? It's a bit of a hike."

And so we visited the tombs of the queens. And Larrimer found what he wanted almost at once.

"Whose tomb is this?"

"It belonged to a son of Ramses III, Amen-her-khopshef. According to the inscriptions he died when he was thirteen."

The tomb is quite simple. An entry chamber and a low corridor leading back to the small room where the coffin rests. There are two small side chambers, empty and undecorated.

"Is the prince still in his sarcophagus?"

"He has not been that fortunate, no."

Henry examined the painted reliefs on the walls, a series of portraits of the dead boy consorting with various gods. "These are quite wonderful. They're not quite like any others I've seen."

"You're right. This is the only tomb in Egypt whose paintings were done in pastels."

He studied them one at a time. Traced symbols and figures with his fingertip. Walked back into the burial chamber and pressed his hands against the cool granite of the sarcophagus. For once he seemed excited, not depressed. "Yes, this is what I want. Can we spend the night here?"

"If you like, yes."

"Good. Let's go back to Luxor now, to get dinner and bring my things back here."

We walked out of the tomb; were blinded by the sun. Henry scanned the landscape as he waited for his eyes to adjust; shaded them with his hand. "Howard, look up there."

On the hillside, a hundred yards or so above the entrance to the tomb, was a small pack of jackals. They were standing guard over the body of one of their own; glared down at us. "They'll probably bury its body and wait a few days until it begins to putrify. Then they'll eat it."

Henry could not take his eyes off of them. "The Sons of Anubis." He tried to make it sound as if he were joking, but I have my doubts. "Will they bother us? I mean tonight, when we come back."

"Not if we don't bother them first."

"They look threatening, even hostile." He turned to look at me. "Are you sure we'll be all right?"

"Believe me, Henry, they want nothing more than to be left alone. They can be vicious if they're provoked, but otherwise they keep to themselves. They're scavengers, not predators."

"Sons of Anubis." He laughed and we headed back to town.

He insisted on dinner at Raki's again; we had lamb stew. Again our table was too close to the music. Larrimer disappeared mysteriously several times during the meal. While he was at the table he ate like a wolf. There was not much conversation.

"Go down to the river. Get us a ferry and some donkeys."

"The donkeys may be a problem this late in the day. Henry, are you certain you want to—"

"I thought we'd settled that."

It was dark by eight. The sky was especially black. He met me at the pier, attended by two boys with his gear.

"It's a good thing you got here now," I told him. "Khmim here wouldn't have waited much longer."

Larrimer gave the boatman a generous tip, "for all your trouble." This was lost on Khmim, who speaks no English. But he was pleased at the large baksheesh. I did not bother to translate.

On the West Bank there was trouble. "Khorassi, the donkey man, won't let us have the animals overnight unless he comes with us. He thinks you want to steal them."

"That's ridiculous."

"Nevertheless."

Larrimer looked cross. His little enterprise was not beginning quite the way he'd imagined. "Well, he can help us with the equipment, then."

"I'm afraid you don't understand." I must confess a certain dark delight in deflating his expectations. "He is not a manual laborer. He is the manager of a business. He expects you to pay him for his time and to rent an additional donkey for him to ride."

"What! That's outrageous!"

"Shall I tell Khmim to hold the boat? We can still cross back to Luxor."

He pouted. "Shit. Tell him I'll pay. But only if he'll help us carry the cameras and things. Shit."

I discussed this with Khorassi, and he agreed. He and I both knew he had no intention of helping; he smiled throughout our conversation at the naïveté of the young American. But he wanted his money. I looked deadpan at Larrimer. "He says he'll help, but he wants his money in advance."

Larrimer shot him a venomous look, then walked over and pressed a note into his hand. "That had better be enough." He stumbled over a rock in the darkness. "Shit. Let's get started. Let's get the lamps lit."

Larrimer and I lifted the packs out of the ferry, strapped them onto the donkeys. He seemed not to notice—perhaps he simply chose not to notice—that Khorassi stood apart, watching us, chatting with Khmim. They exchanged a few wry comments in Arabic and Khmim pushed off. Not much later we headed off ourselves, for the Valley of the Queens.

The moon is nearly new tonight; it will not come up till just before sunrise. The sky was a deep transparent black and the stars were brilliant. Saturn and Mars hung above the eastern horizon. I was terrified Larrimer would start on about the sky again, but he rode in silence. Khorassi, on the other hand, was quite animated as he told me a long, rambling story in Arabic about the way his mother-in-law had tried to poison him when he visited her in Qus. "All women are like that. You can never trust them. I never let my wife cook for me anymore."

The Valley was uncannily silent but still very hot from the day's sun. I kept hoping the jackals in the hills would start howling; this would certainly unnerve my client. But the jackals were off somewhere else or were, for whatever reason, being quiet. Once we were inside the Valley Larrimer came to life. "Well, here we are. Let's get unloaded."

"Amen-her-khopshef is a way along yet. This is his brother's tomb, Kha-em-weset."

"Oh. I thought this was it."

We were there in another five minutes. Khorassi stood back watching us unpack, graciously held a lantern up so we could see. This time Larrimer noticed his inactivity. "Tell him to get to work."

"As soon as the rocks start dancing."

"Tell him."

I told him. He smiled first at me, then at Larrimer, as if we were both simple-minded. Mouthed a few words; smiled again.

"He says he cannot do any more work tonight. He is weak. It seems his mother-in-law, from Qus, tried to poison him. It was last spring, and—"

"All right. All right. Shit."

We placed two lighted lanterns in the tomb, then moved in Larrimer's cameras, plates, flashes, filters. There was also a small crate full of various scientific devices. A galvanometer, a magnetometer, a radiometer, an Edison recording apparatus. He seemed to be missing no chance to detect the presence of whatever it was he was trying to detect the presence of. It took nearly an hour to get everything into the tomb, uncrate and arrange it to his satisfaction. "There. Now I can begin."

"Good. How would you like me to assist you?"

He looked around at everything one more time, rubbed his hands together. "For the moment I'd prefer to work alone. You and the Egyptian can wait outside. I'll call if I need you."

And so we waited outside. Made ourselves comfortable on the hillside. Talked. Khorassi's mother-in-law. Khorassi's wife. His life, he told me in exaggerated terms, had been a hard one. Everyone hated him. My contribution to the conversation was a string of monosyllables. "Yes?" "No!" "Is that so?" He offered me hashish, which I refused. Filled his pipe, smoked, continued talking. I stopped listening; knew that in a few minutes he would retreat quietly, happily into himself. He kept talking, in low whining tones, about his unfortunate life. His voice was the only sound in the Valley.

From time to time a blare of light would show at the mouth of the tomb as Larrimer took flash photographs. After a while this stopped and only the lamplight shone in the tomb. Then, for whatever reason, the lamps went out, too. I assumed Larrimer would not want me to intrude on his researches; decided to wait for his call. The stars above the Valley were dazzling. The Milky Way arched high in the sky; I could trace it through Cassiopeia, Perseus, Taurus . . . A bright meteor crossed through the center of Cepheus; it seemed especially brilliant to me. Khorassi droned on and on and I became caught up in his dream, the stars, the night, the stillness . . .

When I awoke Sirius had risen above the eastern hills. I must have slept for two hours or more. I looked around.

Khorassi had gone and taken the donkeys with him. There was no light coming from the tomb of Amen-her-khopshef. The jackals had returned; were howling. I thought I should look in on Larrimer.

As I approached the tomb I thought I could hear voices coming from it; quickened my pace. My first thought was that Henry must have encountered some tomb robbers. The hills here, like the ones at the Valley of the Kings, are riddled with tunnels they have dug from tomb to tomb, secretly, impossible to detect unless one knows where to look. And the thieves regard these graves as their own special territory. If some of them came upon Henry trespassing in their little world . . . I rushed on to see what was happening.

The voices in the tomb resolved themselves into one voice, the voice of Henry Larrimer. Chanting, intoning as he had done in Seti's tomb earlier in the day. There was some sort of mist or smoke effusing from the tomb. When I reached the door I recognized the aroma: hashish. He must have bought it at the restaurant. Henry's chanting was louder now. He was reciting a verse from the *Book of That Which Is in the Underworld,* from the opening-of-the-mouth ceremony, the one meant to bring life back to a mummy. His ancient Egyptian was spoken with a thick American accent. If there were any gods to hear him, they must have been quite puzzled.

I went softly in. There was a dim light burning in the tomb, too dim to be seen from outside. By its faint light, through the thick hashish smoke, I began to discern what was happening. From the doorway I could just make it out.

Henry was on his knees at the entrance to the burial chamber. He faced the sarcophagus; his back was to the tomb's entrance. The hashish burned in a large pot at his side. He was chanting. That same verse, over and over again. He raised his hands to heaven, then bowed down flat.

Wrapped around him was a leopard skin, the garment of a *sem*-priest. I sidled closer, keeping to the wall of the tomb, hoping he would not see or hear me. I had to learn what he was up to. I had told him there was no mummy in the sarcophagus. What could he possibly hope to accomplish with a spell for reanimation?

It was not until I had stolen within three yards of him that I saw it, on the floor just in front of him. The corpse of a jackal. While I was asleep he must have crept out of the tomb and up the hill to get the dead jackal we saw there today. Its limbs were stiff with death; its mouth was locked open, its teeth bared; its eyes stared blindly into Henry's lamp; its fur was matted, presumably with the saliva of its pack-mates, who had claimed its flesh for their own. Outside, far up the hill, they were still howling; they sounded angry at the theft of their brother, of their meal.

"Henry." I whispered; did not want to alarm him; was afraid of the mental state that had gotten him to this absurd impasse. He ignored me, or was too caught up in his chant. Or in his hashish. "Henry." He hesitated for a moment, then began again, a different chant from the same series of spells.

The smoke was thickening; my eyes began to water. I felt a cough coming on. Lost patience with Larrimer's nonsense. Called his name loudly. "Henry!" Again he hesitated; then turned his head slowly to look at me. There was on his lips what I can only describe as a sinful smile. He said nothing, stared at me blankly for a moment, then turned back to the dead animal on the floor in front of him.

I moved still closer. I had to pull him away from this lunacy. Moved to a place just a yard or so behind his shoulder. The dead jackal's eyes began to glow; they glared at me. I was terrified for a moment, until I realized they must be catching the lamplight. I sighed in relief. But they seemed to glow so fiercely. I had trouble looking away from them. "Henry." He kept on with his chant. And then I heard a growl.

I cannot believe that I saw it. It must have been a trick of the light; the lamp must have flickered. Very slightly, the forepaw of the jackal began to twitch. It twitched again and again, feebly, like the paw of a sick puppy. I cannot have seen it. Its eyes glowed, its paw moved, and a trickle of saliva appeared on its lips. It must have been the light. It must have been.

"Henry, what are you doing? Come on outside where the air is breathable."

He ignored me, began a prayer invoking the Sons of Anubis, the guardians of the dead. "Henry." I took another step toward him, put my hand on his shoulder. "Henry, this is lunatic. Come outside with me." I took a firm grip on his shoulder and shook him. "Henry!"

The jackal snarled at me. Low down in its throat, and without moving at all, it snarled at me. I don't like to admit it, but I was frightened. "Henry!"

Suddenly there came a much louder growl, from behind me. I turned back to the tomb entrance. Standing there was a live jackal, the largest I've ever seen. It bared its teeth and growled. Its eyes were glowing like fire. It seems impossible, but even at the far end of the tomb its eyes caught the light from Henry's lamp, and they burned with it. It blocked the way out, and then two more jackals came in behind it, and then more. The smoke was so dense I could not even see them all, but there must have been half a dozen or more, and all of their eyes were afire. They must have followed the scent down the hill and into the tomb. They wanted the corpse, they were angry.

I moved back away from them. "Henry. For God's sake come to your senses." I shook him again, slapped his cheek.

And he came out of it. Stared at me, then down at the jackal, then at me again. "Howard. Don't interrupt me. It's starting to move."

"Turn around slowly and look behind you. The jackals you robbed want their dinner back."

"But I—" He turned around and looked. "Oh my God. The Sons of Anubis. They are here."

"Nonsense. They are only jackals."

"Look at their eyes, Howard. The light in their eyes."

The jackal on the floor snarled again. Henry glanced down at it in surprise, in alarm. "Howard. Good Christ—"

But before he could say anything the jackals attacked. The leader, the first and largest of them, leapt at me, went for my throat. I only just jumped aside in time. The others rushed after it, came for us.

In the sudden furor I could not see what happened to Henry, though I could hear his screams. I groped around me, found a heavy photographic tripod, still folded and leaning against the wall; took it up as a weapon. Swung it again and again, shattered the skull of one animal after another. At one point Henry and I bumped into each other, back to back; I nearly struck him but recognized him in time. Somehow in the struggle the pot of hashish got overturned, burned quickly and filled the tomb with dense smoke. Still, through it I could see the burning eyes of the jackals; the eyes told me where to strike. The tomb was filled with their growls, cries, whimpers. Then gradually it ended; silence; they were gone.

"Henry. Where are you? Are you all right?"

"I don't know. I think so." He answered me from the far end of the tomb.

"Let me get you outside, where the air is breathable."

We groped our way to each other, left the tomb. Lay down on the hillside. My eyes were still watering from the smoke. Henry's clothes were bloody; he had been bitten. I realized that I was still gripping the tripod; let it fall. "Rest a moment, then I'll dress your wounds. We need to calm down, get our breath." But Henry was already unconscious. Too much fear, too much hashish.

I am too aroused to sleep. Suppose they come back. My vision is clearing slowly; I can see the stars now.

From time to time he cries out. "The Sons of Anubis."

Just before dawn Larrimer awoke for a short while. Looked around groggily. "Howard. Where are we?"

I told him.

"I had a nightmare."

"Jackals attacking?"

"Yes. I . . ." He yawned.

"It was no dream. Go and look in the tomb." I pointed to it with a thumb over my shoulder.

He clambered to his feet, walked unsteadily to the door. The sky was just light enough for him to see inside. "My cameras. My equipment. Are they all shattered?"

"I haven't taken inventory."

He walked back over to me, sat heavily down.

"I told you to leave those jackals alone, Henry."

"But I . . ." He rubbed his eyes, yawned. "Howard! My spell worked!"

"Rubbish."

"That jackal growled, moved. I remember."

"There were growls all right. But from the dead jackal or its living relatives?"

"It was alive, Howard. I saw its eyes."

"You saw them catch the light from the lamp."

He fell silent, pouted; then yawned again. "The others— their eyes glowed, too. I saw them."

"All night animals have reflective eyes, Henry. Cats, bats, jackals . . ."

"I tell you, something supernatural happened here to-night. The Sons of Anubis—"

"Henry. Everything can be explained plainly."

"The dead jackal moved."

"No, the lamp flickered. Or else it wasn't really quite dead."

He sighed, exasperated at my obtuseness.

"Henry, you are letting it run away with you. Interpreting what you saw to make it fit what you want to believe."

"Yes, Howard. Or you are."

It is maddening.

He grinned at me. "I need more sleep."

"Not now. We have to get back to town. There are things I have to do."

He stood up again, walked back to the the tomb door, stepped inside. "Howard." He came out again almost at once. "There are no jackals in here. No sign of them. Only what's left of my equipment."

I went and looked. There were none of them there. "They weren't really dead, then, only hurt."

He smiled a smug smile.

I looked. Lit a lamp and walked all through the tomb. Outside I scanned the hills and they are not there.

Larrimer, not to my surprise, has slept all day. It was with considerable difficulty that I got him the five miles down to the Nile, across the river, and into bed at his guest house. Considerable difficulty. I keep thinking about my ten thousand dollars.

I slept, but only for a few hours. Dreams; nightmares. "The Sons of Anubis." Woke feeling restless. I have a headache. Toyed with the idea of crossing back over to the Valley of the Queens and starting to clean out the tomb. But no, I think I'll leave Larrimer to do that on his own. Later I'll have to inspect the tomb myself; make certain it wasn't damaged. Henry could end up in prison. But that can wait until he's cleaned out the rubbish.

My problem at the moment is that there are too many things preoccupying me. The horror in the tomb last night. And the tomb itself, and the damage to it. And that mummy of Henry's was stuck in the back of my mind.

I wanted to unwrap it. I had not seen Baron Lees-Gottorp's; the curiosity was too much for me. I dressed; had a light, late breakfast in the souk; headed for his room. His landlady, Nora Ali, is an old friend of mine. Her sons have worked on digs for me. And her cooking is famous; the things she does with *gemousa* . . .

"Good morning, Nora. Is my client up yet?"

"No. He sleeps as soundly as a hippo. And as noisily. He has been crying out in his sleep. Things about Anubis. My other roomers are complaining."

I lowered my voice. "He has been introduced to Egyptian hashish."

"Ah." She tried to look disapproving; failed. "You should take better care of your employer, Carter Pasha."

"I will. This one needs watching."

Larrimer had stripped himself. He lay face down on the bed, with his left arm wrapped over his head at an awkward angle. I hoped it would give him a stiff neck. He fidgeted in his sleep, muttered something into the pillow. "The Sons of Anubis." His body was covered with sweat.

The mummy had been stored under his bed. As I slid it carefully out Larrimer shifted his position; his arm fell off the bed and struck it, hard. Part of its chest collapsed. I pulled it quickly away from him.

The mummy had been wrapped with remarkable care. Each finger and toe was wrapped in its own strip of linen. The edges of the bandages were folded neatly under so they would not fray. I began unwrapping with the left hand. First the small finger, gently, carefully; then one by one the others. The skin was dark, dry like leather. The embalmers had done a good job; some mummies had been covered with unguents that actually advanced the flesh's deterioration. This one, so far at least, was perfect. There were no amulets or rings inside the bandages, but I had not expected to find any. I undid the wrappings of the wrist, the arm. No bracelets or amulets. If whoever had found the mummy had stripped and rewrapped it, he had done so with exquisite attention.

Larrimer kicked in his sleep, muttered something about his mother. I went on with the unwrapping.

The right hand and arm. The feet and the legs. The chest and abdomen, which Larrimer had crushed, had to be exposed with special care. If there were amulets anywhere on the body, they would be here; *djed*-columns, sacred eyes, scarabs; all but the very poorest Egyptians were buried with them. I lifted the jumbled layers of linen carefully away, one by one. They were in a complete tangle; the work was delicate, painstaking. The ancient cloth was fragile, partly decayed; pull it too hard, twist it the wrong way, and it would crumble to dust in my fingers. Larrimer started snoring; the sound put me on edge. After a while my hand began to tremble. I thought briefly of Brigit; this was a human body, I was desecrating it, I felt a ghoul. I put this out of my mind. There was a job to do. In the cloth around her chest I found an amulet; a faience falcon. Only that, but it was something.

Finally the entire body was exposed except for the head. It had been an adolescent girl, I would guess around fifteen years old. She had been slender but her breasts had been full. They were desiccated now. The mummification had coarsened her body hair; it was like wire. What would she feel, I wondered, to know that one day she would lie before me like this, exposed like carrion under the sun. It suddenly occurred to me that the baron had found a falcon on his mummy too. That was strange but I was too preoccupied to think about it. I turned my attention to the wrappings on the mummy's head.

For a long few moments I studied them, studied the pattern and the layering so that I could rewrap it when the time came. Then slowly I began to unroll the bandages.

The body of the girl I unwrapped is the body of a girl at rest. Arms folded, legs straight, head reclined like the head of every other mummy. The muscles were tense, and the years had made them hard, rigid; but that is not unusual. But her face . . . This girl died horrified.

I unwound the bandages from the neck upwards. The muscles in her throat were taut. Her lower lip curled down, her mouth was open as if screaming; her tongue protruded, pointed senselessly to one side. Her empty eye sockets were opened wide. I think she must have seen whatever was going to cause her death. Her resemblance to the "unmummified mummy" in Cairo was too much for me. My stomach went numb; I felt as if I'd been punched there, as if I'd have to vomit. Left the room, the building, to get fresh air. Sat by the Nile for a while, trying to relax. To see a thing like that in a museum is unpleasant enough. To touch it, to have it emerge under one's own fingers . . .

Finally I recovered myself, went back in. Nora had seen me rushing out; she expressed concern. "It's nothing, really. Everything's fine."

Larrimer, to my annoyance, was still sleeping, still snoring. I poked him in the ribs. "Henry, get up. There's a lot to do. You have a tomb to clean out."

He yawned, rolled over. I poked him again. "Henry."

The mummy wrappings were in a neat pile in the corner opposite him. He sat up on the edge of the bed and stared straight down into the mummy's face. "Good God, Howard, what can have happened to her?"

"I wish I knew. I wish there were some way I could know." I showed him the Horus-falcon I had found on her. "I'm afraid that's all there was. I'll begin rewrapping her."

He stood up silently; he was still naked. "No, wait. I want to see her." He got down on his hands and knees beside her. Leaned down and inspected her carefully, head to foot. "What happened to her chest?"

I explained. He looked abashed.

"Let me rewrap her now."

"No, please. I want to study her."

"For God's sake, Henry. What can you want to see?"

He turned and looked at me; said nothing. Looked back. "How fragile is she? Can I touch her?"

"Henry."

He placed his index finger delicately on her temple. A few of her hairs fell out. Poked the tip of his finger tentatively into her pubic hair. He pulled back; seemed to find the coarseness unpleasant. "Rewrap her. I can help."

"No, Henry. It's my job."

He sat back on his haunches. "I've never seen anything like it. The fear . . ."

I walked over to him, extended a hand to help him up.

"Just a moment." He had turned his gaze to the pile of bandages; picked one up, examined it. "Didn't you say these were from the time of Ramses III?"

"Yes. You saw the cartouche yourself."

"Well there is a different one here. I don't recognize it."

I took the bandage from him, inspected it closely. The marking was faded, difficult to decipher; but it was definitely not Ramses III. I took it over to the window, for the light. And could just make out the hieroglyphs. "Sekhem-kheper-Ra setep-n-Ra."

Larrimer looked at me, puzzled. "Who is it?"

"Osorkon I."

"Osorkon? But, Howard, wasn't he two dynasties later than Ramses? How could a mummy's wrapping carry both their marks?"

I reread the cartouche. Osorkon. Baron Lees-Gottorp's mummy had had wrappings from the reign of Osorkon. I looked at Larrimer, then again at the mummy's face. "I don't know. It isn't possible. Something is very wrong."

"Carter Pasha."

"Mahomet, my old friend."

The leader of the Abd-er-Rasul family shook my hand energetically, a certain sign he was not pleased to see me. Mahomet is in his eighties, tall, statuesque. His bearing is quite aristocratic, his manners completely polished. His movements are graceful; I think he must plan each one of them so as to appear as relaxed, as feline as possible. Only the slight paunch that shows through his galabea detracts from the picture. The illusion he projects would be perfect, one would be awed or at least impressed, if one did not know that he is a lifelong despoiler of the dead.

I had left Larrimer in the Valley of the Queens, cleaning out the tomb of Amen-her-khopshef and complaining loudly. "Why should I have to do this myself?"

I was wry. "Because you brought the jackals in yourself. This is your ruin."

"Couldn't I hire some boys to do the cleanup work?"

"How much do you value what is left of your equipment?"

"Oh." He became sullen. "Well, what am I paying *you* for?"

"To guide and advise you, presumably. Certainly not to clean up after you."

He looked exasperated; I think all Americans must be spoiled. When I left the Valley he was hurling things out the door of the tomb, not seeming to care where they landed or in what condition. I had not told him I intended paying a visit to a family of tomb robbers; he would quite certainly have wanted to come, and I quite certainly didn't want him along. To get information from Mahomet Abd-er-Rasul is difficult under the best of circumstances. With Henry Larrimer along, interrupting at the wrong moment, saying the wrong thing, asking the pointless question . . . it would be hopeless. Mahomet is a champion among Moslems, for whom it is a measure of intelligence deftly to avoid giving straight answers to plain questions.

Mahomet was all unction as he showed me in. "Please, Carter Pasha, treat my home as your own." This is of course the last thing in the world either of us would want. "May I offer you mint tea?"

"Yes, of course. I'm always honored by your hospitality."

He showed me into a cool, dark parlor; the windows were ornately screened, the ceiling was high. The walls were covered with blue flocked wallpaper and there were bright red velvet drapes. Large amounts of gold and silver were on display; these were the Abd-er-Rasuls, after all. Half a dozen oil lamps gave the room a warm glow. I was comfortable at once in this place of perfect luxury, perfect serenity. I have always loved Moslem houses. No one else seems to have found the knack of building for privacy without sacrificing comfort and airiness. And the Abd-er-Rasuls, as the royal family of thieves, have the finest home in Luxor.

We seated ourselves on two overstuffed divans, and Mahomet clapped his hands once loudly. A boy appeared. "Fetch us tea, quickly. The Inspector of Monuments for Upper Egypt is our guest."

I decided to ignore this gentle goading; put on a blank

expression. "The weather has been quite peculiar. The gossip in the souk blames it on sorcery and evil djinni. And even on some nuns."

"*Mektoub,* Carter Pasha, *mektoub.*" Mahomet has always had an inordinate fondness for the cryptic assertion, "It is written."

The boy returned carrying our glasses of tea. Dutifully served first me, then Mahomet. Mahomet put his arm suggestively around the boy's waist. "Allal is a beautiful boy, is he not?"

I sipped my tea, tried to keep my tone neutral. This was an old game between us. "Quite."

"Perhaps I could send him to you. He is an excellent valet." The boy smiled; Mahomet rubbed his head affectionately, then looked at me.

I couldn't help laughing. "This has been going on for so many years. Surely you know there's no point trying to corrupt me now."

"Corrupt?" He played it perfectly sober. "I merely offered . . ."

Very well, it was to be on his terms. "All I mean is that, since I am no longer in the employ of the Antiquities Service, I can no longer afford servants."

"Ah. Yes, of course." He patted Allal on the backside. The boy took his cue, smiled engagingly at each of us in turn, then quietly left the room. Mahomet smiled after him. "A beautiful boy. The son of my late brother Soliman. Flesh is such a corruptible substance."

I examined an ornamental vase next to my divan and wondered whether this was a reference to his brother's demise or to his own passions. "The tea is quite delicious."

"Thank you, Carter Pasha. There are persistent rumors," he said quite gravely, "that you are still secretly in the government's employ."

I sipped my tea, lied with a straight face. "They are true. And what is your own blackest secret?"

He widened his eyes, hushed his tone, looked around as if making certain there were no spies. "I am also."

"Good. Then we can talk freely, as colleagues."

He laughed. "How else have we ever talked? We have always been in the same trade, here in Luxor."

This also was an old game between the two of us. Mahomet maintains that archaeologists are nothing more than grave robbers, like him, like his sons. To protest that we work for science, for man, does not faze him. He smiles serenely as if to suggest that he knows better, that he understands our reluctance to admit the bleak truth.

My glass was empty. I stared at the leaves in its bottom. "There have been some unusual mummies on the market. Two of them were purchased by clients of mine."

"The German and this red-haired American." Mahomet closed his eyes. There is nothing in Luxor and not much in all of Upper Egypt he does not know about. The legal ramifications of his family business make that essential. If anyone had information about the mummies, it would be he. "You think we Abd-er-Rasuls are involved."

"I know that you are." I put my glass down, looked directly at him. "I was with the German when he made his purchase. The dealer called himself Ahmed Abd-er-Rasul."

"He was a liar." This response came too quickly to be quite convincing. Mahomet clapped his hands and instantly the boy Allal appeared with more tea for us. When he had finished serving us, his uncle again put an arm around him. "Carter Pasha wishes information about Ahmed Abd-er-Rasul. Why don't you tell him what he wants to know."

The boy fixed me with his huge eyes, smiled demurely. Then he looked to Mahomet, as if to make certain he should really tell me. Mahomet sipped his tea. Allal lowered his eyes. "I can tell you nothing that you could not learn from my Uncle Mahomet."

Mahomet nodded, beamed at the boy. "Excellent. You may leave us now." He turned to me. "I hope the tea is not too sweet."

"No, it is quite fine." There had been no chance the boy would tell me any family secrets. I left the lead to Mahomet, who would tell me as much as he wanted to, in his own good time. As a general thing, this was never until the third glass of tea.

But this time he surprised me. "We have heard about mummies coming from somewhere in the Delta. Our nephew Ahmed, who lives in Cairo, has seen some of them. They have been unwrapped and rewrapped, but they are in fine condition otherwise."

"Did he notice anything unusual about the bodies?"

"Ahmed is a silversmith, a very skilled one. He made this ring for me." He held up a finger. "He is the son of my brother Ahmed, whom you know."

The elder Ahmed is bedridden. He is the one who found the cache of royal mummies twenty years ago. "Yes, I know him very well. I hope he is in good health . . . ?"

"He is not the man who sold your German his mummy."

"I am quite aware of that." Ahmed the elder is in his seventies. After he made his famous find he was given a job with the Antiquities Service, which he continued dutifully to swindle until his health failed. But he reported faithfully the doings of tomb robbers—other families of tomb robbers, that is. "And yet the dealer said—"

Mahomet had finished his tea; my glass was still nearly full. He clapped for more. The boy brought it and left silently. "You are not drinking."

I took my glass, drank as ordered. "The dealer used your family's name."

"What of that? Is the mummy you examined genuine?"

I described it. "The mummification is excellent, among the best I've seen."

He was silent for a long moment. "You think this is a thing my family would do? Do you not know what the Prophet has written about those who violently snatch away men's souls?"

I had no idea what he was talking about; this could mean any of half a dozen things I could think of. The most obvious of them I found—find—deeply disturbing. I waited for him to go on. But he sat motionless, waiting for me to respond. After a few moments the silence between us became ridiculous. I groped for something to say; could think of nothing.

"Carter, you have penetrated farther into Egypt—the living Egypt, not the ancient one—than any Christian I have known. Do you not understand that?"

I was still off-balance. My disillusionment with Europe, my fascination with the ancients are well known. "Am I a Christian, then?"

"A man's religion is a much broader matter than the mere question of his beliefs." He laughed to show me he was not joking. He finished his tea in a long swallow; and he was nearly finished with me.

But I decided to take the initiative for once. "You really believe that the Moslem mind is essentially different from the Christian mind?"

"Mind, character, call it what you like. Soul, perhaps. Do you believe in the soul, Carter?"

He is the second person in two weeks to ask me that odd question. I ignored it. "The Moslem soul, then, is different in essence from the Christian?"

"Yes." He shifted his weight on the divan, crossed his legs. "The Moslem soul has learned discipline. It has learned acceptance."

"Acceptance." This was not at all the conversation I had come for. I ran a finger idly around the rim of my glass.

"Acceptance of what we see, feel, experience. Acceptance of what is written."

"*Al Islam*," I said to him. "You are talking about the surrender."

"You see, you do understand. The way you accept and embrace the dead, forgotten world, uncritical of its ways and its order, so we embrace the living one. Its sin. Its pain."

"So did the Greeks. So did Confucius. So do the Christians, for that matter."

He had had enough of this; dismissed it. "We have heard that those mummies that so interest you come from the Delta. Perhaps you should go there to see about them."

This abrupt change left me off-balance. I was annoyed with him. "Mahomet, my friend, how very rude of you to change the topic so pointedly."

"Carter Pasha, I have not changed it. Can't you see that?"

It was exasperating. "Then your revelation is not well expounded. The Delta, those mummies—"

"—are precisely to the point. Surely you can see that. They are precisely to the point."

I left Mahomet not long after this, feeling—as I nearly always feel when I deal with him—oddly unsatisfied. We are old friends, Mahomet and I, but our friendship has always been on his terms. I wish I had the knack to annoy him as he always annoys me. And yet . . . Mahomet had been trying in his oblique way to tell me something. He suspects his Cairene nephew to be involved in the traffic of the mummies; that is clear. But why tell me about it? Why not treat it, simply, as a family matter to be privately disposed of? The one really useful piece of information was that the strange mummies are coming from somewhere in the north.

We had talked late into the day. I stopped at Larrimer's guest house to see if he wanted to take dinner; but he had not come back. It was sunset when I ferried across the river, set out for the Valley to find him. I did not much want to go there, really; not again, so soon, not at night. Muezzins chanted from the minarets in Luxor; the calls followed me across the Nile, echoed among the ruined temples there. *Al Islam,* the surrender. Birds flapped wearily back to their nests, the frogs began their song. All day I had not been able to forget the pain in the mummy's face. The Colossi of Memnon loomed up in the owl-light, and I stopped to regard them. Gods of stone, cold and impassive, are the only gods that have ever made sense to me. Metaphysics and disputation are beside the point completely. I know, I know . . . I have read the papyri; I know that the ancients were as prone to metaphysics as any race in the world today. But at least their gods make sense. It is not the figure that matters; it is the stone. God, what a mood Mahomet has left me in. My little rented donkey brayed impatiently; I moved on.

Larrimer was asleep again, inside the tomb. I half expected to find more hashish, but he was simply exhausted. I woke him, brought him out under the sky. After today, after the jackals and the mummy and Mahomet's conversation, I would not have felt right leaving him in the tomb.

The tomb itself seems to have escaped damage. I don't know how. But at least Henry won't be going to jail.

He awoke irritable. "Couldn't you have let me sleep?"

"The air is better out here."

"You sleep in tombs all the time." He rubbed his eyes. "Look at the sky, Howard. I've never seen such a black sky or so many stars."

"The moon is new tonight. Later on there will be meteors, off the shoulder of Orion."

Larrimer fell asleep again almost at once, on the hillside. There is no sign of the jackal pack. I have sat here for hours watching the constellations. The Milky Way is beautiful tonight; it seems almost to shimmer. The meteors came just after midnight, long slow streaks like tears across the sky.

Chapter Three

Cairo is always crowded and seems even more so to me now than it did a month ago. Some of the streets are almost completely impassable. There is no religious festival; I don't know how to account for all the people.

Henry Larrimer is, I think, quite intimidated by it all, but then Cairo is an intimidating city if there ever was one. He has never quite explained why he didn't stay longer in the capital his first time here, why he didn't see all the sights, book his guide here, learn the city. But the look on his face is explanation enough; every time we turn a corner and encounter another mobbed street his face registers something near to panic. Is it simply the crowding, I wonder; or is it the general strangeness; or the fact that they are Moslems . . . ?

The train from Luxor broke down only three times instead of the customary half dozen; pulled into the station here at two A.M. Fortunately the night clerk at Shepheard's is an old friend of mine; we were given a good suite of rooms with a minimum of fuss. My bedroom overlooks the Ezbekiyeh; Larrimer's has a view of the river.

One of the breakdowns—the longest, as it turned out—

was near Beni Hasan. We spent the afternoon inspecting the
rock-cut tombs there. Henry looked into every corner,
pressed his fingers against every wall as if stone were new to
him. His cameras, or what remains of them, were packed
away on the train; he seemed impatient for them. Fortunately we hadn't the time.

I have no doubt he would have chosen one of the tombs
there, spent the night in it, as he tried to do in the Valley of
the Queens. Or to be more precise, despite the Valley. I
have asked him several times, and he refuses to tell me
precisely what he expected to accomplish that night in the
tomb of Amen-her-khopshef. It shook him; he is still
shaken from it. He seems less . . . well, less enthusiastic
than he did before. Still, he clings to the project, to his
photographic survey, and to his "experiments." And still
refuses to discuss them.

It seems so obvious to me that he is after ghosts, after the
world of spirits. He believes they are there, he wants to find
them. I can see it in his eyes every time we enter another
tomb; he wants there to be ghosts. And yet at the same
time—since that night in the Valley—he is quite frightened. I have no doubt that most of what disturbed him
sprang out of hashish, not out of ectoplasm. There are no
spirits in Egypt, only believers in them. Henry is trying to
make this place into something it is not. Egypt has a way of
remaining what it is despite the mystics and the crackpots.
Stone, mortar, paint; temples, statues, tombs. A strange
and beautiful place, but a human one, finally comprehensi-
ble only in human terms. I watch him. At each new tomb he
is filled with both fear and delight. He seems such a boy to
me.

I don't quite know how I feel having a client who fancies
himself a sorcerer; but there is no way I can think of to feel
comfortable about it. Still, there is not much I can do about

it, except try to keep myself from getting caught up in it. I could simply leave him, of course; but I need—want—the money.

My old teacher Flinders Petrie used to tell a story. There was a psychic, a mystic, a diviner of hidden secrets, named Piazzi Smyth. It was his theory that the Great Pyramid of Giza contains in its walls and angles and dimensions the key to all the great moments in human history. Measure from one corner to the nearest crack (using a unit called the "pyramid inch," a neat fabrication) and you get the date of Christ's crucifixion. The height of a stone gives you Napoleon's birthday. From a given chink in the stone to a certain bump tells when the world will end. And on and on. Twaddle.

One night Petrie, who was excavating at Giza, had trouble sleeping. He decided to take a stroll around the Great Pyramid. And there cloaked in the night he found Smyth, armed with a heavy tool kit, chiseling cracks and filing down bumps in the stone to make it conform with his theory. Petrie had a good laugh and told everyone who would listen. And Smyth left Egypt, to spread his faith where it was less susceptible of disproof. The last I heard of him he was lecturing in America.

I used to ask Petrie whether Smyth was an outright fraud. "Or did he believe in his ideas so deeply he couldn't resist gingering up the evidence?"

Petrie had no patience with this sort of question. "What difference does it make?"

It seemed to me to make all the difference in the world. I told him so.

"Rubbish. Smyth is gone now, and the chinks he made have already weathered off the pyramid's face. But the pyramid is still there."

These days my temperament tends toward Petrie's impa-

tience with the mystics. There is too much I do not
understand in the physical world for me to spend much time
worrying about other, hypothetical ones. Yet absurd as it is,
I find Smyth's story rather sad, especially if he really
believed what he preached. I find him on my mind a good
bit lately, because of Henry Larrimer. I like Henry, I
genuinely do. I may even indulge him to the point of calling
him Hank one day. But I don't understand what he thinks
he will find here. I don't even know if he knows himself
what he is looking for. But I find unhappy the thought that
his cameras and galvanometers and what not are merely his
own equivalents of Smyth's chisel and file.

All of which would be fine, if I could only be certain I
won't get caught up in his delusions myself. That night in
the Valley . . . between the drugs and the force of Henry's
personality, I got caught up in it. I could swear I saw the
dead jackal move, saw the fire in its eyes. I know it is not
possible but I could swear it. I can't admit that to Henry, of
course. I keep telling him that he has imagined an encounter
with a pack of jackals into a mystical experience, that he
ought not to get so carried away, and so on. I will not let
him know that I got caught up in his dream, or nightmare.
And I must make certain it doesn't happen again.

Cairo. This morning Henry insisted I take him on a
walking tour of the city. "I want to see everything."

"In one day? This is the largest city in Africa."

"Everything important. The mosques, the Citadel."

"There are hundreds of mosques."

"I know. I heard the muezzins at dawn. Show me the
really beautiful ones." He smiled that smile of his, flashed
his green eyes. "You are my guide, after all."

And so we looked at mosques, one after another of them.
The Blue Mosque, the Mosque of Mohammed Ali. And at

each one Larrimer's enthusiasm was further dampened. Everywhere we received unfriendly looks from the faithful. For a while Henry seemed—or pretended—not to notice; but it finally got to him. "Why do they look at us as if we were thieves?"

"We are infidels. It comes to the same thing in their view. The caliphs used to dress criminals in the clothing of Christians before hanging them."

He admired the Mosque of Kait Bey. "It's beautiful, the most beautiful we've seen. The Bey must have been a wonderful man."

I was matter-of-fact. "He had his court scientist tortured and executed for failing to turn lead into gold."

"Oh."

At the Bab-el-Azab I described in animated terms the slaughter of the Mamelukes. Blood stains can still be seen on the walls there after ninety years. I saved the Mosque of Caliph el-Hakim for the end of our tour. It was unused for centuries; now it is a ramshackle, melancholy lamp factory. "El-Hakim was a tyrant, the worst of them. He founded a sect of fanatical Moslems called the Druze."

"I've never heard of them." He looked around stonily.

"Their devotion to the word of the Prophet is lunatic. El-Hakim had all the dogs in Cairo slaughtered and all the vines cut down. Women were forbidden to leave their houses, even to escape fires. For his own mad reasons he ordered the whole population of the city to work by night and sleep by day. Violators were disemboweled on the spot."

I suppose I overdid this sort of thing a bit; the alarm with which Henry views the Cairenes is at least partly my fault. But Cairo is not a friendly city for an uninitiated Westerner; I'd rather have him frightened than wandering around on his own. Luxor lives on tourists; Cairo tends to ignore them, at

best. At worst . . . And Henry Larrimer of the Pittsburgh
Larrimers is exactly the sort of character apt to be victim-
ized. Wide-eyed, trusting, agog with gullibility. It's
better for me to prey on his naïveté myself and keep him
cautious.

To the extent that I overdid this, it is because I don't much
like Cairo myself. The city's history is red with blood, more
blood than any Western capital I can think of. Then
again—and in this I am probably naive myself—I cannot
think of Cairo as being quite a part of Egypt. It is not part of
my own Egypt, at any rate, not the ancient and wonderful
place. Cairo was built up out of the Nile mud by the Arab
conquerors, who chose to ignore the old capital of Memphis,
only twenty miles away; chose to erect their own. Cairo is not
tempered by age, by longevity like the rest of the country.
The serene contemplation of eternity, a gift of the ancients,
is missing here. It always seems to me such a rash place,
shrill, frenetic. But then I grew up in the countryside; I never
find cities very cordial.

There is a little shop off the Ezbekiyeh run by an ex-priest
from Switzerland who sells the latest in photographic equipment. I had promised Larrimer he would be able to replace
his broken cameras there; first thing this morning I took him
there. And he is now a compleat photographer again.
"Thank heaven," he sighed. "I was afraid we'd have to
abandon the survey."

But to his dismay none of the other apparatus he wants can
be obtained in Cairo. He questioned the proprietor repeatedly; finally accepted the fact that the scientific devices are a
rarity here. "I'll have to order them from the Continent," he
complained to me. "It could take months."

"Yes, Henry." I was all sympathy.

"All that time wasted."

"There is still the photographic survey."

He looked at me glumly.

"Couldn't you make notes during the survey, then revisit the more promising sites next season?"

This brightened him up a bit. I left him busily testing shutters, polishing lenses. It was the opportunity I needed to slip across the square to the Museum. I wanted to talk to Maspero.

He was not in his office; his secretary was uncertain where he'd gone. I made myself comfortable behind his desk, settled in to wait. Examined, for what seemed the hundredth time, the room, the view.

Monsieur le Directeur's office overlooks the most imposing room in the Museum, the hall of colossi. It is dominated by an enormous seated sculpture of Amenhotep III and his queen in rose granite, staring out into eternity with that expression of timelessness the ancient sculptors did so well. (Though I must confess that at times the expression seems not so much timeless to me as simply blank.) The hall is filled with other statues, nearly as impressive; monumental sarcophagi are everywhere; there are half a dozen pyramidions. None of this is well displayed. In fact most of the exhibits in the Egyptian Museum have the appearance of having been dumped unceremoniously where they stand. The building is only two years old but already the interior seems piled with ancient dust. But the things themselves are so beautiful they make up for it all. The hall of colossi in particular has something of the air of a warehouse, and yet the pieces are so overpowering. I sat in Maspero's chair, stared down at the huge gallery. Wondered what it would feel like to have all of it mine, as it is all Maspero's. For whatever reason it made me feel uneasy.

"You look highly proprietary. Should I remove my things?" Maspero had entered noiselessly.

"Monsieur le Directeur." I stood and we shook hands. As always Maspero beamed at me, worked his discreet charm. I quite forgot he was the man who had sacked me only a month before. That is charisma.

He pumped my hand energetically. "I sent you a wealthy American. Did you get him?"

I laughed. "He's over at Shepheard's now, playing with some new cameras. He . . . had an accident with the old ones."

He looked at me quizzically.

"I'll tell you about it later. How are things in the Service?"

"As always." He shrugged. "Lord Cromer wants to cut back our exploration fund. It seems the governor's palace is not grand enough to suit him."

"I'm sure you can charm him out of it. You always do."

"This time he means to do it." He made a sour face. "You English. You insist on governing Egypt as if it were India. There is no recognition of the country's true nature. Or its true value, for that matter." Maspero's constant complaint.

"Why accuse me of membership in the governing class? That is one sin of which I'm afraid I never will be guilty." He avoided my eyes, but I could not resist going on. "Lord Cromer is not exactly noted for Francophilia. He thinks there are too many of you in the Service."

He had caught my drift; shifted the subject. "Tell me about Henry Larrimer of the Pittsburgh Larrimers." Offered me a cognac. "It is early in the day, I know, but with Lord Cromer at my throat . . ." He began walking about, launched an animated diatribe.

I listened to Maspero's complaints, half-amused. "Surely you wouldn't suggest that the governor would purposely work against the best interests of the country?"

He had been swirling his cognac in its snifter; he stopped, eyed me curiously. Was I working for the government? A spy? "No. Of course not. Of course not. But Howard, surely there is no point to leaving Egypt's treasures in the ground."

I was wry. "That's where the Egyptians put them."

He sat down; grew cautious. "Lord Cromer accuses us archaeologists of being no better than grave robbers."

"He has a point. So do the Abd-er-Rasuls, by the way."

He stiffened. This had been unfair of me. Also unwise; I was putting more distance between myself and the service when what I wanted was the reverse. Maspero sipped his brandy deliberately. Then relaxed, sat back in his chair. Then he started laughing. "And so we are. We are all thieves, Howard. All of us. We are sinners. We are ghouls, in love with death like Baudelaire." He grinned. He didn't mean a word of it.

I kept my tone without expression. "Don't include me. I'm nothing but a well-paid guide. My days as an excavator are past."

Maspero's eyes twinkled. "So they are. So they are."

So that was that. There was no prospect of my reemployment. I had hoped, since he'd appointed no successor . . . But it was half my own fault. I let it pass. "There have been some strange mummies on the market at Luxor. I was wondering if any had appeared down here, as well. You'd be the man who would know."

"Strange?" He pretended to study some letters on his desk. "Strange in what way?"

I described the one I had examined. "My information is that they come from somewhere in the Delta. So I think that if they've made their way as far south as Luxor, some of them must certainly have turned up here."

Maspero's manner became careful, studied. "Wrappings from two different dynasties."

"Yes, the Twentieth Dynasty and the Twenty-second."

"Where did you hear that they come from the Delta?"

I hesitated, decided to tell him. "Mahomet Abd-er-Rasul."

"Do you believe him?"

"Yes."

He looked doubtful. "Well, you know him better than any of us."

Us. The word jarred me. I am no longer a member of Maspero's "us." "Mahomet suggested to me that his nephew may be involved. A Cairene silversmith. I thought I would visit him while I'm here, to see if he really does know anything."

Maspero was staring at me, looking as grave as I have ever seen him. He seemed not to have heard me. "We have three of them." He spoke slowly. "They turned up on the market here. The sellers claimed to have got them from anonymous parties, nameless men from unknown cities. From your description, ours are more horrible even than yours. They are all in wrappings from the Twentieth Dynasty, so we assumed . . . You remember the 'unmummified mummy'?"

"Yes. I remember it."

"We assumed that they must be related to it in some way. But the confused wrappings on the mummy Larrimer bought . . . That changes things."

For a moment neither of us had anything to say. There are so many possibilities, and they are all so awful. Finally Maspero stood up, slowly. "Why don't you come and take a look at them?"

There is something about the Egyptian Museum that prevents haste. The great age of the exhibits, the dimness and the shadows, the echoes of one's footsteps through the galleries and halls; it is not a place to hurry through. We walked among the sarcophagi and the statues of men dead for millennia, reaching for something to talk about, wanting to take our minds off the subject at hand.

"What is Larrimer like?" I don't think he much wanted to know, really.

"Henry? There isn't much to say about him. He is pretty much what he seems."

"And what does he seem to you?"

"Young and full of energy. It's horribly demoralizing."

Maspero laughed, relaxed a bit. "When we met he gave me the impression he has a mystical bent."

"*Bent* is the word." I described Henry's night in the Valley of the Queens; was careful not to mention the dead jackal or the spells. It was simply a matter of hungry jackals searching for meat. Telling it that way—putting it into words, concrete and demystified—made me feel better.

"But what was he trying to do in there? And was the tomb damaged?"

I decided to ignore the first question. "No, only Henry and his things."

"Thank heaven. Amen-her-khopshef has always been a favorite of mine."

"Of everyone's. I won't leave my client alone again. Too much of value could be lost."

Maspero narrowed his eyes, stared at me. "You do mean our tombs?"

"And Henry too. He is a likeable young man when he isn't hunting spirits in tombs."

"He told me he came to Egypt hoping to find adventure. I hope you are providing it."

"He is doing a fine job of providing it for himself."

Maspero chuckled.

We had descended the stairs into the basement. There are electric lights, but they are strung far apart and the bulbs are dim. Worse, a good many of them are burned out. *Le*

Directeur chooses to disburse his funds for exploration, excavation rather than for upkeep. I suppose it is a wise decision but the Museum, especially its darker corners, can be a depressing place. The basement corridors are wide, but they are crammed full of statues, stone embalming tables, mummy cases, wooden crates, all of them thick with dust and cobwebs. Most of the crates are not even labeled; there could be anything in them. Treasures, papyri; some of them, for all anyone knows, could be filled with Nile mud.

The most unsettling thing about the Museum, though—at least for me—has nothing to do with dust or gloom. It is the birds. They live in the building, dozens of them. They fly in through open windows, then cannot find their way out again. Or perhaps they simply like the cool, dark rooms. At any rate they stay. And thrive; I have no idea how they live, what they survive on. I am not certain I'd care to speculate. But they do thrive. Build nests in the shadows from stray twigs and cobwebs and whatever else they can find, and multiply. Their chittering and the flapping of their wings are constant sounds; thanks to them the galleries are never quiet. Once, in the room where the royal mummies are displayed, one of them had the boldness to dive at me; nicked the top of my right ear; drew blood. This is common. They swoop down off the dimly lit heights, alarm the tourists. The suddenness of their unexpected appearance in this place, the illogic of their occasional attacks is quite unnerving. And even here, even in the black corridors of the basement, I could hear their chittering. It made me tense.

I snapped at Maspero. "Why don't you clean the damned birds out of here once and for all?"

"I never hear them anymore. They are part of the background, like traffic."

"They are vicious. The atmosphere here makes them vicious."

"Howard, calm yourself. You are letting your imagination get the better of you."

"I just wish they'd stop their damned chittering, that's all."

The basement is honeycombed with storerooms, most of them filled to the ceiling with exhibits, boxes. A large rat ran out of one of them, down the corridor ahead of us and into another. It would not normally have bothered me but I was on edge. "This isn't a museum. This is a zoo."

"Relax, Howard. We are almost there."

We were at the end of the corridor; the last storeroom opened off to our left. We entered.

Against the wall opposite the door rested a plain white coffin. There were no markings on it, no inscriptions. I recognized it at once: it contains the unmummified mummy, the man who was embalmed alive. The coffin was closed but I remembered all too clearly its awful contents. On the floor in front of it lay the three newly acquired mummies. Their heads lay pointing toward the coffin, their feet toward the door, toward us. All of them were twisted, contorted; they had all died in the same manner as the man in the coffin at their head. In all three cases the embalmer's slit along the side of the chest cavity was clearly visible. All three mouths were open in what must have been screams. The left leg of one was wrapped around the right leg at what seemed an impossible angle; its death throes must have been very strong. They were the bodies of children. Two small girls perhaps six years old, and a boy of eight or nine. The boy's eyes were shut as if he were wincing. Each of them wore a small falcon pendant around its neck. The wrappings lay at their feet in neat piles.

I knelt next to one of them, one of the girls. Touched the skin. It was leathery, resilient. A perfect job of mummifying. For a long time I stared at her face, at the pain there.

"Well?" Maspero was standing beside me.

"It is the same. The one Larrimer bought is the same. The girl was older. Her body is tense, but it seems relaxed compared to these. And the expression on her face is the same."

"And the embalmer's cut in the chest cavity?"

"I don't know. Larrimer accidentally crushed the chest."

There was nothing in the room but the coffin and the three mummies. The room seemed huge. There was a pool of light striking them. The room had no windows, no electricity; I could not tell where the light was coming from. Looked around. There was no light outside the door. "You should crate them up. The rats will get at them. Or the birds."

We walked back through the winding corridors. Maspero stumbled over a small block statue, turned his ankle. When we reached the stairs he threw the switch to turn off the basement's lights. I looked back over my shoulder into the tangle there. "The lights don't seem to make much difference."

The staircase is narrow but with a high ceiling. When we were halfway up a pair of birds flew swiftly over our heads, down toward the basement. Then they wheeled around, flew back up to the ground floor. I felt the rush of air as one of them brushed past me; raised instinctively my arm to cover my eyes.

"Relax, Howard. They are not interested in you. Or in the mummies, for that matter. They are mating."

"How much farther do we have to go?"

I had decided to bring Henry with me on my visit to Ahmed Abd-er-Rasul, as protective coloring, lured him with promises of good buys on precious things. We entered the souk of the silversmiths early, not long after dawn. Looked for Ahmed's shop. Could not find it.

An Arab boy, for a small tip, told us what we needed to know. "Ahmed Abd-er-Rasul moved away years ago. He was not welcome here anymore."

"Why not? What did he do?"

"He is not a good man."

I squatted down, looked the boy in the eye. "Where does he live now?" I held out a fifty-piaster piece.

The boy could not take his eyes off it; tried to bargain for more. "No one knows."

I stood up, made as if to go. "Then there's nothing you can tell us. Thank you anyway."

"Wait!" Fifty piasters was more than enough. "He lives in the Coptic quarter now. He is a Christian."

I remembered the silver crucifix around his son's neck. "Where in the Coptic quarter?"

"No one knows."

"Then thank you just the same." I handed him the coin. The Coptic souk is small and the people there are helpful. There was no sense paying for more information.

Henry was confused. "Why this Ahmed so particularly? Surely there are good dealers right here."

"I know his family."

He thought for a moment and it dawned on him. "The tomb thieves? The Luxorite tomb thieves? Is he one of them?"

"Yes, he is."

"Then I can't wait to meet him."

"You can do me a favor. When I raise the subject of the mummy you bought, just follow my lead."

"Why? What game are you up to?"

"No game, Henry, I'm just after information."

"I can't wait."

But after two hours of walking he was complaining bitterly. "How much farther, Howard?"

"I thought you wanted to learn Cairo."

"My feet hurt."

"Look. Over there is the street of the whores."

Henry stopped walking, peered down the alley. "Not very inviting, is it?"

"That depends on what you are looking for."

"Are you suggesting a visit? I thought we were after silver."

"So we are. The Cairene whores are notorious for the diseases they carry."

He looked again, made a sour face. "They seem to be on the plump side, too."

"I believe the word is 'voluptuous.'"

Henry laughed. "Why did you point the place out to me?"

"Oh, you know my puckish sense of humor."

Not long after this we reached the Coptic quarter. For a mere two piasters a boy led us to Ahmed's shop. "Here," the boy told us. "He lives here. He is not a good man."

No one seems to think much of Ahmed. "Oh? Why not?"

"He is not a Copt." On that cryptic note the boy left us.

A small sign read, "Ahmed Abd-er-Rasul. Silversmith. Antiquities." Below this legend was a cross. There were small square windows, protected by iron bars, containing a wonderful pair of silver pitchers. The handles were elaborately carved dragons.

"They're beautiful!" Henry's delight showed in his face. "The dragons look almost Chinese."

"Let's go in."

As we entered a small bell rang; but no one appeared to greet us. We were left on our own, a sure sign there was nothing of value in the room. It was dark, gloomy. Heavy curtains covered the windows and the door to the room beyond. There were glass cases containing newly manufactured "antiquities"; the dust on some cases was so thick it was difficult to see their contents. At one end of the longest case sat a cardboard box filled with papyri; the top one had a thick coating of dust. Henry glanced at it. "Can you read it?"

"No. It is in Coptic. There are thousands of Coptic papyri on the market. The old monks made records of everything."

"These are genuine, then?"

"Most likely. And not worth much. They are probably the laundry lists of an extinct monastery. The country is black with them."

"I'd like to visit one sometime."

I ran my finger through the dust on the counter. "To see the ruins or the desert?"

He smiled. "Both."

Splendid. Another place to hunt ghosts. I should have learned by now.

From the room beyond a boy entered. It was Azzi, Ahmed's son. So this was the same man I met in Luxor; he was exactly who he claimed to be, not an imposter. Azzi and I recognized one another at the same instant. I could see the flash of concern in his face; what would he make of my being here? Then he put on his mask. "Carter Pasha, I believe. How interesting to see you again."

"Azzi." I nodded to him, smiled. "And how are your father and brother?"

"Quite fine, Carter Pasha." He looked to my companion.

Before I could introduce him he stepped up and shook Azzi's hand. "I am Henry Larrimer, of the Pittsburgh Larrimers." I really must talk to him about this. The boy's puzzlement was obvious.

"My father will join us in a minute. He has been detained. May I offer you some mint tea?"

I was struck by a change in Azzi's manner. That night in Luxor he had worked at making everything mysterious. But here in his father's shop he was the perfect little business host, courteous, deferential, but not too much so. "Tea would be wonderful, thank you. Henry?"

"Yes, please."

"Then excuse me for a moment, gentlemen. Please browse as you like."

He went back into the next room. I looked around. "Would you care to browse the dust?"

Henry laughed. "He doesn't make a very impressive thief."

"This is the Cairene branch of the family." I gestured toward the street. "Tombs are in short supply here."

"Still . . ."

"I think you'll find that the family business is a sore point here."

He had no idea what I was trying to tell him.

"Henry, this is the Christian quarter."

"Yes, I know, but—"

Azzi came back through the curtains. While he was gone I had heard him talking to someone. I smiled at him. "Azzi. Will your father be joining us soon?"

"When the tea is brewed, I think. Have you seen our fine collection of antiquities?"

"We have been browsing, yes." I refrained from commenting on the quality of the pieces.

Henry piped up. "What we really came looking for is silver. Those pitchers in the front windows are magnificent."

"My father will be pleased that you appreciate them."

I had not come here to make business small talk. "Does your father travel to Luxor often?"

"My father travels a great deal."

"To Luxor? I would enjoy to meet him there again."

"My father travels all through the country. On business."

"Does he go to the Delta very often?"

He ignored my rudeness, turned to Henry. "Would you like to inspect the pitchers, sir?"

"Yes, very much."

He unlocked one of the windows, removed one of the pitchers from its place, handed it to Larrimer, who looked it over quickly and handed it to me. It was heavy, heavier than I'd expected; a substantial piece. On the bottom were engraved three Arabic letters. "These are not your father's initials."

"No, sir." He seemed surprised that I'd noticed. "My brother Dukh made the pitchers under my father's supervision. Dukh is the most skilled apprentice in Cairo." He smiled a businessman's smile.

"So I see."

In the next room the teakettle whistled; he excused himself and went to tend to it. Then the curtains parted and Ahmed Abd-er-Rasul stepped into the room, smiling effusively, his hands extended to take mine. "Carter Pasha. How wonderful of you to visit my shop."

"It is a pleasure, Ahmed. This is my client, Mr. Henry Larrimer."

Ahmed beamed. "Of the Pittsburgh Larrimers? What a joy to meet you."

Henry actually seemed pleased at Ahmed's eavesdropping, and oblivious to the gentle mockery. Or perhaps he was simply charmed by Ahmed's good looks and manner.

"You must come into my parlor for tea."

The parlor was as sumptuous as the front room was stark. Velvet curtains, brocaded wallpaper, overstuffed furniture, an ornate china tea service on a low table. On a perch in a corner an African grey parrot sat motionless, murmured something unintelligible. There were wonderful vases, boxes, curios everywhere. Ahmed obviously does a good business. He gestured us to a plush sofa. "Have you heard from Baron Lees-Gottorp?"

"A previous client," I explained to Henry. "No, I haven't. I assume he must be back in Germany by now."

"How unhappy for Egypt." He was studying Henry—trying to guess if he is as soft a touch as the baron? "He was so knowledgeable."

"And acquisitive." I could not resist adding this.

"Yes indeed."

Azzi served our tea. It seemed to me that he fussed particularly over Henry; but then Henry was the potential customer, not I. He looked flustered. "What was this baron like?"

Ahmed took his tea from the boy's serving tray. "Blond, blue-eyed, muscular. German. A skilled collector of antiquities."

"I see," said my client, who obviously did not.

Ahmed turned back to me. "You have not heard from the baron, then?"

I thought I had caught his drift. "He unwrapped his mummy while he was still in Luxor. I believe he was disappointed. But he chose to make nothing of it."

"Then you yourself did not assist with the unwrapping?"

"I did not. I'm afraid the baron decided he could do quite well without my services."

Ahmed frowned, sipped his tea. "I am sorry to hear that. You have no idea where he is, then?"

I could not imagine why he should be so preoccupied with the baron. And of course he would not tell me. The Moslem penchant for indirectness can be maddening at times. "As I said, I think he must have gone home by now."

Something disturbed the parrot in the corner. It whistled shrilly; screamed, *"Mektoub! Insh'Allah! Mektoub! Imshi, imshi!"* Ruffled its feathers angrily and returned to silence.

Larrimer was delighted by this. "What a wonderful bird. What do you call him?"

Azzi went to the parrot, stroked its stomach. "His name is Imshi."

"Imshi." Larrimer obviously has no idea what it means. "Can I hold him?"

Ahmed smiled. "He has bitten the finger of more than one Westerner."

"Mr. Larrimer purchased a mummy much like the one you sold to the baron." I had let Ahmed direct the conversation long enough.

Ahmed was impassive; sipped his tea. "Much like it? In what way?"

"The date, the style of the wrappings. And it too is the body of an adolescent."

"How interesting. Did you find anything on the body?"

The parrot screamed again; I ignored it. "We have not unwrapped it. The wrappings are so beautiful . . ."

Fortunately Henry had sense enough not to contradict me. "It really is quite beautiful. This is delicious tea, Ahmed."

"Thank you very much."

I sat forward on the sofa. I did not want to lose the conversational thread. "As a matter of fact, we were hoping to find a second mummy like it. Two would make a wonderful display."

"Yes." Henry was enjoying this.

"Is your tea all right, Carter Pasha?" Ahmed was the perfect host.

"Quite fine, yes."

He turned to Henry. "I understand you are also in the market for silver."

"Well, I'm browsing seriously, at any rate. I'm quite taken by the dragon pitchers your son made."

"My son Dukh."

"Yes. I'd be interested in buying them if the price were right."

"I'm sure we can come to some arrangement. More tea?"

Azzi had been off in the corner playing with the parrot. He refilled our cups.

There was an interval of silence while we tasted our tea; it was strong, almost too strong for my taste. I decided to take the lead again. "Do you have another mummy? Or know where we can get one?"

"I do not have one, no. The tea is strong. Would either of you like sugar?"

Henry took sugar; I had hoped he would follow my lead to press Ahmed for another mummy, but he sat there drinking his tea. The parrot screamed, *"Imshi! Imshi!"*

Henry laughed. "He really likes his name."

"Yes." Ahmed had decided it was time to get to business. "What would you consider a fair price for the pitchers?"

So began the process of haggling. Henry was better at it than I'd expected him to be. He hesitated; found fault with the goods; pretended to lose interest in them; ignored Ahmed's complaints and protestations; all done quite masterfully. In the end he got the pair of them for two hundred Egyptian pounds, quite a good buy.

Ahmed also seemed pleased. "My son Dukh would be quite pleased to know that such a gentleman as yourself had found merit in his handiwork."

Larrimer was flattered. "I'd like very much to meet him and pay the compliment myself."

"That is not possible, I'm afraid. But I shall give him your regards when I see him next. In the meantime, gentlemen"—he rose; nodded first to Henry, then to me—"I thank you for visiting my shop." He was dismissing us.

I could not let this happen. "About those mummies. Mr. Larrimer would be willing to pay quite well for a second one."

Ahmed looked to Henry.

"That's right. A pair of them, if the wrappings matched well, would be much more valuable than just one."

"I see." He looked at the parrot. "Unfortunately, as I have said, I only had the one to sell."

I pressed. "Then if you could tell us where you got it . . . Perhaps we could go to the source."

"An anonymous seller, Carter Pasha. You know how awkward it is to deal with them."

It was a gentle slap. "Yes, I know. Still, they can be traced at times."

Ahmed laughed. "So they can. I will see what I can do." He turned again to Henry. "How much did you say you would pay?"

"I didn't. I'd have to see the mummy first."

"Naturally. Well, perhaps my seller will turn up again. I can reach you at Shepheard's?"

"Yes."

"How long will you be in Cairo?"

I wanted him to move quickly. "Only two more days."

Ahmed shrugged, made his face blank. "Then I cannot promise much. But we will see."

Back at the hotel (Henry had insisted we take a carriage, not walk) I wrote a quick note to Maspero at the Museum: "Ahmed Abd-er-Rasul. Silversmith in the Coptic quarter. Have him watched. He will lead us to more mummies." The "us" was quite deliberate.

Larrimer watched over my shoulder as I wrote. "Do you really think it will work?"

"Ahmed smells money. You were very good with him, by the way. Thank you."

"Is it really so important that you find the source of the mummies?"

"Yes." I did not want to say more.

"Why?"

I sighed. "Someone is rewrapping them. Valuable archaeological evidence is being taken."

"I see."

There are of course more serious possibilities. I did not
want to talk about them with Henry; with anyone. I feel less
and less easy about all of it.

Early this morning I took Henry to the Museum. It was
before the usual opening time but the attendant recognized
me and admitted us. The huge galleries were empty but for
us; our footsteps, our voices echoed among the gods and the
pharaohs. I showed him all the great treasures, the statue of
Khafre from Giza, the colossi of Akhenaten, all the rest. But
I avoided the Mummy Room. Mummies have been rather too
much on my mind.

In the hall of colossi he got down on one knee, studied a
black pyramidion. "I'd like to photograph the pyramids,
Howard."

"All of them? You still want that?"

"Yes. Monsieur Maspero told me it's never been done."

"Not photographically. But Napoleon's savants covered
all of Egypt. The engravings in the *Description de l'Egypte*
are quite wonderful things."

Henry ran his finger along a hieroglyph carved in the
stone. "Who did this belong to?"

I read the cartouche. "Amenemhat III."

He stood up, brushed off his trouser leg. "Engravings are
not photographs, Howard. Monsieur Maspero seemed to
think it would be a valuable project."

A pair of birds swooped into the hall, from where I am not
certain. Henry glanced up at them briefly, then back at me.
Their presence seemed to faze him not at all. There must
have been more birds in the darkness up near the ceiling. I
could hear the sound of their wings, their chittering. "The

birds are always shrill.'' I looked at Henry. "For some reason it is never songbirds that get trapped in here.''

"Howard.'' His tone was as serious as I have known it. "Monsieur Maspero thinks a photographic survey of the pyramids would be a valuable thing.''

Something made me speak very softly. "He is correct, of course.''

"Good. I want to be of service.''

We had been walking among the colossi, came to the feet of the largest of them, the one of Amenhotep III. The king gazed out far over our heads, oblivious.

"What would be the most practical way of going about it?''

I thought for a moment. "North to south, I suppose.''

"Where would we start, then?''

"Athribis. In the Delta.'' I leaned against a toe of the pharaoh. "It is small, little known. I don't know much about it myself, really. But it is the northernmost pyramid.''

Henry paused, looked around. "I'd like to see the mummies now.''

"The ones in the basement?'' I had not told him about them. How could he know?

"Is that where the Mummy Room is?''

"Oh.'' I had been off-guard. "No. No, it's upstairs.''

We walked to the broad staircase. It is lined with beautiful papyri. Henry studied them, commented on the illustrations, asked me to translate now and then. The Mummy Room is not far from the head of the steps.

There are the royal dead. Each in a glass case; there is a purple pall covering each one from the chest down, out of reverence, out of modesty. I waited by the door; I have never found the room congenial. Henry walked among the cases, read each name card—Thutmose, Seti, Amenhotep, Ramses; stared into each of their dead faces, as if they might tell him a secret. The light reflecting off one of the cases caught Henry's eyes, large, sad, gentle.

He stood for a long time over one of the cases. I did not need to ask which one. "I've never heard of this pharaoh," he said. "Tell me about him."

"Seqenenre." All I could see in the room was Henry, bowed over the dead king. "He died in battle, helping to drive the Hyksos out of the country. He was killed with an ax."

He pressed his hand against the glass of the case, moved his face near to it. "Yes, I can see the gashes it made in his skull."

I was still at the door. "And you can see the pain in which he died."

"Couldn't the embalmers have taken the pain out of his face?"

"No. They couldn't do that."

Henry looked over his shoulder at me, then back down at the mummy. He stared at it for a long moment. Then moved on through the room.

"There are more in the basement?"

"Nothing important," I lied. "Only the minor ones are stored down there."

"Oh."

"I'd like to go upstairs and use the library. Would you mind wandering about on your own for a while?"

"No, not at all. Go on."

I headed for Maspero's office. As usual he was not there. I found the proper volume of the *Description de l'Egypte*, took it down, found the engraving of the Athribis pyramid.

I suppose it is rather shameless of me to have manipulated Henry in this way. I want to go to the Delta for my own reasons; for the mummies. Still, Henry wants to photograph pyramids, and Athribis is as good a place as any to begin with it. So why do I feel vaguely guilty . . . ? I could never explain to him my real motivation.

"Howard. Good morning." Maspero had entered just behind me.

"And how is the Antiquities Service this morning?"

"I am quite fine, thank you." We laughed. "Unfortunately, so is Lord Cromer. The man is a devil. He never rests. He has actually gone and hired an architect to redo the state mansion. An Arab named el-Fendar, a notorious pederast. The whole thing disgusts me."

That again. Maspero's complaints are as constant as the birds' twittering.

"Will you join me in a brandy?"

Maspero is a politician at heart. There is nothing he would like better than to rule Egypt himself. But the British Empire is in charge; the best he can hope for is to run the Antiquities Service, a thing he does with remarkable skill. There is not much he wants in Egypt that he does not get. He is a master politician, and his charming, cheery manner is a politician's device. That it is genuine, that he really is a pleasant man, is beside the point. He knows how to use his personality, and it never fails. Lord Cromer and his people never have much of a chance, really, but they keep on trying just the same.

It is as if there are two Egypts, the living one ruled by Cromer, the dead one by Maspero. And the subtle warfare between the two never ends. Perhaps that is why I always feel a bit uncomfortable sitting in *le Directeur*'s chair. Maspero was a brilliant excavator in his day; he has been reduced to bureaucracy. Glum thought, that that might ever happen to me. I prefer my lonely work on the banks of the Nile. A statue has only one face.

He swallowed his brandy in one long gulp. Then his eyes rested on the open volume on the desk. "You are interested in Athribis?"

I sat upright in the chair. "It is our next stop."

"But I thought . . . Larrimer told me that he wanted to start his survey in Luxor."

"So he did. But that was before the 'accident' with his cameras. We are here in the city to replace them; then he wants to move on. Besides, I think the Theban tombs frighten him now, more than he wants to admit."

"But why Athribis? No one ever goes there. I've never been there myself. Will you have some more brandy?"

"I haven't had any in the first place."

"Oh." He filled his own snifter to the lip. I have never known a politician or bureaucrat who was not also an alcoholic.

"It is Henry's plan to photograph all of the pyramids in the country."

"All of them?"

"Unfortunately, yes. Athribis is the northernmost of them; it seems a logical place to start. We can just work our way south. So we are going to the Delta." I said this pointedly.

"But Howard . . ." He took a long swallow of cognac. "The pyramid at Athribis is not much more than a pile of stones. It has never been excavated. No one even knows who built it."

He bent over to inspect the engraving more closely. It shows a small step pyramid; the eastern face is crumbling.

"I've told him all that. He insists." I tried to make my tone accusatory. "He says you told him it would be valuable."

"And so it would, I suppose. Still . . ."

We both studied the engraving wordlessly for a moment. I had heard of Athribis—there are the ruins of a town there also—but as Maspero had said, it is quite off the usual archaeological track. "It looks crude," I said. "It must date from a very early period. Earlier than the Step Pyramid at Sakkara, do you suppose?''

Maspero's eyes twinkled. ''Before the real 'Age of Pyramids'? Conventional wisdom puts it in the Fifth or Sixth Dynasty.''

I turned the book to face me. ''Surely all the pharaohs of those dynasties have known resting places.''

He chuckled. ''Ah, Howard. You love the romance of Egyptology more than the conventional detail. You are the guide for Henry Larrimer.''

This made me defensive. ''I only suggested—''

''That this pyramid was built by an unknown pharaoh in a time before anyone built pyramids. Yes. Exactly.''

He had made me feel quite testy. ''If you can take it as given that a Third Dynasty king named Zoser simply invented the pyramid one day, why can't you accept the possibility that it might actually have been done by an unknown king a generation or two earlier?''

Maspero drank more brandy. ''Where is your evidence, Howard? Where are the inscriptions to support you?''

I sat back. ''Where are the inscriptions to support any other view? There has been no excavation, remember?''

Maspero tugged thoughtfully at the end of his moustache. ''Will you have time for any serious excavation while you are there?''

''I don't know. It is unlikely. He'll probably want to take a few photographs and move on.''

''Are you sure you won't have some cognac?'' He had finished his second glass, poured a third.

''Thank you, no.''

''Suppose,'' he said dryly, ''you could persuade Larrimer of the excitement of a dig, the thrill of discovering the unknown.''

So that was it. I stared at *le Directeur* as he savored his

Napoleon. "The Antiquities Service wishes me to dig, but not at its own expense. Is that correct?"

He smiled; the brandy seemed, at long last, to be satisfying him. "That is precisely it. I could have a permit for you by tomorrow."

"Larrimer would be bored in two days."

"Play on him. Excite him. Tell him thrilling stories. Tell him there might be gold."

I was amused by this. "Are you suggesting ways to handle Henry Larrimer or Lord Cromer?"

He hesitated for a moment; then broke out laughing. "Howard, you are so cynical. Why did you come here today?"

"Can I not stop in to visit an old friend without having my motives suspected?"

"No."

His mind works like that. Unfortunately, so does mine. He is right, I am too cynical. "All right, then, I wanted to learn what you know about Athribis."

He pursed his lips, managed to look thoughtful. "That is all?"

I stared directly at him. "All right, then. What did you learn about Ahmed Abd-er-Rasul?"

He put on a straight face. "This is the Antiquities Service, not the police department. How could I have him followed?" Maspero does injured innocence very well.

I ignored his protestation. "Where did he go?"

"Howard, the police are all busy. It seems that children are being kidnaped in alarming numbers north of here. How could I trouble the authorities with a matter as trivial as some mummies?"

I stared at him. "Gaston, where did he go?"

He sighed resignedly. "To the train station. To the northbound platform. Then my man lost him in the crowd."

"Which train was due to leave?"

"There were two, both to Alexandria. One via Benhir, the other along the Western Desert. He could have taken either one of them."

"Larrimer and I will be on the Benhir train tomorrow evening."

Monsieur le Directeur understood me perfectly; was not certain how he wanted to react; lapsed into silence. He pretended to study the engraving.

I would not be shaken off. "We are going to the Delta. To Benhir."

"Yes." He avoided looking at me. "There is something . . . unsavory going on." This was careful understatement. "Officially I am concerned. It is part of our function to monitor the antiquities trade. You know that."

"Yes. You have that responsibility."

"Unofficially, I am consumed with curiosity."

"Yes."

He finally looked at me. "While you are in the Delta ask questions. Poke, probe, see what you can find."

"I will be working on Larrimer's survey." I did not want to make this easy for him.

"If you could discover the source of those mummies, the Service would be very grateful."

Thus was our bargain struck. We shook hands. I found Henry, still in the Mummy Room, and brought him back to Shepheard's.

I want my job back. I am a fool. Taking back my job will mean giving up Henry Larrimer and his ten thousand dollars. But for whatever reason I want my job back. The prestige, the recognition. I want it known that I am valuable to Egypt.

Chapter Four

THERE WAS ONE delay after another at the station. Our train was to have left at eight P.M.; did not pull out until nearly midnight. Then an hour out of Cairo we stopped. No explanations; no apologies; *mektoub*.

The train was dimly lit; one oil lamp per compartment. The flame danced in the drafts made by the train's movement. Light from the first-quarter moon came in through the windows, gave us a pale illumination. Then it set and the gloom dominated. Henry found the holdup depressing; fidgeted constantly. "We might as well be outside."

"Why not take a walk? It should be all right as long as you stay near the train."

"I'd probably be bitten by a cobra."

Our compartment was shared with a Coptic priest, a middle-aged man with a full grey beard. He wore dark blue robes and a turban. Henry's fussiness seemed to annoy him. He remained politely quiet until Henry finally nodded off. "An American. Am I correct?"

"Yes, very much so."

"They expect the whole world to be like the lobby of a New York hotel."

"This one at least is learning."

We introduced ourselves. He is Father Khalid, an arch-priest from Cairo, traveling on Church business.

"Howard Carter? Inspector of Monuments for Upper Egypt?"

I was flattered he had heard of me. "A private guide, now."

"I see." I wondered if he did. "You and your companion are traveling to Alexandria?"

"No, only as far as Benhir."

"Excellent, so am I. We must dine together. Tomorrow is market day in Benhir. The food will be excellent."

I promised to have dinner with him. Henry was quite sound asleep by now, snoring softly. I wanted to nod off myself.

But Father Khalid was suddenly talkative. "I do not travel to Benhir often. But these are exceptional times."

"Exceptional? How do you mean?"

"Religiously active."

I was lost; I was also not especially interested. But I tried to be polite. "I'm afraid I don't follow you."

He lowered his voice; he was obviously letting me in on something he thought important. "There are 'missionaries' all over Egypt. Romans, Lutherans, Baptists. Mostly Romans. The country is polluted with them."

I didn't understand his concern. "Western religion has never made many inroads in Egypt. Why should the competition worry you now?"

"The times have changed; this is a new century."

I had an uneasy suspicion he was about to go mystical on me; decided to head him off. "Have you lost many parishioners to them?"

"No. Practically none."

"Then I don't see—"

"They come here and they call us heretics. They cry that the Coptic Bible, the one true Bible, is filled with apocrypha. They preach about the fires of hell with such force even the Moslems are alarmed."

"That must be something to hear." His heat amused me.

"And they are plundering our heritage." I waited for him to continue; this was too cryptic to go unexplained. But he put on a grave expression and stared at me.

I prompted him. "Your heritage."

"Our ancient monasteries."

"Oh." I was not certain why he should care. The Copts have never shown much interest in the ruins left by their forebears. "So they have been excavating. Is that really much of an issue? I mean, they might always find something of real value."

"You miss my meaning. They are not simply—"

With a loud snort Henry woke up. There was a frightened look in his eyes; I think he must have had a nightmare. He yawned, stretched. "My neck has gone stiff."

I introduced him to Father Khalid. For once Henry did not make a point of his Pittsburgh lineage. He shook Khalid's hand energetically. "You're the first Coptic priest I've met."

"Archpriest." Khalid was dry.

"Uh, yes, archpriest." Henry's puzzlement showed in his face.

I filled him in on our conversation. "We've just been talking about some of those ancient monasteries you're interested in." I turned to Khalid. "Mr. Larrimer is anxious to visit one."

"I see. There is a fine little one near Benhir, the best preserved in Egypt. It is what I'm going there to inspect."

"Inspect?" I was as curious as Henry: a priest, or archpriest, who inspects ruins.

"We have heard reports that the Western missionaries have

actually taken up residence in our old retreats. The one in
Benhir, and a number of the larger ones in the Wadi Natrun. I
am told that the monastery of Saint Pilate is now full of
German nuns.''

I remembered Sister Marcellinus and her friends; it must
be they who were living there. So they came not from the
Delta but from the desert west of it. I was about to tell Khalid
what I knew about them when Henry spoke.

"Did you say Saint Pilate?"

"Yes."

"Pontius Pilate?"

"Yes."

"But— But he—"

"There is so much you Westerners have forgotten about
the beginnings of the Church. Pilate refused to condemn
Jesus; he even tried to save his life. There is an ancient
document called the *Paradosis of Pilate* which tells the story.
The Roman procurator died a Christian martyr.''

Henry's incredulity showed on his face. There was an
awkward silence. I had found irritating Khalid's condescen-
sion; but of course there was no polite way to say so. In the
first century after Christ men wrote hundreds of gospels,
epistles, paradoses, and what have you, and ninety percent of
them are pure nonsense. They tell the most fantastic stories
about the private lives of Christ and the Apostles. Among
them, one could find authority for almost any creed, however
absurd. But nonetheless, the Copts have a way of sneering at
sects of more recent date, as if to base one's beliefs on
modern fabrications is somehow less respectable than to base
them on ancient ones.

The locomotive's whistle blew and with a sudden buck the
train began to move. Henry looked around as if he found the
motion impossible to believe in. ''Thank heaven. I thought
we'd be here all night.''

Khalid was about to make a remark about pampered

Americans; I could see it in his eyes. I wanted to keep the peace. "You were going to tell us about those monasteries. Why should it bother you that anyone is living in them?"

"Not just anyone, Mr. Carter. Westerners." His manner had changed; the tone turned pious. "Those are holy places, the places where our faith was born and nurtured. Our ancient fathers are buried there. Do you see that? To go there looking for relics, looking for ancient manuscripts, that is one thing. To find them enriches us all. But to go there for the purpose of spreading an alien faith . . . that is desecration."

Priests. It is when they grow most serious that they seem to me most naive. I could not resist goading Father Khalid a little more. "It is still Christianity."

But he refused to be baited. "I have been talking far too much. What business takes the two of you to Benhir?"

I deferred to Henry. "We are beginning a photographic survey of the pyramids. In future seasons we plan to cover the entire country, all of its temples and monuments."

Henry's obvious enthusiasm did not spread to Khalid. "*All* of the pyramids?" He looked incredulous.

"Yes." He said it with obvious pride.

"I see."

"The Athribis pyramid will be the first one we photograph. Then we'll work our way south. Howard has most of the trip mapped out already."

The priest had been listening politely; suddenly he seemed interested. "Athribis? That is the location of our old monastery. Perhaps we can visit the ruins together."

Henry smiled, told him we would be delighted.

"Have you been out to the ruins before?" I had to ask.

"No, only to Benhir itself. On pastoral business, you understand." So much for his great concern about the ancient monastery.

There was a severe jolt and the train stopped moving.

Khalid muttered an Arabic obscenity under his breath. If Henry heard it, he did not realize what it meant. The oil lamp swung wildly on its hook; went out. We were in darkness. None of us seemed to know how to react. After a moment Khalid broke the silence. "Has either of you a match?"

"I haven't. Henry?"

"No, sorry."

There was a rustle of robes as the priest stood up. "I'll go and find the porter." He left in what seemed to me unnecessary haste. Can he be afraid of the dark?

In the shadows beside me Henry began to fidget.

"Would you like to take a walk, Henry?"

"Yes. Yes, I would."

We found our way to the end of the car, stepped down. There were lights in a few compartments farther up the train, but most of the windows were dark. We were not far from an orange grove; the sweet smell of the trees came to us clearly. Henry took a long breath. "It's hard to believe we're still in the same country."

"Everyone says that when they come to the Delta. Wait till you see it in daylight."

The Damietta branch of the Nile was a few hundred yards to the right of the tracks. Frogs croaked loudly. In the sky above us the stars twinkled brilliantly. Jupiter and Mars hung over the western horizon.

"It's chilly." Henry rubbed his arms. "Let's go back in."

"I'd like to stretch my legs for a minute or two. Will you keep me company?" We walked along the length of the train. The stars lit dimly the sides of the cars. "The chill is from the soil. The earth here is quite damp."

"Look, there are strawberries here. Right beside the tracks."

"They're probably tart."

He picked one, bit into it. "You're right. But even so, they're wonderful. I haven't had strawberries for months."

We reached the front of the train. There was no sign of the driver. Henry climbed up to look into the cab. "Where is everyone? In the States there'd be all sorts of commotion."

I tugged at his trouser leg to get him down; Egyptian workers can be very territorial. "Delays like this are routine here. Everyone is probably asleep. I'd be sleeping myself if Father Khalid hadn't been so talkative."

"I like him." Poor, naive Henry Larrimer. "I think it's wonderful that he's so concerned about the Coptic heritage."

"Rubbish. You heard him admit that he's never even been to this monastery before."

"Yes, but he—"

"What really worries him is that some of his faithful might defect to the missionaries. His archaeological concern is only a pretext. If he makes enough fuss about desecrating sacred ground and so on, he might embarrass them into leaving. It probably won't work, but I wish him luck. Anything to keep Egypt from becoming more priest-ridden than it already is."

"You are a cynic, Howard."

"Not at all."

"What do you believe in, then?"

"I believe in the truth. 'The Cynic questions everything in order to learn what is true.' "

Henry laughed, to my extreme irritation.

"You can laugh at Greek philosophy and call me a cynic?" I snapped at him; the night has been long and tiring.

"Relax, Howard. Calm down. It's just that that's the first time I've heard you say anything that wasn't purely practical. It seemed so out of character."

"I yield the lamp of learning to no man, sir." We both laughed. He was right, of course. "Would you care to see the Damietta Nile by starlight?"

We walked to the river. A large cargo boat sailed northward past us in the darkness. There was no sign of anyone on board her. We conversed idly, walked along the bank. Henry kept steering the conversation back to religion; he seems determined to discover what I "believe in." I am equally determined not to discuss the matter, for obvious reasons. I kept returning to small talk. Finally we heard the locomotive starting up again; rushed back to the train. Khalid was asleep in the compartment. There was still no light. I went and found the porter, got matches from him. By the time I returned, Henry was sleeping too.

I feel restless. I wish I were back in Luxor.

Benhir. Market day. The town is thronged, the streets are impassable. Every open patch of ground is covered with things for sale. Fruits, vegetables, pottery, metalware, linen. Henry seems, once again, intimidated. I tried my best to convince him that the thieves and the slave traders are confined to Cairo, but he refused to leave our inn. I wandered through the town on my own, smiling at people, eating. Fresh grapes and oranges; juicy apples from towns farther north; breads and rolls still warm. It is all quite wonderful, even more so than market day in Luxor. Luxor is a business town; deals, trades, haggling are everyday things. But here it is like a holiday.

The train did not get here till after dawn. I have had less than three hours' sleep. But I don't mind much. Henry on the other hand claims exhaustion; has slept most of the day. From the train I took him to an inn at the north end of town, the end closest to the ruins of Athribis. But he did not like "the look of it." We spent an hour and a half looking for lodgings more pleasing to him. The place he settled on is, to my eye at least, identical to the first one; in fact the innkeeper is the brother of the man who owns the first place. But Henry, in his mysterious American way, prefers where we are now. The place is crowded; we are sharing a small room.

"I'm hungry." Henry woke up just as I returned for a siesta.

"The market is full of delicious food. Enjoy it."

He glanced out the window; looked glum. "No, I don't think so. Aren't there any restaurants?"

"They are as crowded as the streets."

He sighed. "Did we have to come here on market day?"

I stretched out on my bed. "You are the one who was so anxious to leave Cairo." This was not fair; after all, I am the one who made him so frightened of Cairo.

Of Father Khalid there has been no sign all day. He left the train as soon as it stopped moving, with only perfunctory good-byes; vanished into the crowd. I have no idea where he went, where he is staying, whether he will try to contact us. But then priests enjoy acting mysterious. It is their job in life.

While I was writing this Henry disappeared; I had assumed he'd given up and gone out into the town. But he just came back, grumbling.

"Damn. I gave a boy fifty piasters to bring me some apples, and he ran off with the money. Damn."

Henry, Henry, Henry. "The boy spoke English?"

"No, but I used sign language."

"Come on. We're going out. I'll buy you what you want."

He smiled that naive American smile that he smiles so nicely.

"I can't have you starving to death. It would make me look bad. Come on."

So he got his apples, and some bread and cheese, and a glass of mint tea, and now he is asleep and snoring again; and I can finally get my own siesta. I have been yawning for an hour.

Just as we were leaving the inn, I caught a glimpse of a blond head, a block or so down the street. I am not certain, but it looked to me like Brigit Schmenkling.

All afternoon clouds have been building up; the sky is dark grey now. The differences—climatic, geographical, cultural—between the Delta and the land upriver are always startling to me. Tourists often seem not to notice. Henry sees the vegetation everywhere, finds it unremarkable. This, despite his comments of last night. Perhaps he is used to a lush landscape; I don't know. There are vineyards not a hundred yards from our inn, and rich mandarin orchards within eyeshot. Roses grow wild in the streets, thousands of roses. Egypt is still, as it was anciently, two lands.

Henry slept longer than I did. I went for a short walk along the river. The Nile here is slower, narrower; it branches a hundred times before it finds the sea. It hardly seems the same water that flows through Luxor. "The waters out of nowhere," that is what the ancients called the Nile. Perhaps they had a point.

When I got back to the inn I found Henry locked in conversation with Father Khalid who, it seems, was serious about wanting to dine with us. "Mr. Carter, I have reserved a table for us at the one worthy restaurant in Benhir. You will be my guests." It was a statement, not an invitation, but then he is a priest.

The restaurant was open to the air on three sides. On a warm day it must be wonderful, but today the air was damp. Uncomfortable winds kept coming up. At one point the menus nearly blew out of our hands. Then it began to rain, slow, heavy drops. But despite the weather the restaurant was crowded and the customers were lively. There were musicians; when their sheet music blew away they improvised.

Henry found it all quite disagreeable. "This is not a fit atmosphere for dining."

"This is Egypt, Mr. Larrimer." Khalid was the soul of hearty hospitality. "You should learn to savor it."

"How can I savor what keeps blowing away?" He smiled to show how deeply he was irritated. I jumped between them, made idle chat about the menu. We ordered a fish casserole.

Before our food was served a bottle of wine arrived at our table. "Compliments of the caïd," the waiter explained.

Khalid read the label. "Alexandrian chablis. He must not like us."

A moment later the caïd himself appeared at our table, a tall, elegant, handsome man in his late thirties. He had deep brown eyes and a thick mustache; wore a galabea and sandals. I would have thought he'd be chilly.

"Mr. Carter, I believe. Mr. Carter of the Antiquities Service." We stood as he introduced himself. "Soliman Aziz Nakideh. But please call me Soliman. Provincial politicians aren't entitled to much respect." He smiled; did not mean a word of it.

I introduced Henry ("of the Pittsburgh Larrimers"; the caïd was suitably puzzled) and Khalid. "Will you join us in drinking your wine?"

"Naturally." We sat down together.

There was a good deal of small talk. How was the train ride? How do we like his town? Would we be here long? And on and on.

"I keep hearing about children vanishing from Delta towns. Has it been a problem here?"

But the caïd backed away from it. "No. Not here." And quickly changed the subject.

The food began to come—bread, cheese, soup—and it was outstanding; market day is the day to dine in small towns. Our main course was finished before he finally came to his point. "You are here to investigate the Christians. Is that not so, Mr. Carter?"

"Investigate?" I gestured at Khalid. "As you can see, I am on excellent terms with the Christians."

Soliman laughed at my little joke; like Victoria was not amused. "The Western Christians. The Romans. The Antiquities Service has sent you to investigate their activities." It was an accusation.

I had not had a chance earlier to explain about myself; did so now. "I am here solely as Mr. Larrimer's guide."

He looked from me to Henry and back again. "The Christians have brought great benefits to Benhir. Money, jobs. Our men and boys have been employed for weeks on the work at the pyramid."

"The work?" This was the first thing he had said that had caught my attention. No one may excavate anywhere in Egypt without permission from Maspero. If he had issued a permit for digging at Athribis, he would certainly have mentioned it when we talked. He had specifically wanted me to dig there myself, with Larrimer's money. Or had *le Directeur* been having some harmless fun with me?

"Yes, Mr. Carter, the work. It has been going on for a month now. I believe it is very nearly complete."

I was anxious to press for more information, but Khalid interrupted. "No, Your Excellency, it is I who am here to investigate."

The caïd smiled briefly at the use of so flattering a title; and because his suspicions were confirmed. He glanced at me with a knowing look on his face; Khalid and I were so obviously together. "I see."

"We have heard that they are desecrating our ancient shrines." Khalid obviously expected Soliman to confirm this, but he sat in silence, drinking his wine. Khalid prompted him. "That they are inhabiting our ancient monastery at Athribis."

"That is what you have heard." The caïd was stony.

"Yes. Is it true?"

He took another long drink of his wine, drained the glass. He was finished with us. "I do not know where they live." He looked around the table, challenging us to question his obvious lie. "Perhaps you should ask them yourselves."

His rudeness had caught us off-guard; no one was quite certain what to say.

Soliman stood up, singled out Henry, shook his hand. "It has been a great pleasure to meet you, Mr. Larrimer. Of the Pittsburgh Larrimers, no less. I am most impressed." Even Henry detected the mockery. The caïd turned with a flourish and rushed into the restaurant's kitchen.

I watched him go, puzzled. "Why should he have gone in there? Do you suppose he wants to poison us?"

Khalid adjusted his robes. "He owns the restaurant."

"Oh. Then it is a good thing we've already eaten."

Henry took a last spoonful of casserole. "I don't understand why he took such a dislike to us."

I explained the rules governing excavation. "If he has been a party to illegal digging—or even if he simply knew about it without reporting it to the Service—it will cost him his position. And he'll likely end up in jail."

Khalid approved of this. "No amount the Romans bribed him with could make up for the disgrace."

"At all odds," I said, "I am quite anxious to get out to Athribis."

"Tomorrow?" The priest is as eager as I am.

"Tomorrow is Friday. The Moslems will be at prayer. We won't be able to rent donkeys. Unless you know of a Christian with animals . . . ?"

He shook his head. "Benhir is a Moslem town. There are only a few dozen Copts here."

Henry also seemed keen for adventure. "How far is it? Could we walk?"

"It is only a mile or so. But Henry, your cameras are so heavy."

"We'll manage them."

His "we" annoyed me; they weigh a ton. "Will you walk with us, Father?"

"Of course. I'll meet you at your inn, at dawn."

Father Khalid is staying at the first inn we visited, the one Henry disliked. So I suppose in a way it is a good thing we are not stopping there.

It was almost nightfall when we finally left him, got back to our inn. And almost at once Henry proposed a stroll through the town. "It'll be better now," he explained cheerily. "Most of them will have gone to bed."

So I showed him the town, what there is of it. Typical, unpretentious, ordinary . . . We saw all of it by early-evening moonlight.

A man approached us from a shadowed alley. "You wish to purchase antiquities?" We went with him, expecting the worst; the Delta's damp climate has destroyed most of what once existed here. The ruins are weathered, dilapidated; genuine antiquities are almost nonexistent. The man's place of business was a small mudbrick hut near the river. He lit a lantern and in its dim light I saw five mummies on the floor, wrapped as the others had been wrapped, bodies wrenched like the others. Five of them, all children and adolescents; five. I turned and left without saying a word. Henry called after me, puzzled, alarmed perhaps at my behavior. But the sight of them gave me a sick feeling in my stomach. It has not gone away.

Henry did not follow me; has not yet come back. I pray he has not bought another of them. I could not unwrap it. I could not touch it.

I am sick with apprehension.

Larrimer came back very late. I was in my bed when he returned. Empty-handed, thank God. He obviously suspects that something is going on, something more important or at any rate more mysterious than I have admitted to; pressed me for information. I put him off; claimed it was just the unexpected sight of the mummies that had upset me.

"Surely you're used to seeing the things by now." He wouldn't let it drop.

"No. Not mummies like that. Most of them are the remains of people who died peacefully, or at least expectedly. But these . . ." I did not wish to talk about it; rolled over, pretended to sleep.

The clouds are still heavy today, but there has been no rain. The sun shone, a pale specter of itself, through the greyness. Father Khalid was here at six o'clock, ready for our little expedition. "I hope you slept well."

"Very well indeed," I lied.

"And you, Mr. Larrimer?"

"Miserably. Mr. Carter snores."

I do not. Khalid had brought a loaf of bread with him; we ate it, took up Henry's photographic things, and set off.

The day was just breaking as we left the inn, and there was a thick morning mist. The muezzin was calling the faithful to the town's sole mosque. His sad chant seemed to follow us; we turned corners, traveled farther and farther but it was still there. It might have come out of the earth itself, like the mist. We passed more and more Moslems, walking to him like dreamers, dressed severely in black. They appeared out of the mist and vanished into it, paid no attention to us. We were rocks in their stream, that is all.

Henry listened intently to the call. "What is he saying? What do the words mean?"

"Un-Christian things." Khalid was abrupt.

"But holy ones?" Henry was being perverse.

And Khalid was suitably annoyed. "Have you read their Koran? Full of slaughter, blood. It is an ugly book."

"So is the Bible. Look at the story of Agag. Or of Cain. Or of Sodom and Gomorrah, for that matter."

"The difference is that the Bible—the Coptic Bible—is true." Said like a priest.

Henry laughed; he obviously did not think his game worth pursuing. "You're unusually quiet, Howard. Are you feeling all right?"

"The dampness makes my bones ache. I wish I were back in Luxor." No point telling him what really preoccupies me.

"You should drink more wine." Khalid's advice was unsolicited. "It warms one so. It is the blood of the earth."

I was not in the mood for small talk. "Now there is a pagan sentiment if I have ever heard one."

Athribis is on the only northbound road out of Benhir. Though "road" is an exaggeration; it is not much more than a wide track. The mud carried the marks of cart wheels, deep ruts. A great many workers must have traveled this way recently. The road winds among orange groves; the fruit on the trees gave the only color to our grey morning.

Henry sneezed. "How far is it?"

"Only a mile or so, Mr. Larrimer. We should be there soon."

Ahead of us there was a slithering sound, then a splash.

"A cobra!" Henry was suddenly tense.

I tried to reassure him. "No, they don't like water. It was most likely a frog."

But he remained on edge.

Here and there the road widened into small clearings. They were littered with food tins, roughly dressed stones, broken tools, discarded ropes. There were even articles of clothing. I took all this in with dismay. "Whatever they have been doing here, it has been quite a job."

In one of the clearings, among the rubbish, I found a badly weathered granite sphinx, a foot or so long. On its side, so badly eroded as to be almost invisible, was an inscription. I strained my eyes to read it, got a magnifier out of my pack.

"Can you make it out?" Henry was leaning over my shoulder.

"I'm not certain. It is quite ancient. This is a serekh." I traced the square frame with my finger. "The earliest pharaohs used it the way the later ones used the cartouche, to encircle the royal name."

"It's nothing but a square."

"No. That's all that's left of it. A serekh is a stylized depiction of a palace facade." I looked around at him. "*Per-aha*, 'the great house.' It is the origin of the word *pharaoh*."

Henry squatted down to see more closely. "Can you make out what it says?"

"Part of it is missing. But I can make a guess." I pointed to the hieroglyphs as I translated. "I think it must read 'Khasekhemui.' Here, you see these two figures on the top of the serekh?"

Father Khalid had been standing apart from us, wearing a disapproving scowl. I suspect that like many priests he dislikes to be reminded that his faith is a relative upstart. He walked slowly over to us, glanced at the sphinx. "It isn't much of a find, is it? Why don't we move on?"

I stood to face him. "If my reading of the glyphs is correct, it is quite a valuable piece."

"You wish to stay here and look for more?"

Henry was eager to do it. "Why don't we, Howard? I find this exciting."

I took a long, slow look around the clearing. "No. This was lying on the surface. It was dropped here, probably by one of the workmen. It is likely from Athribis. That is where we should look for more. Let's go." I put the sphinx in my backpack and we set off again.

The clouds began gradually to break apart. Beams of sunlight pierced them, touched the earth, then faded again as the clouds continued their shift. They opened up more and more. It would be a sunny day after all.

Soon we rounded a bend in the track; came upon a broad open area, the site of ruined Athribis. Coming in the middle of all those trees it seemed odd. A large flat space, five hundred or more yards across. Littered with the remains of small temples, toppled statues eroded by the dampness. Only one small chapel, at the far side of the field, seemed fully intact. The base of an obelisk rose to a height of nine feet or so, then broke off; of the upper section there was no sign. The ground was mud. There was not really very much to look at; if there had not been work crews here lately I'm certain the whole place would have been grown over. I stared across what had been a city once, slowly from left to right. This place had been alive, vital for more than three thousand years, and it is still a human place; there is still humanity here, or at least the traces of it.

Henry was the first to step out into the city. He ran like a boy into a playground. "Howard, this is marvelous! I can't wait till we dig it up!" He pulled his camera excitedly out of his pack, fumbled with it. "I want pictures of it all."

Khalid followed him more slowly, as befit his priestly dignity; looked from side to side as he walked; seemed to take in everything. "The monastery is beyond the clearing." He pointed. "Behind those trees there."

"We'll get there soon enough. I want to see everything here first. Howard! What are you waiting for?"

I stood, not able to move or speak. Scanned the ruins from left to right, right to left. Along the left side was a large square area, extending into the trees, thirty or thirty-five yards on a side. That would be the place. But there was nothing there. There was nothing there. "Henry."

He ran back to me, set his camera down on a square stone. "What's wrong?"

"Henry. Look at the ruins. Look at them."

"I . . ." He was puzzled; did as I asked. Father Khalid was twenty yards away from us now; a breeze made his dark robes billow like sails. Henry looked back and forth. "I don't understand. What is wrong?"

"Think, Henry. We came here for a reason."

"Why yes. We . . ." Then he realized it. He looked out once more across Athribis, searching as I had been searching, a look of growing alarm on his face. Found the flat empty space where the pyramid must have been. "No. It can't be possible. There is nothing there. Howard, it can't be possible."

Why should they have done it? Why should they wish to destroy such a thing? Scattered on the ground were hundreds of stones, thousands of them, thrown about at random it seemed. To think of it made me bitter. "What do you mean? Why should it not be possible? Enough labor, enough time . . . It wasn't a large pyramid. And they had all those men from Benhir to work for them."

The clouds had broken up completely by now; the Egyptian sun blazed. The damp soil glistened. I felt numb. I wanted to believe that it was not possible, that we were mistaken, that the pyramid was somewhere else, hidden by the trees. But the thing had been done; it was so plain. I sat down on the stone, next to Henry's camera. Buried my face in my arms; I did not want to see.

I sat like that for a moment or two; not long. Something is happening in Egypt, I don't know what, but it frightens me. The new century, perhaps. I don't know.

"Howard, there's someone here."

I stood up; the bright sun made me wince for a second. Father Khalid had sailed off through the ruins, reached the far side. There were two men standing there, too far away for us to see much of them. They wore black. Roman priests, the ones from the monastery. In a very short time Khalid was engaged in an energetic exchange with them. He paced; his arms waved. They appeared to remain calm in the face of it.

I turned away from them. "Let's leave them to each other. We have a lot of work to do."

Henry kept his eyes on Khalid. "Work, you say."

"This has all got to be photographed. We have to document what they've done here, send it all to Maspero."

"Look. One of them is, coming this way."

"Splendid." One of the men had left Khalid, was hurrying toward us. He moved quickly; at times he ran. When he was halfway to us I recognized him. Or rather her: it was Brigit. She wore a man's clothing and her blond hair was cropped short; from a distance she looked like a young man.

"Mr. Carter!" She called my name repeatedly, waved her hands. In only a few minutes she was with us, out of breath and red-faced; her hair, short as it was, was wildly disheveled. She panted, smiled. "Mr. Carter."

"Brigit!" I took a few steps to meet her.

She seemed unable to catch her breath; hugged me impulsively. "I wasn't sure you'd want to see me again."

"Don't be ridiculous. We became good friends in Luxor. Where is your uncle?"

Henry cleared his throat loudly.

"Oh, excuse me. This is Mr. Henry Larrimer, of the Pittsburgh Larrimers." Henry smiled, ignored my irony. "And this is Brigit Schmenkling, Baron Lees-Gottorp's niece. I believe I told you about them."

"Yes, of course." They shook hands, smiled at one another. "It's a pleasure to meet you, Brigit."

"Likewise, Mr. Larrimer."

"Call me Hank."

"Hank, then. I'm very glad to meet you."

Brigit was still out of breath. I gestured to our stone. "Why don't you sit down for a moment? Your uncle is here, too?" I did not much want to see the baron again.

"My uncle? No. No, he isn't."

"He isn't? But . . ." I was lost.

"And how have you been, Mr. Carter?"

"Oh, I'm quite fine. But . . . but your uncle?"

"The baron is presumably back in Berlin by now." Her manner was offhand.

I stammered. "But . . .?"

Brigit explained patiently. "He took Dukh Abd-er-Rasul. They hit it off remarkably well that night in Luxor. When the baron met him again in Cairo . . . well, that was that."

"I don't understand. You mean to tell me that your uncle left you stranded here? I mean . . ."

Brigit had finally caught her breath. She hesitated for a moment. Then, very softly, she said, "Do you mean you actually believed he was my uncle?" She seemed quite astonished.

I felt a fool, I wanted to crawl under a stone. To be so green, to be so trusting, and to have it shown up by a sixteen-year-old girl . . . I tried to find something to say; could think of nothing.

Henry on the other hand was quite breezy. "No wonder Ahmed kept pressing you for news of the baron."

"Yes. Yes, of course." I was still abashed; turned back to Brigit. "Are you all right? I mean, did he give you any money?"

"No. He and Dukh just . . . went to Germany. I think they had arranged to meet in Cairo, but they played it as if the whole thing was a coincidence. I think they wanted to spare my feelings. Or perhaps they simply enjoyed playing at conspiracy, I don't know. Then they were gone."

Henry seemed more amused than shocked. "So they abandoned you in Cairo?"

"It wasn't so bad. The hotel bill was paid for another week, and I had all my clothes and so on." She glanced down at the black male clothing she was wearing; laughed. "Don't judge by the way I look now. My things have all been shipped to the Wadi Natrun. Father Rheinholdt lent me these."

I glanced across the ruins to where Khalid and the other men were still arguing, pacing, gesticulating. "That is Father Rheinholdt?"

Henry nudged her back to her story. "So how did you eat?"

Brigit smiled. "It wasn't difficult. I just kept having my meals at the hotel and charging them to the room. After I left, they'd send the bill to the baron in Berlin."

I pressed her. "Who is Father Rheinholdt?"

"That is him there. I met him in Cairo. He was staying at my hotel, made a big fuss over me, kept telling me how much he wanted to meet Baron Lees-Gottorp—who had already gone."

Henry laughed again. He seemed to find Brigit's style very entertaining.

"Well, one night he got into trouble. He had been preaching in the Street of the Whores; preaching rather vehemently, I gather. He has a bad case of the Gospel. The women claimed he was driving away their customers and called the police, who arrested him for disturbing the peace. I heard about it later that night at the hotel. And since he was a fellow German and had been nice to me . . . To be honest, Mr. Carter, I was feeling lonely and a bit frightened. I thought if I could get him out of jail . . .

"So I learned where they were holding him and went there. Put on my best official personna. 'I am Fraülein Brigit Schmenkling, amanuensis to His Grace Baron Rolf Lees-

Gottorp, of the Kaiser's Imperial Army,' and so on. I improvised at considerable length. I think the jailor had been smoking hashish; the building smelled of it. Anyway, my bluff worked and I got the priest out. Using the name of Lees-Gottorp.'' She smiled broadly. ''It would really gall the baron if he knew. The Lees-Gottorps have been staunch antipapists since the Reformation. Father Rheinholdt says it was a daring thing for a woman to do in a Moslem country.''

''It was. You're lucky the jailor was numb with hashish.''

She laughed. ''I am Rheinholdt's secretary now. He needed one. The old one left him while they were in Cairo. Claimed he found the work 'distasteful.' God knows what he meant by that. Perhaps he was a Lutheran.'' She smiled; Henry laughed again.

Through all of this Brigit had been glancing periodically over her shoulder, at the two priests across the field. Now they were gone, presumably to the old monastery. Brigit stood up, brushed the brown mud off her black trousers. ''I'd better be going now. He might need me for something. But when the Copt told us he was here with Mr. Howard Carter of the Egyptian Antiquities Service . . . I had to come and see you.''

''I'm glad you did. I'm so relieved to know you are all right. But why don't I come with you? I know how to handle Father Khalid.'' I wish I really did. I shall have to be very firm with him. I simply can't have him using my name like that or, worse yet, misrepresenting me so. ''He means to have you all ousted from the monastery, you know.''

''Yes, I know. It was the first thing he told us after he invoked your authority.''

''My authority. That is a good joke.''

''Anyway, it doesn't matter much. We'll be leaving in another few days. Our work here is finished. Besides, the place is damp and drafty. It's . . . well, a ruin.''

Their work is finished. Finished indeed. I stared out at the scattered remains of the pyramid. ''Brigit, what on earth has been going on here? And why?''

Suddenly her manner grew cautious. ''I don't know, really. I've only been here for a few days.''

''But the pyramid. I mean . . .''

I was pressing too hard. Henry realized it, interrupted me. ''Why don't you join us for dinner in Benhir tonight.''

Brigit hesitated, put her smile back on. ''I'd be very happy to.''

Henry gave her the name of our inn. ''About seven o'clock?''

We shook hands with her and she walked off, back to the monastery. Neither of us said much until she disappeared into the trees. I looked around, sighed; it was not yet noon and already the day had been so long. ''We'll need photographs of what they've done to the pyramid. Maspero will have to be told. He will want pictures. He will want proof. No one . . . nothing like this has ever been done before.''

Henry quietly went to work assembling the tripod, readying the plates. I walked out to inspect the destruction. A few stones are still in place; not many. His camera assembled, Henry joined me. ''Where shall we start?''

''I don't know. There is so much rubble. I suppose we'll have to photograph as much as we can and hope we miss nothing of importance. I'd like to spend a few days making at least a cursory inspection of the remains. There may be a few inscriptions, I don't know. I'm afraid it is all lost now.''

Henry's manner was sober for once. The day had gotten to him. ''Spend as much time as you think you need. I want to help you. I know this is important.''

''It shouldn't take Maspero more than a few days to get a team out here, once he gets word. Then we can get on with your survey.

''Of course.''

I turned a stone over with the toe of my boot. "This will make a fine frontispiece for your book."

Father Khalid arrived at our inn at almost the same time Brigit did; and immediately began regarding her suspiciously. She was still wearing her priest's suit. I had not much wanted to see Khalid again so soon. It is my nature to avoid confrontation. But on the other hand, the sooner and more emphatically I told him that I would not have him using—or misusing—my name, the more comfortable I would feel.

He encountered us in the lobby of our inn. Put on a mock smile and bowed slightly to Brigit. "The young lady priest," he said ironically. "I had a long conversation with your superior this afternoon. I hope you are as comfortable in our house as he is."

Brigit smiled back at him. "As a matter of fact I find it cold and damp. You should keep it in better repair."

I decided not to let things go any further than this. "Fraülein Schmenkling tells me that you claimed to be traveling with me, that you used my name as your authority in ordering the missionaries out of Benhir."

"I naturally assumed that the Antiquities Service would be concerned, yes." He was all innocence.

"I am no longer with the Antiquities Service, as you know perfectly well." I should not have been quite so abrupt; I realized that even as I spoke. But it has been a long day and I am drained. I began to move past him.

Khalid put on his priestly manner again. "If I acted out of turn, of course I apologize, Mr. Carter. But I know you love ancient things. I only thought that . . ." I was past him, walking away. "May we not dine together again?"

I turned. "I'm afraid I have a prior commitment."

Henry and Brigit, somewhat bemused, followed me out of the inn. Henry tried to be a peacemaker. "You were rather hard on him."

"He has been trading on my name. I can't have that. If word should get back to Cairo that I am here representing myself as an agent of the Service, my career in Egypt would end in a minute."

He was doubtful. "I can see what you mean. But Khalid doesn't strike me as a man one should cross."

"You talk as if he were the pope."

Henry laughed. "No, if he were the pope I wouldn't be concerned. The fact is he's a Coptic archpriest here on legitimate—and important—church business."

He had a point and I knew it. But did not want to admit it. "The Copts don't really count for much."

It was a warm clear evening. The moon lit brilliantly the town's white buildings. The air was still; sounds carried from the far distance. The muezzin called the people to their nightfall prayer. The streets were crowded with them.

Henry wanted more fish, so despite his grumbling there yesterday we found our way back to the caïd's restaurant. I entered first. Soliman, who was playing host tonight, saw me and frowned. Then he recognized Brigit, and he instantly became the ideal maître d'hôtel. Fussed over us, seated us personally; insisted we take a table near the musicians, which I did not really want. He was especially solicitous of Brigit. How is the young lady tonight? And Father Rheinholdt and the others? Is there anything the caïd or his town could provide for them? And on and on, at absurd length. Brigit was obviously flustered. But finally he went away and left us to our menus.

"He didn't want me to dine with you. I'm not certain why." Brigit glanced absently about the restaurant.

I didn't follow her. "The caïd? I thought he seemed delighted."

"Father Rheinholdt."

"Oh." This was unexpected. "And why not?"

"I think he believed Khalid about you. I think he is afraid."

"Didn't you tell him that I am not with the Service?"

"Yes. He didn't believe me. I think he was afraid to believe me. Is what he—we—did here illegal?"

I hesitated; decided to be frank. "Yes. Very much so. I sent word to Cairo on the evening train."

Brigit lowered her eyes. I do not think she knew how to deal with this awkward situation. "He is afraid I'll tell you more than you already know."

"They pulled down the pyramid. What else is there to tell, Brigit?"

"Nothing. I've only been here a few days. I . . . He screamed at me, told me not to come." For the first time all evening she looked directly at me. "I think I'm afraid of him."

Henry had taken all of this in. He was, characteristically, smiling. "Why don't you leave him?"

Brigit was morose. "And go where? And do what?"

"Well, I need a secretary at least as much as Father Rheinholdt does. You could help with the cameras, handle the plates, take notes on the photographs I make . . . We've got several seasons of work ahead of us. I can pay you very well."

Brigit was nonplussed; she had obviously not expected anything like this. She turned to me. "Mr. Carter?"

"Well there would certainly be enough work for you to do. You could be a real help. It's a fine idea."

We were interrupted by the caïd with a bowl of fresh fruit "for which, I assure you, there will be no charge."

Brigit was puzzled by all the attention he had paid us. Henry explained it to her. "Like your Father Rheinholdt, he assumed we were here to investigate the goings-on at Athribis. He seems highly relieved to see you dining with us. He must take it as a sign that all is well."

I bit into a succulent pear. "The priests could hardly have done what they did without his cooperation. And his silence. I imagine they made him a rather considerable baksheesh."

From somewhere down the street came a number of loud shouts. We tried to ignore them but they continued, loudened. Henry was annoyed. "Damned open-air restaurant."

"You are the one who suggested coming here." I smiled. "Besides, it will pass in a moment."

But it did not pass. The cries became louder and more vehement. Within a few moments it was impossible to hear anything else. I craned my neck, tried to see down the street. "It sounds like a riot."

The caïd, an expression of deep concern on his face, hurried to our table. "Carter Pasha, there is trouble at the mosque. Please come at once."

"Trouble? What kind of trouble?"

"At the mosque, sir. Please hurry."

"But why me? What can I do?"

"You are the government. You are the Antiquities Service."

I rolled up my eyes in exasperation. "Working for the government is like original sin. You can never get the stain off your soul." Henry laughed at me. We stood and rushed after the caïd.

The mosque was two streets away, a small one but with exquisite leaded-glass windows with elaborate geometrical designs. A mob of several dozen people had collected in the street. Most of them, from their clothing, had come for their nightfall prayer. But from the tone of their cries, their mood was quite virulent.

The caïd took hold of my sleeve, led me into the thick of the crowd. The shouts were deafening. I had no idea what I was getting into. A number of the men in the mob gave me venomous looks.

We reached the center of it. Lying on the ground, soiled,

bruised, was a priest, the one I had seen dining out in Luxor. There was a vicious bruise on the right side of his head. Standing over him, looking completely impassive, his robes covered with dust, was the imam. Soliman shouted something, trying to quiet the throng, but it was lost among their screams. He shouted again; they ignored him. The imam watched him with an air of detached amusement; glanced curiously at me. Then he raised his arms high overhead. The cries began gradually to trail off. In a few moments everything was quiet.

"Father Rheinholdt." Brigit had followed me into the mob. I had not been aware of her presence; turned in surprise to find her there. Henry was standing just behind her. They both stared down at the stricken priest.

The imam did not speak English. I asked him in Arabic what had happened. He stared, expressionless, at the priest and said, "He came here to desecrate the mosque. Such infidels as he . . ." He stared directly at me. "You know what Mohammedan Law directs us to do with them."

I know indeed. "So now that the work is over, he has gone from generous employer to despised infidel?"

The imam stared at me icily.

I knelt down beside the priest to examine him. A stream of blood trickled down the side of his head, formed a little pool in his ear. He rocked his head from side to side feebly, as if he were trying to empty it out. He moaned something unintelligible.

Soliman addressed the imam. "This is Mr. Howard Carter of the Antiquities Service."

I stood again, bowed slightly. "Late of the Antiquities Service. I am anxious to do what I can here. Can you tell me exactly what happened?"

The imam conferred quietly with a few old men, whom I took to be the elders. Then he turned back to me and explained, in a perfectly matter-of-fact manner. "He came

running into the mosque. Did not remove his shoes.
Screamed at me, at the elders, at the faithful. Called us
blasphemers, barbarians, idolaters. He called us idolaters.''
He had been watching Rheinholdt, who was now quite
motionless but groaning softly; looked back at me. "You
will have been in many mosques, Mr. Carter. Tell me, have
you ever seen an idol in one of them?''

A circle had opened around us and Rheinholdt. From
somewhere in the second or third rank of onlookers, someone threw a rock. It hit Rheinholdt in the ribs and he cried
out. The side of his head was now matted with dried blood.
A man in the front of the crowd spit on him.

The imam looked down at him. "He was raving like a
fiend." He adjusted his robes, stroked his beard, went on
with his story. " 'Where are they?' he cried again and again.
He pulled a boy up from the floor and shook him fiercely.
'Where do you keep them? I have more right to them than
you.' I still have no idea what he can have meant.'' He
shrugged, looked down once again at the priest, and smiled
what can only be called a gentle smile. "Do you understand
al-Islam, Mr. Carter? Do you understand the surrender?''

"I believe that I do, yes.''

"And would you mock it, assail it as this man did?''

"Leave him to me. Will it satisfy you if I vouch for his
future behavior?''

He conferred again with the elders. "There are three saints
buried in the mosque. Their graves have been defiled.''

I was tiring, losing patience. "Look at him. You can see
the spilled blood. Do you want him dead?''

Calmly, "He is an infidel.''

I had had enough. I said very firmly, "So is Lord
Cromer.''

His expression changed; once more he turned to the old
men. "You may take the priest. And now you must excuse
me. I will need to change out of the filthy robes before the

prayer can continue." With a casual air he turned and reentered the mosque. Slowly, by ones and twos, the men in the crowd followed him.

There was no place to take him but to our inn. It was night; the people who were not at prayer had gone to their houses. The moonlit streets as we carried him were quite deserted. Rheinholdt was not a large man; to look at him I would not think he weighed much at all. A hundred and fifty pounds at very most. But as Henry, Brigit and I carried him through Benhir he seemed impossibly heavy. It took more than twenty minutes to get him the few blocks to the inn.

The caïd followed us, pointedly not sharing our burden. I turned back to look at him. "Perhaps you should go and bring a doctor."

"There is only one doctor in town."

"Bring him, then."

"He is at evening prayer."

"I see."

"I could not interrupt him. Not for anyone, but certainly not for this man." The look on Soliman's face was difficult to interpret. Father Rheinholdt had enriched him, I suspect by a good measure. I think he realized that in the street before the mosque this particular source of revenue had dried up. At the same time his association with the priest will have compromised him in the eyes of Benhir's faithful. And there was still the Antiquities Service to be dealt with; he must have realized I had informed them of the pyramid's destruction. On the whole Soliman did not look like a man with happy prospects.

I could not resist needling him. "Should you not be at prayer yourself?"

He did not answer me; fell a few paces farther behind us. At the inn he hesitated at the door, bowed, and without a word walked off, headed back to the mosque. Or perhaps simply to his restaurant.

In our room we got water and disinfectant and cleaned the priest's wounds. He is a handsome man, blond, lean; a smaller, trimmer version of the athletic Baron Lees-Gottorp. There was a first-aid kit among our traveling things; Henry got the smelling salts and bandages. Rheinholdt winced at the salts, then opened his dark swollen eyes and stared directly into mine. A look of slight alarm entered his face, and his body stiffened a bit. He glanced anxiously about the room; saw Brigit. "How did I get here?"

Brigit smiled but moved no closer to her employer. "We brought you."

" 'We'?"

"The three of us. This is Mr. Howard Carter and Mr. Henry Larrimer."

His eyes fell on Henry, who was unpacking bandages. Suddenly, inexplicably, Rheinholdt became frightened again. He looked wildly from one of us to another. "No!"

"Calm down, Father." I tried, not very successfully, to sound like a doctor.

"What are you going to do to me?"

"Bandage those bruises. What did you think?"

He looked around still again, quite uncertainly. Sat up on the bed and inspected the room still more carefully. Then seemed to relax. Stared at me. "Bruises."

I pointed my finger to the side of his head. He reached up, touched the worst of the wounds; winced.

"You should be glad it isn't worse. Moslems have a rather severe way of dealing with unbelievers. Especially ones who interrupt their worship."

"Barbarians. I hate them."

"And they hate you. More to the point, though, they outnumber you. What on earth possessed you to act so foolishly?"

Henry had prepared the bandages. He came over to the bed and began wrapping them about the priest's head.

Rheinholdt fell silent for a moment; began to look glum. "It was that priest, that Khalid. This is all his doing."

"I beg your pardon?" This struck me as a strange way to talk about a fellow Christian clergyman. But I do not think I was completely surprised. "Father Khalid . . . ?"

"He sent me there." Henry pulled a bandage too tight. Rheinholdt winced, then went on. "Or rather, he tricked me into going. We had a long conversation this afternoon, and he must have guessed why I am in Egypt. He played on that."

"And why are you here?"

He had been talking more or less freely; now he stopped, became suspicious. "Howard Carter." He studied me. "Brigit tells me you have left the Antiquities Service. Is that correct?"

"It left me. But at any rate we are no longer connected."

"I see." He still looked suspicious.

Henry had finished bandaging his head. "There. You look like Lazarus fresh out of the tomb." I'm afraid my sense of humor is beginning to rub off onto Henry.

But Rheinholdt was not amused. "That is an extremely distasteful remark."

Henry grinned. "But appropriate, don't you think? We thought your ribs might have been hurt, too. Do they feel all right?" He pressed his hand on the side of Rheinholdt's chest.

The priest screamed, glared at Henry as if he were an assassin. But Henry smiled, breezy as ever. "I'm surprised you were able to sit up. We'll have to bind them."

I wanted to press Rheinholdt while he was still off-guard. "You were saying, about Father Khalid . . ."

He braced himself under Henry's ministrations, avoided looking directly at any of us. "There are certain relics here. A clay bird and some cloth. Do you take my drift, Herr Carter?"

"Yes. I do." Or at least I thought I did. There is not a town anywhere in the Delta that does not claim to have been the home of Jesus, Mary and Joseph while they lived in Egypt. And the apocryphal accounts of their lives here are so numerous and varied that anything, almost literally anything can be passed off as a relic to a sufficiently impressionable visitor. One book mentions the young Christ planting a sycamore grove; so now every town in the Delta with sycamores growing claims to have been visited by the Lord. The cloth Rheinholdt was after would be the white cloth that the Christ child is said to have miraculously dyed many colors. The clay bird was new to me.

"Herr Carter." Father Rheinholdt was beginning to look a bit fanatical; this was obviously a hot topic with him. "I don't think I shall be able to stand alone. Will you help me to the mirror? I want to see what I look like. What they did to me."

Henry had finished bandaging his ribs. The two of us helped him to his feet, eased him toward a small mirror on the wall at the foot of the bed. He tried to stand erect in front of it; could not. Then he studied his face, quite closely. Smiled at himself. "Do you think there will be any scars?"

No one answered him. But Henry chuckled. I have no idea what he was thinking.

"Brigit." The priest turned awkwardly around, supported himself with a hand against the wall.

"Yes, Father?" Through all of this Brigit had kept her distance. Her face was quite expressionless. She still did not move.

"I shall not be able to return unassisted. I'd like you to go out to the monastery and get help. Two of the nuns, perhaps."

"Yes. Of course." I could see in her face that she did not want to go.

Henry walked her to the door. "Why don't you come back with them? We have a lot more to talk about."

I had a suspicion that Rheinholdt would not begin to open up to me until we were alone. "Better yet, Henry, why don't you go with her? For company."

Both Henry and Brigit seemed to like the idea; they took two lanterns and left. I watched them cross the inn's lobby and go out into the night.

Rheinholdt was still standing, quite unsteadily. "Please, help me back onto the bed." When he was resting again he looked about the room half-suspiciously, as if he were unsure we were really alone. His tone suggested conspiracy. "Herr Carter, are you really no longer in the employ of the Antiquities Service?"

"Rather emphatically not, I'm afraid."

"But you do know about Egypt's ancient past?"

I answered him rather stiffly. "It has been my profession."

"Then"—he hushed his voice even further—"you understand about those relics I mentioned."

I leaned against the table, tried to sound casual. "I presume you are after relics of Christ. The cloth whose color he changed I have heard about. The other one—"

"The clay bird," he prompted.

"—yes. That one I am not familiar with."

He adjusted his weight on the bed; sighed. Now that the shock was wearing off, he must have been in a good deal of pain.

"There is some morphia in our first-aid kit."

"No. Thank you, no. I need only your conversation." For the first time all night he smiled. It changed his appearance completely. There is a cold handsomeness to the man, like chiseled stone. But now he was smiling; now the force of his personality animated him and even through the bruises he looked engaging and friendly. I wanted to like him; I wanted to trust him. "About that bird . . . You have really never heard the story?"

"I'm afraid not, no."

"Well, it is recorded in the *Gospel of the Infancy of Christ,* which some sources attribute to St. Thomas. One day the young Christ and his playmates fashioned animals out of the clay in the streets. Asses, birds, oxen, and the like. Then Christ breathed on the ones he had made and gave them life. They walked, ate, drank; obeyed his commands. The birds flew about and returned when he called them."

I tried to keep my tone neutral. "You believe this?"

"It is in the Gospel."

"The apocryphal gospel." I could not resist correcting him.

But he dismissed it. "A good number of the Church fathers accepted it as genuine. Eusebius, John Chrysostom, dozens of them."

"So the clay bird you believed to be in the mosque—"

"Is one of them, yes. Khalid described it to me in detail. It is a sparrow. The Gospel specifically mentions sparrows. He told me that they desecrate it, mutilate it during their services."

"He fed you a line."

He looked glum. "So I realize. And a good line, at that."

"I think you will find that the Moslem attitude toward other religions is largely one of indifferent contempt."

"For the one true religion—" His zeal was coming back.

But I cut him off. "Which they believe to possess. Even if you believed Khalid's story, did you have to go bellowing into the mosque when it was most crowded?"

Rheinholdt smiled at me again. I think he was pleased at his own audaciousness. "I think there is a good chance that they really do have those relics. If I had gotten them, these bruises would have been worth it."

"Does the Church really want more martyrs?" I was wry. Khalid had laid his little snare all too shrewdly. He must have sensed the strain of fanaticism in Rheinholdt, played on it, blown on the coals until the fire came out. "More to the point, didn't it occur to you to wonder why Khalid should not go after such precious things himself?"

"He said he was afraid of the Moslems. He said they could hurt him and his church too deeply to take the chance. But his motives are beside the point. Herr Carter, I have proof that this is where the Christ child grew up."

I kept my voice soft; did not want him to get too excited. "You have."

"Yes."

"May I ask what?"

I was certain he was going to tell me about a sycamore grove. Or an ancient scrap of colored cloth. Or something equally meaningless, equally equivocal. But I was mistaken.

"Herr Carter, I have one of the animals."

"I beg your pardon?" I had to hear it again.

"I have one of them. An eagle or a hawk. Crudely fashioned. It is four inches long. Made of clay. It flies, it eats. I have it in a cage."

He was in earnest; for a moment I was half-tempted to believe him. But my common sense came back to me. "A clay eagle brought to life by Christ."

"Yes. Exactly."

"But . . . but it would be nineteen hundred years old."

"What the Lord Christ raises up, stays raised." He said this quietly, confident of its truth.

"And you would be willing to let me examine it, of course."

"Of course." He looked at me squarely. I think he must actually believe it. We must get Brigit away from him. "I have it in a cage."

I was at a loss for anything to say. I stared at him. A drop of blood had seeped through the bandage on his forehead.

"A bird cage. It pecks at the bars quite fiercely."

"Yes. Naturally." I have never felt so uncomfortable with anyone. I had no idea how to deal with him; groped for conversation. "Where did you find it?"

"At the pyramid." He was matter-of-fact. "It was scrambling about the north face. I think it was trying to get inside."

There was a quick knock and the door opened. Henry and Brigit had returned. I could not have been more glad to see them. Behind them were four nuns carrying a litter. I recognized one of them. "Sister Marcellinus."

She looked at me quizzically. "We have met?"

"Yes. Early one morning in the Valley of the Kings."

She stared at me blankly.

"You were chasing a scarab, as I recall it. And you had an old magical papyrus, a love spell. You dropped it as you were leaving. Surely you remember . . . ?"

"No, I am afraid I do not. You must be mistaken." She looked at me with hatred, uncomplicated hatred in her eyes; then glanced at Rheinholdt. Who was looking at her with something like the same expression.

I put on a wide smile. "But I recall it so clearly."

She turned her back on me, helped get Rheinholdt onto the litter.

He looked rather imperious as they lifted him, carried him toward the door. "Come with us, Brigit. I have some notes I shall want you to transcribe."

"Yes, sir. I'll be along in a moment. I just want to say good night to my friends."

"Hurry up. I shall need you." The five of them left rapidly.

Brigit shook Henry's hand, then mine. "Hank tells me the

two of you will be camping out at Athribis for the next few days.''

''Yes. We need to survey the damage. There is a lot of work to be done.''

''Good. I'll see you there tomorrow, then.'' She waved good night to us and hurried off to catch up with the others.

Henry sat on his bed, stretched. ''She is going to join us. She just needs time to find the right moment to tell Rheinholdt.''

''I'm glad to hear it, Henry. Father Rheinholdt is not quite sane.'' I recounted for him my conversation with the priest. ''He obviously tore the pyramid down thinking he would find these miraculous animals inside.''

Henry considered this. ''You don't think he might really have one?''

''Don't be ridiculous.''

''Do you take Egyptian magic any more seriously than you do Christian magic?''

''Henry.'' I tried my best to sound like a disapproving teacher.

''No, I mean it. If there are magical creatures around here, how could we know for certain they originated with Christ?''

Henry can be as maddening as any Moslem. I wish I knew how seriously he meant all this.

And so . . .

And so it appears that an archaeological treasure—a minor one, I admit, but nevertheless a thing that can never be replaced—has been sacrificed to this man's religious obsession.

I need a long sleep.

Athribis. The pyramid site.

We both slept late this morning, much later than we'd intended. We had asked our innkeeper to wake us at eight

o'clock; but for reasons not stated he let us sleep. *Mektoub*. It
was nearly noon when we got up and well past three when we
finally got our things moved out here. Two boys from Benhir
helped us, then demanded ruinous amounts of baksheesh.
Henry, who is becoming expert at such things, gave them a
tenth of what they asked for and sent them away satisfied.

He stood looking glumly at our folded-up tent. "It's too
bad there are no rock-cut tombs around. I've never been
much good at putting these things up."

"There is a small stone chapel over there." I pointed to
the far end of the field. "It would probably be quite usable,
unless the roof is missing. Why don't we look?"

The chapel is dedicated to Khonsu, the god of the moon.
Henry traced the god's likeness with his finger in the
weathered stone. "Do you think he'll mind us moving in?"

"Not likely. We'll be giving him more attention than he's
gotten in two thousand years."

"I'm not so sure about that. This looks like a good place
for lovers."

We stepped inside. It measures about twelve feet by
fourteen and, unlike many tombs and shrines, is cool and
well ventilated. There are reliefs on the walls, not very good
ones, of the moon god in his various guises. There is more
than enough room for our equipment and provisions. We
stowed our gear and began a preliminary survey of the ruins.

Henry reminded me he was new to field archaeology.
"What should I look for?"

"For now, it's hard to say. Anything that looks interesting
or promising."

"Is it possible for one pile of rubble to look more
interesting than another?"

"I know it sounds vague, Henry, but we don't have to be
all that thorough. The team Maspero sends will do the real
work. But we shouldn't overlook anything obvious. Statues,

potsherds, amulets, anything with inscriptions . . . Try to imagine what it must have looked like here before they pulled down the pyramid. Look here.'' I pointed to a pile of bricks from the pyramid. "These were obviously just put here. It looks like there is something under them.''

We removed the bricks, one by one. "Be certain to check them for inscriptions. Especially cartouches or serekhs.''

At the bottom of the pile was a large stone, a foot and a half square and perhaps three inches high. In the center of it, badly eroded, were two low stumps. I inspected all of the exposed surfaces; there was no writing on them. "Help me turn it over. The bottom is probably blank too, but it's worth a look.''

"What is it?''

"This is a statue base. Those two stumps were the feet.''

"Oh.'' He stared at it for a moment, then helped me turn it. "It must be very old.''

"It is very worn; that's all we can say. It's limestone. Soft. Weathers easily.'' I checked the bottom surface carefully. "Nothing. But you see the sort of thing we want to look for. The next one we find could easily be inscribed.''

All afternoon we zigzagged across the field together, on the assumption that what one of us missed the other would likely spot. We inspected hundreds of stones, bricks; found a small sphinx, much like the one I found yesterday, but uninscribed. Stone after stone was badly eroded, told us nothing. I began to feel frustrated. "Damned Delta weather.''

Henry had been down on one knee, examining a small chunk of black stone. He stood up, stared into the sky. "I don't like it either. Look at all the clouds. You're right, Howard, we might as well be in another country. The sky seems too heavy here. Not at all like the sky over the desert. Nowhere near so transparent.''

I only half listened to this. "Henry, is that a piece of basalt?"

"Hm?" He came out of his rhapsodic mood. "This? Oh, I don't know. I think so."

"Let me see it." I ran my eyes along it. "Here. Where's the magnifier?" He handed it to me. I pointed to the inscription. "Here. It is another serekh. You see the two animals perched atop it? It is the same as the other one. Khasekhemui."

"This is a piece of a statue?"

"Yes, I think so. The front part of its shoulder. See if there are any more fragments." I had been kneeling on the ground; sat back. Reinspected the piece. "Khasekhemui."

"I've never heard of him. Was he a minor pharaoh?" He was scrambling among the stones. "It doesn't look like there's any more of it here."

I joined him in the search. "Not minor, just very ancient, and so ill-remembered. He ruled in the Second Dynasty, just before Egyptian civilization really bloomed."

"So"—he did some quick reckoning—". . . 3,000 B.C.?"

"Give or take a hundred years, yes. Here, I've found another piece." It was the upper part of an outstretched arm, an unusual pose for a piece of Egyptian sculpture, but not unknown. "It's a pretty good fit with the shoulder you found."

We went on searching. "You were saying about Khasekhemui . . . ?"

"Yes. There is some evidence—indirect and circumstantial, but enough to be convincing—that it was Khasekhemui who gave Egyptian religion the final shaping into what we know. Those two animals above his serekh are the key. You see—"

"Look here!" Henry had found two fragments of a leg.

"But they don't look quite proportional. A bit too big, or too thick, to go with the other pieces we found . . ."

"I can see what you mean. But this is a very early piece. The craftsmanship wouldn't necessarily be as expert as what you're used to seeing."

"Is this an important find, Howard?" Henry was positively beaming.

"If it ties Khasekhemui to the pyramid, it's priceless." I looked about glumly. "Or what little there is left of the pyramid."

"You sound so bitter when you talk about it. *Mektoub*, Carter Pasha."

He smiled; obviously wanted to make me laugh. But I could not. All that senseless tearing down. I sighed. "Let's see if we can find anything else. You want to hear about Khasekhemui?"

"Yes, definitely."

We kept sifting through the rubble. "In archaic Egypt— before the culture took its final shape under the Third Dynasty—there was a considerable amount of religious tension. There is even evidence for a religious civil war, on a rather destructive scale. There were two opposing cults, one dedicated to the solar falcon Horus, the other to his enemy Set. The separate cults may have come from the Delta and from Upper Egypt; that seems likely. Anyway, various early pharaohs crowned their serekhs with either the falcon of Horus or the Set animal, depending on their allegiance."

"The Set animal?" Henry walked back to the statue, inspected the serekh.

"No one's certain what it is. Part donkey, part camel, part giraffe . . . Strange looking, isn't it?"

He looked closely at the fragment, and realized what I was explaining. "This serekh has both."

"Exactly. It is evidence—indirect but concrete—that

Khasekhemui forged some kind of religious fusion, presumably the source of Egyptian religion as it was practiced for three thousand years.''

Henry stood up, peered away at the piles of brick and rubble. ''And this was his pyramid. What secrets it must have contained.''

How like him to go overboard. ''All we can say with certainty is that we've found a statue and a small sphinx here bearing his serekh. But that doesn't make it his pyramid, Henry. Now, if we could find a brick from the pyramid with his serekh stamped on it . . .'' I turned a brick over with the toe of my boot. ''Or better yet, the pyramid's capstone, with appropriate inscriptions. Pyramid building is generally thought to have begun only in the Third Dynasty.''

He turned suddenly back to me. ''Egyptian religion is pretty much the same thing as Egyptian magic, isn't it?''

''I suppose so. They were inextricably connected. But, Henry—''

''Then we've got to get back to looking.'' He ran off toward the actual spot on which the pyramid had stood and began turning bricks over, tossing them about with enthusiastic abandon.

''Henry! Now that we know what we're looking for here, we've got to be more systematic.'' He ignored me, went on playing gleefully among the bricks. ''Henry!''

I finally got him calmed down, but it was a chore. I do not like this at all. He is beginning to act mildly fanatical again. Much as he did before that awful night in the Valley of the Queens. I never know what to expect from my employer.

Toward dusk Henry gathered wood from the forest and banked an enormous bonfire in front of our chapel. ''Big fires are more fun.'' The evening air carried a slight chill, and the white light of the gibbous moon made it seem even colder. The motionless evening air brought faintly from Benhir the muezzin's call to nightfall prayer.

I pulled on a sweater, moved as close to the fire as I could. "We should hike into the town. Maspero will have sent me some sort of message by now."

"Instructions?"

"More or less. I'm quite certain he'll want to act quickly, before the site can be damaged still further."

We took up lanterns and walked to town. The moon, the lamps lit our way well and we made good time. The air tonight is perfectly still. We will have rain tomorrow.

But when I called at the train station there was no message for me. I had the clerk double- and triple-check it. But there was nothing.

Henry seemed surprised at my disappointment. "You actually expected a government bureau to act quickly?"

"For something as important as this I did, yes."

"Poor Howard."

"Let's go." I didn't speak to him on the way back to camp. I hate it when Henry—of all people—treats me like a naive child.

When we got back to Athribis Brigit was waiting for us. She stood next to the fire; the flames turned her eyes wild, made her hair a brilliant bronze. She was wearing the same black things she had had on yesterday. "This is a fine, high fire you've made here. Shall we sacrifice to the gods?"

Henry laughed. "That depends. Which one did you have in mind?"

Brigit widened her eyes, extended her arms toward the flames. "Between the fire and the moon," she intoned, "there is room for a thousand."

I was in no mood for this sort of thing; was still cranky from Henry's goading. "How was your day, Brigit?"

"Oh, all right, I guess." She came out of her mock

trance. "Father Rheinholdt has been in his cell all day. I could hear him talking to himself."

"Casual conversation? Or is he too in a mystical mood?"

"Nothing special." She shrugged. "Just some random muttering. He only came out once, to get some food for his pet bird, I think."

Henry jumped on this before I could. "He has a bird? What kind?"

"I've never seen it." Brigit seemed startled by Henry's urgency. "He keeps it in his cell. No one ever goes there except the nun who cleans it. Why do you ask?"

I decided not to let Henry spill any beans. Brigit finds the priest intimidating enough as it is. "It's nothing, Brigit. Henry numbers birds among his hobbies, that's all."

Henry glanced at me, puzzled; but followed my lead and dropped the subject.

I decided to shift to a safer topic. "I'm surprised that the priests and nuns sleep under the same roof. It seems . . . irregular."

"Oh, the monastery has two wings, separated by a wide courtyard. The wing the nuns and I occupy is in poor repair. They never stop complaining about it."

"How many are there?"

"Do you mean priests or nuns?"

I was glad Brigit was in an informative mood tonight. "Both."

"Well, there are three priests who seem to be there more or less permanently, and a half dozen others who come and go. The nuns . . . I don't know how many there are in all. They keep coming and going, too. Traveling around the country, I think."

"But Father Rheinholdt is in charge of it all?"

The questioning was finally making her suspicious. She looked from one of us to the other. "Yes. Why? Is anything wrong?"

''No, not at all. It's just that they seem so mysterious. It's difficult not to be curious about them.''

Henry took the lead now. ''We made what Howard thinks may be an important find today.''

''May be,'' I emphasized.

''Would you like to see it?''

''Very much.'' Brigit's smile was back.

Henry brought the fragments out of the chapel, unwrapped them, explained to Brigit—in qualified terms, I was glad to note—what I think they may indicate. She got down on one knee and pressed her hand against the black stone, traced the outline of the serekh with her fingertip. The gesture was so much like Henry's customary response to ancient stone that I was a bit startled.

She pressed her hand into the hollow of the shoulder a second time. ''Hank, it's beautiful. Do you think you'll find the rest of it?''

Henry said nothing, looked to me.

''We searched fairly thoroughly today. If there are more pieces to be found, they must be widely scattered. They could be anywhere. They could be in the Nile.''

Brigit lowered her eyes. ''I'd like to help you search. I'd like to find—retrieve—something of beauty from the old world.'' Then she looked directly at me. ''I'll be leaving the priests in another day or so.''

''We'll still be here.''

Henry seemed to get caught up in Brigit's enthusiasm. ''Would you like to see where we found them? It's over there, near where the pyramid was.''

''Yes, I'd love to.'' She stood up, dusted off her trousers. ''You coming, Howard?''

''No, I don't think so. The long day is catching up with me. I think I'll turn in. Good night to both of you.''

''Good night, then.''

Brigit made a mock bow and clicked her heels like a good

Prussian soldier. They took up a pair of lanterns and walked off into the ruins.

I yawned three times. Speaking about my fatigue seemed to sharpen it. I took our third lantern into the chapel with me, lowered the flame, crawled into my sleeping bag. And I think I must have gone to sleep almost at once.

And then awoke again, quickly. The flame of the lamp was higher now, glowing brilliantly. Its light dazzled my eyes. Then it grew rounder, paler; white; it became the face of the moon. "Idiot," I muttered to myself. "Dreams." The face in the moon grinned at me, wider and wider, then began to laugh at me the way Henry does sometime. The moon's face transformed itself into the face of one of those mummified children; blood poured out of its mouth as it screamed. Then again the face in the sky changed, into the face of Henry Larrimer. He opened his mouth. "Of the Pittsburgh Larrimers," he said, and out of his mouth flew a thousand pieces of ancient basalt. Arms, legs, heads, all of them tumbling toward me out of the sky. I would be crushed.

I sat up in my sleeping bag. "Dream. Idiot." I was sweating. My breathing was fast; it took a long while to get it back to normal. Took a full, deep breath. Coughed. There was something in the air. Smoke. I could see it outside in the still air around the bonfire. Could see it inside too, more thinly. Good Lord, Henry, not again. It was hashish.

It took me a few moments to get a grip on myself. There were voices. Henry and Brigit outside the chapel, talking by the fire. I wanted to lie down, go back to sleep. But I was on edge. I listened to them.

"I was eleven then." Henry was talking softly. If I had cried out in my nightmare they hadn't heard me; went on with their conversation. "It seems to me I didn't stop crying for months."

They were both out of my sight, beyond the edges of the open door. I could see the fire, nothing else. My senses were still confused. At moments it seemed as if the voices were coming to me out of the fire.

"I never knew my mother at all," Brigit said. "And my father . . . I was better off with 'Uncle Rolf.' "

"I'm getting cold."

"Come over here and sit next to me."

There was the sound of footsteps, then silence for a while.

"I've never stopped wanting my mother back. I've never stopped missing her." Henry sounded weary. "If I could see her again, even for a moment, or hear her voice . . . That is why I came to Egypt. I thought that here . . . if anywhere in the world . . . I don't know what I thought. Talking about it like this, actually saying the words, I feel absurd."

"You shouldn't."

Henry. What a pity. I felt so terrible eavesdropping on these private things. Poor Henry. What did he hope to find here? How could he hope for . . . The flame in my lantern flickered, made the stone gods on the walls seem to move; reminded me where I was. Hope is a manufactured thing; we make it ourselves. It is not the gift of any god.

"It's freezing out here, Brigit. Let me get you a sweater."

"No, I'm all right. The fire is more than enough. Does Mr. Carter know . . . what you came here looking for?"

"No. He must suspect, of course. He's seen all the things I brought. Measuring devices, detectors. But I could never tell him about it. His mind is so practical. He'd laugh at me."

"Laugh at grief and loneliness?"

"I know him, Brigit. He has no use for anything that isn't practical."

This hurt me. Very deeply.

"I know him too, Hank. I have seen, or at least I have glimpsed, his spiritual side. It is there. He hides it but it is there. He might laugh at your apparatus, but never at you yourself."

Thank you, Brigit.

"I don't know." Henry seemed very tired; or perhaps he just thought he had said too much. He gently backed away from it. "I wish I could believe that. I'd like to be closer to him."

Lying there in the half-darkness, hearing those disembodied voices, enclosed by the ancient stone of the chapel, I have never felt so alone.

"It's freezing, Brigit. Are you sure I can't get you a sweater?"

"The cold never bothers me. I hardly feel it."

"I'm freezing."

"Here. I'll warm your hands."

I felt exhausted. I felt as if I'd been awake forever. I lay back, curled up in my sleeping bag. I wanted to leave them to themselves; I wanted to sleep. Closed my eyes.

Then awoke. Something disturbed me. Voices. My lamp had gone out; it seemed I had had my eyes closed for only an instant but my lamp had burned out. In the dark I could not get my bearings. There were anxious voices.

"Howard! Howard!"

"Mr. Carter! Come quickly!"

I crawled out of my bag, scrambled unsteadily to my feet. The glow from the bonfire filled the chapel's doorway. Then Brigit was outlined there. "Mr. Carter, Hank has seen something."

The bonfire too had burned lower; was less than five feet high. Beyond it, at the perimeter of its light, Henry was down on all fours, digging madly through a large heap of brick and rubble. Turning over bricks, throwing them aside with a frenzy that made it seem that to reach the bottom of the heap was all he wanted in the world. He glanced over his shoulder. "Howard! Hurry up! We can't let it get away!"

I rushed to his side. "What, Henry? Let what get away?"

"One of the animals! I saw it. It ran here among these stones." He looked wild; his eyes were opened wide. "It crawled into a crack!"

"Henry, stop a minute. Slow down." I tried my best to calm him down. "Now tell me exactly what you saw."

He had been breathing rapidly; eased off. "We were sitting by the fire. I saw it walk around the far side. It seemed to be warming itself. It looked . . . it looked like the Set animal, the one in the carvings. It stared at the empty pyramid site and lowered its head sadly. It was only six inches high."

"Henry." I tried not to let my voice sound too disapproving; turned to Brigit. "Did you see it too?"

Henry answered for her. "No. I cried out when I saw it, and it bolted for the rocks. Brigit never had a chance to see it."

"I see. Well, calm down. We'll move the rest of the stones and see what is there."

"You don't believe me." He looked crestfallen; glanced at Brigit with a just-as-I-told-you attitude.

"I just want to see for myself."

So Henry moved the bricks and debris, carefully, one piece at a time. He handled them himself; would not let me touch them. And then he came to the last stone. Lifted it carefully aside. And there it was.

Good Jesus, there it was. Hiding behind the last of the stones, looking as if it were terrified of us, looking around wildly for someplace to run. The Set animal, alive, breathing, moving; made of clay. It stared directly at me; I went numb. "Jesus."

"We've got to catch it!" Henry reached for an empty canvas sack. "Don't let it get away!"

The animal opened its mouth; cried. The sound was more like a whistle than anything else. It cried repeatedly.

Henry lunged for it. It bolted and, for whatever reason, made straight for me. My reflexes were almost too slow. I shot out an arm, caught the thing by a hind leg. It whined shrilly, nipped at my fingers.

"Here." Henry held out the opened sack and I put it inside. "God, Howard, this is terrific. We have proof! We actually have proof!"

I was numb; my limbs felt like rubber. "Proof, Henry, yes. But of what?" He held the sack out to me, wordless. "No, I'm in no condition to deal with it now. Put it somewhere safe and we can examine it in the morning. And for God's sake, Henry, don't smoke any more hashish."

I came back into the chapel; got back into my sleeping bag. And was much too agitated to sleep. There was Henry, with his drugs and his fantasies, and once again I had been pulled into the center of it.

After a few minutes Brigit came in. "He's asleep already."

"Good."

"He was so excited. I thought he'd be awake all night."

I propped myself up on an elbow. "Drugs. We are none of us in our right senses. That animal can't be what it seems."

"Why not?"

"Brigit." My schoolteacher voice is becoming second nature to me. "I take it Henry told you about the clay animals Rheinholdt is after?"

"Yes."

"And you don't think the drugs, combined with that suggestion, could . . ." I wanted to convince myself, not her. I did not care what she believed. I could hear the animal outside, crying.

She smiled. "Let's go and look, then."

"No, I'm too tired. By morning it will have turned to something ordinary."

"How long have you lived in Egypt, Mr. Carter?"

I yawned. "Thirteen years."

"And until tonight you have never glimpsed the bits of magic that still exist here, off in the corners and in the shadows?" She smiled again.

And as always her smile, her manner disarmed me. "Yes. Of course I have. Why do you think I stay here?" I kept my voice low.

"Of course you have seen it. I have been here for only a matter of months, and I already know what a special place Egypt is."

Baron Lees-Gottorp was a fool to abandon this girl. "But Henry is . . . Don't you see it? Henry is trying to make Egypt into something it is not. Into what he wants it to be. He came here wanting to find magic."

"And you came wanting not to. What if his image of Egypt is closer to the reality?"

I had let this go too far. "Ghosts, Brigit? Voices of the dead? Contacts with the spirit world? That sort of stuff belongs in maiden ladies' parlors, not here."

"He's trying to find what is here, Howard. He has already found part of it. You can't deny that." It was the first time she had used my Christian name. Outside, the animal squealed. "I mean, you make it sound as if he were traipsing around with ouija boards and tarot cards. I think you're just afraid to admit he was correct about something. You treat him like such a boy."

My elbow was sore from the pressure; I sat up. For an instant I thought I heard Henry walking about. I listened, but everything was quiet. "How much hashish did he smoke tonight?"

Brigit sat down beside me. Her features were outlined by the dying firelight. "Not as much as I did. That isn't the point."

"It is precisely the point. If there is—as you put it—magic off in the shadows, the way to find it is with science. With method and reason and hard work. Chasing pipe dreams won't help."

She leaned back against the wall. The stone must have been cold, because she sat upright again. "It helped tonight. You don't want to believe what's out there, do you?"

She was making me feel old, and irritable. "I accept Egypt for what it is. Henry is trying to use it. That is the difference, and it's an important one." I hesitated; looked away from her. "No, I don't want to believe it. In the morning it will be gone. Nothing but a dream."

Outside, the fire crackled loudly. I thought I heard footsteps. Then there was nothing.

Brigit had glanced at the door; looked back at me. "Dreams are reality, Howard. And so are nightmares. That is the whole point."

This was exasperating. "We are talking at cross-purposes."

Suddenly the light from the dying fire was blocked. We looked to the doorway simultaneously. The outline of a man was there, pitch black against the glowing background. Brigit spoke first. "Hank. We thought you were asleep."

The figure leaned casually against the side of the doorway, stretched out an arm to the opposite lintel.

"For heaven's sake, Hank, say something."

The figure yawned exaggeratedly. "Your Mr. Larrimer is still asleep."

In the near-darkness I could feel Brigit stiffen. "Father Rheinholdt."

I stood up. "Good evening, Father. Surely it is rather late for you to be out here?"

"This place draws me irresistibly. Evidently I am not alone in that."

"Let's go outside. You can warm yourself by the fire."

He did not move; continued to block the doorway.

"I'd like to go outside," I repeated.

He moved slowly away. He intended his manner to be threatening, I am certain. But it came off simply odd.

The fire was low, less than a yard high. We would have to refuel it soon. Henry was curled up on the ground beside it, snoring faintly. Next to him were the fragments of sculpture we had found. I should have repacked them before I went to sleep. Rheinholdt tapped one of them with the toe of his boot. "You have had good hunting."

"We have made a promising start, yes."

He was trying to sound light, conversational; instead he sounded preoccupied. "Do you think you will find the rest of it?"

I shrugged. "Who can say? There are times when I wish I had made one of the exact sciences my profession."

"And give up the adventure?" Rheinholdt smiled at me. There was a branch of wood on the ground at his feet; he stooped down, tossed it into the fire. Suddenly abandoned any pretense of friendliness. "You told me you were here only for photographs."

"What we came to photograph is no longer in existence. That changes things."

"I know why you are here. It will not do you any good. I have connections. I can do as I please here."

Rubbish. "You mean to tell me that you have a permit for what you did here?"

"I have," he said slowly and carefully, "met with your superior, Monsieur Maspero."

"My late superior," I corrected him.

The fire crackled; sparks floated upward. He took a step backward. "Why do people from Protestant countries always take Catholic priests to be fools?"

He turned to Brigit. "And you. My secretary. The girl I helped, helping them now."

Brigit had been standing apart, keeping her distance. She could only assume that the priest knew of my message to Cairo. She had no idea what she could say. I could see the confusion in her face. All she could manage was, "No, I wouldn't do that."

Rheinholdt laughed. "You all take us for fools." Then he put on a benign, priestly smile. "You wish to keep your position with me, then?"

Brigit looked at me; at Henry, asleep on the ground; then back at Rheinholdt. Summoned her nerve. "No. Mr. Larrimer has offered me a position." True as it was, in the circumstances it sounded feeble. "At a higher salary," she added weakly.

The priest's smile broadened. His suspicions were confirmed. "Of course. It is all as innocent as that. You play the innocent very well."

I could not let pass this opening. "She would make a fine priest, don't you think? She's even dressed for it."

But he ignored my irreverence. He was glaring at Brigit. "You can come back with me now and get your things. I don't want you coming back after that."

"But the rest of my clothes, the things you had sent to the Wadi Natrun . . ."

"I shall have them sent here for you, in care of Herr Carter. They will be here inside a week."

I did not like the idea of Brigit going off into the night with this man. "Why don't you get your things tomorrow, Brigit? Carrying them through this darkness—"

"That will be quite impossible, Herr Carter," Rheinholdt snapped at me. "I have important business tomorrow. She can get her things now or do without them."

"Then I'll come with you."

''No, it's all right, Howard. I can manage.'' I could see in the girl's face that it was not all right. But Brigit seems to pride herself on her independence, and I didn't want to intrude on it. There was really nothing to be done.

The animal in the sack had been quiet through all of this. Now, at this unfortunate moment, it resumed its struggles; let out a cry. Rheinholdt glared at it, startled; obviously recognized the sound. He took a step toward it, but I cut him off, picked up the sack myself. ''We caught a rabbit. For dinner tomorrow. It will make good eating.''

He stared at me for a long moment. Then, without looking at her, he said, ''We should go, Brigit. It's getting late and I want to be rid of you.''

There were clouds building up in the north. I did not like the look of them. ''Well, hurry back. We're in for some unpleasant weather.''

They left together without exchanging another word. Brigit took one of our lamps or they would have been in total darkness.

I brought the animal into the chapel with me so it will be dry when the rain comes. Have been tempted to look at it again. Cannot. It is only a lizard or a field mouse. In the morning I will see. I am afraid to look at it now. This one dream, at least, has become far too real.

The fire is dying down. I should look for more wood.

Rain. Cold heavy rain, and clouds so grey and thick they are almost black. The air has a sharp, chill edge to it. The floor of the chapel is damp with it.

When I awoke Henry was already up. ''My head. Good God. Where's the first-aid kit?''

I had trouble shaking off my sleep. ''You've got what you asked for. Damned hashish.'' My back ached from the damp stone. I rolled over, tried to sleep some more.

"Howard, get up. Where's Brigit?"

"She'll be back. She just went to—" I was suddenly awake. Yawned. "What time is it?"

"After nine."

"She went back to the monastery with Rheinholdt last night. To get her things. She was going to come right back here."

"Rheinholdt was here? I thought that was just a dream. Howard, I have an awful headache."

"So do I." I glared at him. "And I didn't even smoke any of that damned stuff. I just inhaled your offal."

He was sitting, with his back against the chapel wall and his knees up. He crossed his arms on his knees, buried his head in them. "I feel like shit."

I stood up, stretched. Every joint in my body was stiff. "Brigit must have seen the rain coming and decided to sleep at the monastery." As I said this I realized how unconvincing it sounded. "That must be where she is."

I walked to the chapel door, stared out across the plain. Everything was mud. Puddles, pools everywhere. The rain was coming down in vast grey sheets. Our pieces of sculpture were half-buried in the mud. I should have packed them away last night. I should have waited up for Brigit. But I don't remember much after she left with Rheinholdt. Must have fallen asleep as soon as I finished last night's journal entry; without wanting to. Damn Henry and his drugs.

My ears were filled with the sound of rain pounding the mud. It was like nothing I have seen since I left London. I walked out into it, pried the pieces of basalt out of the mud; brought them inside. Henry was sitting motionless. "You should go outside. The rain is icy. It'll wake you up in no time."

He groaned; did not move.

"Henry. Get up."

He ignored me.

I had some apples in my pack; got one and bit into it. The chapel's doorway was a grey rectangle. I sat against the back wall to watch the rain.

The chapel had faced the pyramid. Does not, I thought sadly, face it anymore. The priest saw to that. But then, after five thousand years of this climate, it can't really have been much of a sight. Weathered; weathered with a vengeance. And now gone. I hope the priest is pleased; I hope he found something, anything to make him feel this destruction was worthwhile. Because if he has it, I can get it away from him. I can, or Maspero can. The world will be poorer by one pyramid but perhaps there will be something, some small thing to compensate. I stared out the door, tried to envision the pyramid as it would have looked, cold grey water streaming down its stepped sides. No one will ever see that again.

There was a sound outside, a splash. Henry looked groggily up. "Brigit?"

"No, Henry. Brigit has had sense enough to stay at the monastery."

"No." He stood up, leaning against the wall for support. "I don't think she would have done that."

There was not much I could say to this.

Henry walked to the door, stared out as I had been staring out. "Good Christ, look at it. People always talk about rain bringing life. But look at it. There's nothing moving out there, nothing but the water itself. Rain is death."

"You're just hung over; don't take it out on the weather. There are hundreds of things moving. Frogs, snakes, spiders. You just can't see them." I put on a cheery tone that I hoped would annoy him. "Think of it as cleansing the landscape or something."

He stepped into the doorway, blocked my view. He was

dark grey framed by bright grey. "I hate it. What happened last night? With Rheinholdt, I mean."

I told him. He continued staring out the doorway as he listened. Then he half turned, as if it were the rain that really held his attention and he did not want to take his eyes off it. "He said he didn't want Brigit there anymore."

"Yes. He seemed relieved to be getting rid of her, in fact."

"But you think Brigit spent the night there."

"The rain—"

"Howard." He walked into the room; paced its length. "We are dealing with a man who does not mind tearing down pyramids to suit his caprice. Do you really think he'd hesitate to turn a girl out into a rainstorm?"

This is what had been at the bottom of my mind since I woke up; I had not wanted to let myself think it. Could think of nothing to say.

There was another loud splash.

"Howard, did you leave the animal outside?"

"No, it's right here."

We both looked around the chapel. And there was no sign of it. Looked again. Nothing. We both knew at once what must have happened; neither of us had to speak it.

Henry stared fixedly at me. "We have to go to the monastery."

"Yes."

"To get Brigit. To confront Rheinholdt. I want the girl and the animal back. I mean to get them both." Spoken like a true American millionaire. But of course he was right. We had to go. Despite the rain and the sickness and the body aches.

I looked around; looked at our supplies. "We don't have rain gear. I never thought we'd need it. We could wait . . ."

"I'm going now. Will you come?"

"Yes. Of course. Our things will be all right here."

Under normal conditions the walk to the monastery would not have taken us more than fifteen minutes. Through the rain and the mud it took more than an hour. As we passed among the trees Henry slipped on some wet grass, turned his ankle; found a stick to lean on and kept walking.

The monastery is small, a few dozen cells, a refectory, a chapel. There was no one there. They had left in the night; in the rain. We looked in each cell, one after the other. Not all of them had been used. The unused ones were filled with bats; the stench of their droppings was horrible. Even the cells that had obviously been occupied recently had a few bats in them; it had taken them no time at all to reclaim their own. The rain slowed down some. There was no sign of Brigit, or of anyone at all.

I was waiting for Henry to say, "Why did you let her go?"; was prepared to make excuses about muddled thinking, drugs on the air. But none of that was needed. I groped; there had to be something to say. "Well, at least Khalid will be pleased."

Henry started limping back in the direction of our chapel.

"Why don't we stay here until the rain stops? And dry out?"

"No."

So we walked. More water could hardly matter.

"We will have to go and get her, Howard."

"Yes."

"Where is it they were going? To the Wadi—?"

"To the Wadi Natrun. In the Western Desert."

"Yes. We will have to go there."

"I know it." I wish I didn't feel so guilty. It is the priest's doing, not mine. "We can pack in a few hours, Henry. But we'll never get our things back to Benhir until this rain stops."

He stopped walking, looked at me. "Once, Howard, just once couldn't you call me Hank?"

I sighed; walked over to where he was standing. Put my arm around his waist. "Here. You can lean your weight on me. Hank. Let's go."

Chapter Five

HENRY IS ASLEEP in the back of the cart. He has spent three days taking morphia for the pain in his ankle, which is swollen and wonderfully colored. And I have been active continually, without ever accomplishing much.

Our driver is named Akim es-Sihri. He claims to be sixty-two years old, but he looks to be in his nineties. As we ride through the water-soaked Delta he talks on and on. About his youth; about his wife, who died young; about his children, whom he does not much like; he has a small melon farm which he works himself, with help from three granddaughters.

"Why did you never remarry?" I like to keep him talking. His voice is deep for an old man, reassuring.

"My wife told me in her death throes that if I ever took another woman to my bed, she would come in the night and snatch my soul away and leave it in hell."

I said nothing.

"Believe me, she could do it."

"Of course."

He must have caught the edge in my voice. "You laugh. Other archaeologists have come to el-Qatta to break into the old tombs there. They never stay long." There is a thick, heavy fog surrounding our road; es-Sihri's voice echoes faintly among it. Three times this morning the cart got mired in the wet soil; I had to push it while es-Sihri urged the donkeys on.

The heavy rain did not stop for three days. No one in Benhir could remember anything like it. The streets were little lakes. The canals and the Nile's arms swelled all across the Delta, fashioned from the lush farmland an enormous marsh. The people in Benhir were outwardly quiet, withdrawn. But every now and then one of them would do something quirky, and betray his mood. Some of them, I think especially the older ones, must have been near panic before the downpour finally ended. A man who lives near the edge of town beat his two infant sons to death. The mosque was in constant use; the prayers, like the rain, kept coming.

Yesterday morning, despite the rain, I hiked out to Athribis. It is covered in water. The stones will be buried in mud, inscriptions eroded more badly than before. The elements began the destruction millennia ago, and they will end it. The priests were only a footnote.

Through all of this Henry remained in bed, nursing his ankle. But he could hear the torrent pounding on the roof, could feel the thick dampness coming in through the walls. Saw my drenched clothing every time I returned from an errand. And though he tried to act casual, he was obviously worried. "It's almost Biblical, isn't it? What do you think will come next, lice or boils?"

"It will stop soon." The weather also affected me; wore me down. Dampness makes my joints ache; I am getting old. I tried to cover it, but I'm afraid I was not very good at it. "There are records going back five thousand years, and there is no mention of any flood but the regular, yearly one as the Nile rises each summer.''

"Perhaps everyone drowned in it."

"You're in an apocalyptic mood, Henry. Can it just be the rain that brought it on?"

"Hank. And you know what brought it on. Have you had any word from Cairo yet?" He winced; his leg twitched. "I keep getting shooting pains."

I pulled off my wet shirt. "Is it still tender to the touch?"

"A bit, but it's getting better. Is there any word from Maspero?"

"No."

He looked away from me. "The caïd hasn't let any of your messages leave Benhir."

"I know it." I pulled off my boots; they were water-logged.

"Will he let us leave?"

"I think so. If he really believes I'm a government official, he'd hardly dare to—"

"To what?"

I didn't answer him. The caïd, absurd as he is, must be feeling rather desperate to keep news of his dealings from the authorities in Cairo.

"Howard, I feel like Custer."

"Who?"

He told me about the unfortunate general's downfall, in rather too vivid a style.

I found a towel, dried myself. "Well, to the best of my knowledge Moslems don't collect scalps." I grinned at him. "Though if they did, I'm sure a nice, shiny red one would be a real prize."

Through the three days, I was out of the inn a good bit of the time. Getting food, trying to make sense of our situation; looking for the caïd, who avoided me quite carefully;

searching for a way to leave Benhir unnoticed. I think the time Henry spent alone, convalescing in our room, made him anxious. He is a gregarious man; he enjoys company, he needs it; but I think it was more than that. Last night, having found Akim es-Sihri and come to terms with him, I went back to the inn and found him writing a long letter. Except for the notes he makes in tombs and the like, I have never seen him write a single word.

"Writing to your father?"

"Yes. He hasn't heard from me for months."

"I don't think I've ever heard you say much about him."

He stared at the letter. "We're a strange family, I guess."

I was toweling my hair; stopped and looked at him. "All families are strange, one way or another."

He looked at me. "Was yours?"

I resented his asking, though of course I had given him the opening. Dismissed it. "I live in Egypt now, not England."

I was afraid he'd press me, but for once he let it drop.

"I've found us a ride west. We leave as soon as the rain stops."

"If it ever does. Why don't we just take the train?"

"Well, for one thing there is no direct service between Benhir and the wadi. We'd have to go either to Cairo or Alexandria, then double back. For another thing, I think we should avoid the caïd's notice if we can. Just as a precaution.

"Akim es-Sihri will drive us to el-Qatta, on the western rail line. From there we can take the train to Khatatba. The Egyptian Salt and Soda Company runs a narrow-gauge railroad from Khatatba into the wadi. You should be able to stay off your sore foot most of the way."

He rubbed it, winced. "Good."

Early this morning the rain stopped. The sound of it has been constant for so long, when it stopped the silence woke me up. I lit a match, looked at my watch. Three o'clock. I pulled on some dry clothes. Packed my things quickly. Hank was still asleep; snored softly. We will be out of morphia soon. I hope he has not gotten too used to it. I left the inn as quietly as possible; walked the two blocks to es-Sihri's inn.

He was already up, harnessing the donkeys to the cart. "Carter Pasha."

"Good morning."

There were wisps of mist rising from the ground already. Akim swirled his hand through one of them. It coiled in the air; dissipated; did not quite vanish. "We will have fog."

"Good. It will cover our leaving."

"Go and bring your friend."

"He can't walk. We will have to stop and get him."

"Then sit with me and we can talk as we ride."

The cart looked to be as old as es-Sihri. I was sure it would squeak and rattle, but it was silent. The donkeys' hooves made sucking sounds in the mud. "Who is your friend, Carter Pasha?"

I told him about Hank.

"An American." He sounded disapproving; fell uncharacteristically silent.

In a few moments we reached the inn. Brought our packs out to the cart and secured them with rope. Then brought Hank out. He was groggy with morphia; laughed at us when we asked him to be quiet. Fell asleep in the cart almost at once.

Es-Sihri and I climbed back up to our seats, and our journey began. He looked back over his shoulder at Hank. "You see what I mean about them? Not good for a goddamned thing."

The donkeys took us at a slow, sleepy pace. Through the town, past the caïd's restaurant, the mosque, the train station. Everything was mud. The donkeys made only the slowest progress. In places the road was still under several inches of water. On the steps of the station sat a small boy, leaning against a post, sleeping. The sound of our approach

woke him. He stared at us, wide-eyed. Began shouting.
"Aiee! Carter Pasha! Carter Pasha! Aiee!" Ran into the
thickening mist to spread the alarm.

Es-Sihri flicked the donkeys with the reins. They picked
up what speed they could. "Why are they watching for
you?"

I did not want to go into it. "It's a long story. The caïd
thinks I am still with the Antiquities Service."

He kept his eyes on the road, the donkeys. "You are."

"No." I started to explain about myself, yet again.

But he let me off. "You are a Westerner. You are British."

There would have been no point arguing. He did not need
to add it, I could hear it in the silence of his pauses: You are
an infidel.

After a few moments, from a good way behind us, came
what sounded like gunshots. Akim seemed unaffected, kept
us moving at a steady pace. But I was alarmed. "They will
follow us."

He grinned. He has very few teeth. "They don't know
which road we are taking. They can't see us, and the water
will cover our tracks."

We rode on into the fog and Akim told me at great length
about his wife, whom he had married when she was thirteen.
She had had large eyes like many Egyptian women, and full
breasts. She bore him four children and died giving birth to
the last of them, a son who died too. And she made love with
the wild passion of a cat. "Did you know that our ancestors
worshiped cats?"

"Yes, I know that."

"Well my wife could have been one of them."

There were more gunshots, farther behind us but still
clearly to be heard. In the back of the cart Hank was roused
to consciousness, or at least semiconsciousness. "Where are
we? How did I get here?"

I introduced him to Akim es-Sihri.

''Good morning.'' He yawned. ''Thank you for letting us ride with you.''

''Akim speaks only Arabic, Hank.''

''Oh. *Sabah el-kheir,* Akim es-Sihri.'' Hank has learned a few Arabic phrases and now fancies himself a linguist.

''Naharak said. Eish halak?''

Hank turned to me, blank-faced. ''What did he ask?''

''He wants to know how you are feeling.''

''Oh.'' He looked glum. ''Tell him that I feel very well, thanks. Do we have any more morphia?''

''No.'' This was a lie. He has spent too much time using it already.

''Oh. Shit. Well, I guess the pain's eased off some. I can stand it.''

''Good.''

''I . . . uh . . . I dreamed someone was shooting at us.''

''That was no dream.''

He looked around us, seemed to notice the fog for the first time. ''Oh. Howard, I always thought the weather in Egypt was fairly constant and predictable.''

''It is. Or it's supposed to be. But all autumn things have been quite strange.''

''Perhaps a sorceror is tampering with the elements.'' He yawned again.

''Yes. Or perhaps it is the beginning of the end of the universe.''

Akim ignored all of this; acted as if it had not occurred. ''The ancient cemetery at el-Qatta is a foul place. You should stay away from it.''

Protesting that this was not our goal would do me no good. ''What is so awful about it?''

''Our ancient ancestors did not die.''

''Their bodies did. I've seen too many of them crumble to dust to believe anything else.''

''Bad embalming.''

"That is all?"

"That is all. Would you continue to occupy a defiled body if you had the choice?"

We had been traveling for a good while. The sky—or rather the fog—was beginning to lighten. There was no road visible in the mud ahead of us. I was grateful Akim, or his donkeys, knew the way. "No." I wanted to drop it. "No, I don't suppose I would."

"Well." There was a faintly triumphant note in his deep voice. "Well, then you see. El-Qatta was one of the great centers of embalming. The bodies in the cemetery on which our village sits are perfectly preserved."

This was not a thing I wished to discuss. I said nothing, pretended I was trying to see through the fog. Now that daylight was coming, I could hear occasional bird sounds. "All this water. There will be thousands of frogs soon. And then the birds will multiply to eat them."

"Let me tell you a story." His eyes were fixed on the donkeys. He seemed not to have heard me. "It is about myself. This is not the first bad rain I have seen in my life. I had almost forgotten about it until three days ago."

I was only half listening to him. "The sun will burn off the fog. It will take hours, it's so thick. And then dry the land. Things will grow better for all the rain."

"Carter Pasha."

I turned to face him.

"I want to tell you about what happened to me when I was a boy. About how my brother vanished in one of the old tombs."

"Oh. Of course. I'm sorry, Akim. I've been without much sleep. Please tell me about it."

"It happened when I just had turned thirteen. My brother Ahmed—the one who disappeared—was eleven. We used to go to the old tombs. Partly to play; we would find adventure there. Partly for the money. One used to cut through the mummies' bandages and find things to sell. Or bandages themselves; huge rolls of ancient bandages preserved in large pots; we would find them and sell them. There must be plenty of them still there. Once the great Belzoni himself bought some of my things. He rubbed his fingers through my hair and said, 'You are quite a little archaeologist.' And he took me back to his hotel room. I was very proud of that, Carter Pasha.

"The oldest tombs in el-Qatta are shaft tombs. The shafts go straight down a hundred feet, a hundred and fifty feet. Very deep. And at the bottom there are suites of rooms, scored out of the rock. You know the kind of tomb?"

"Yes. Yes, of course I do."

"You know them, then. Well, it used to be great fun for Ahmed and me to go to these tombs. We had an enormously long rope with knots in it. We would lower this into a tomb and one of us would climb down, to see if there was anything there. Then the other would join him in the deep tomb and we would go to work.

"Well on this day it was my turn to do the exploring. There were heavy clouds, and our mother told us not to go there, to stay on the farm, it was going to rain. We hated our mother, so we went to the cemetery anyway, knowing how much it would upset her when she learned about it. Our mother never wanted us to go to the tombs. By the time we arrived there the clouds were almost black. I lowered our rope down the shaft of the tomb, and anchored it to a boulder, tied my galabea up around my waist, and began to climb down. And before I had gone down more than ten yards, there was a terrible flash of lightning, and thunder shook the earth. Heavy raindrops began to fall, then stopped again. But in the flash I saw that the floor of the tomb was littered with objects, and so I descended. I called out to Ahmed, 'There are things down here,' but he did not answer me.

"There was more lightning. My rope trembled in the vibrations from the thunder. The wind kicked up, and the column of air in my shaft began to vibrate like the air in a titanic flute. A deep, low moaning sound, as if the earth were in great pain and could bear silence no more. I could feel the air around me singing.

"Finally I was at the bottom. I unloosed my galabea and looked around me. The shaft was small, only six feet by six feet. The floor was scattered with pots and boxes. In one corner was a mummified arm. I picked it up, examined it to see if there were any bracelets on it. There were none. I took out my tinderbox and lit the end of it; it made a fine torch. I carried it by the hand. 'Ahmed!' I looked up the shaft and called him. The sky was black. There was no answer. I decided he must have been frightened by the lightning and run home.

"I was alone. There was not much I could do. I was only a boy, you understand, and could not carry much alone. Only the light from the burning arm enabled me to see. Suddenly there was more lightning, flash after flash of it; it must have lasted thirty seconds or more. Then the real downpour began. Rain poured down the shaft into the tomb. Up above, it must have been like the Nile flood. My galabea was soaked and my arm was flickering and sputtering. I did not want it to go out, did not want to be in darkness. So I ducked into the first of the burial chambers that opened off of the shaft.

"The room was filled with things. Pots, most of them broken. Boxes. Statues. And there was a coffin. I walked over to it. Touched it. It was covered with dried mud. I looked around; so was the floor. That should have told me. But I wanted to stay and see who was inside the coffin.

"It took me a few minutes to pry the lid open. And there she was. A young girl no older than I was myself. She was wrapped beautifully, with her arms straight down at her sides. The bandages over her face were layered in a delicate geometric pattern. You know the style?''

"Yes. I know it all too well."

"Well. I touched her in a few places to see how firm she was, and she was very firm. I don't mind admitting to you, Carter Pasha—you are a man of the world—that I ran my fingers over her private parts. She was quite a beautiful mummy.

"It was then that I noticed, to my alarm, that my feet were wet. I must have been standing in an inch of water. It had not occurred to me that so much water could enter the tomb. If the rain kept up it would be flooded. Terror filled me. What a horrible way to die, drowned in a stone tomb a hundred feet below the earth.

"There was nothing to do but climb out. The rope would be soaked by now, difficult to grip well. But I had no choice. I stood at the entrance to the shaft, holding my burning arm high up, and looked back over my shoulder into the chamber. No, I could not leave her there to be ruined by the water. She was too beautiful, the most beautiful mummy I had ever seen. I had to take her with me.

"The rain was pouring heavily down the shaft, but it was not just rain. The upper entrance to the shaft was in low ground; water from the whole cemetery was pouring into it, cascading down the shaft. I did not know how many rooms there were beyond that first chamber, but they were all filling up. By now I stood in water four inches deep.

"What I wanted to do I would have to do quickly. I tore a long strip of cloth from the bottom of my Galabea, lifted her out of her coffin, tied her to my back with the strip of cloth and walked into the shaft. The arm guttered and went out in an instant. It was black as night. I groped until I found the end of the climbing rope, gripped firmly above one of the knots, and began to climb.

"The water struck me, rushed past me, roared in the shaft. I gripped the knotted rope with my hands and feet and slowly ascended. From time to time there would be more lightning and I could see how far up the shaft I had gone. It was slow, Carter Pasha. I was frightened, and I was working against the pressure of all that falling water, and the weight of the mummy kept shifting on my back.

"It was when I was thirty feet up the shaft that I felt it. She was moving. I could feel her moving. Her right arm, which had been at her side, inched up farther and farther, inched up the side of my body. My flesh tingled. I wanted to scream. I gripped the rope as tightly as I could. Her arm crawled up the side of my chest. I thought that she must be reaching for my throat. Then her arm extended as far as it could, pushed out past the side of my face, and stopped. Her fingers were spread apart. She had stopped moving.

"I could not stand the tension. I had to see. I turned my head slowly to look at her, to see what condition she was in. As I turned my face to the right, it pressed against her arm. When I inhaled, bits of rotted cloth clogged my nostrils, made me cough. Then I saw her. Her jaw gaped open, and her empty eye sockets stared directly into my face. Our faces were not more than two inches apart. I stared into her eye holes; wanted to scream and cry, but I was thirteen years old. There was more lightning; I think it must have struck the earth somewhere near the shaft I was in. In its light I could see every line in her face. Even the inside of her skull was illuminated. I felt her left arm begin to move, to crawl up the length of my body. Then I lost my grip on the rope and we fell to the bottom of the shaft, landed in a foot or more of water.

"Fortunately I landed on top of her, or I am certain she would have killed me. But the bandages from her body, wet from the flood, clung to me, wrapped themselves around me like the legs of a spider. I could contain it no more. I shouted, I howled like a madman as I struggled to pull myself free of them. It seemed to take forever to get them off. All the centuries of dust in them turned to paste when the water touched them. I pulled and tore and finally got free.

"The water was now up to my chest. I slipped a few times on the muddy floor before I got to the rope again. And I do not remember much more than that. I remember being at home and not telling my mother what I had done, because I knew she would scold me for disobeying her, and her anger would have been one storm too many on that day."

He lapsed into silence; watched the donkeys. Did not look at me. I had the feeling he was ashamed to have told me all of this. If it was true—Akim is a polished storyteller—it must have been horrible for him. Horrible, but I doubt there was anything supernatural about it. All that water on her dead, stretched flesh . . . It would have caused contractions, movements, the appearance of life. I have heard similar stories from other people.

But was his story true? It could easily have been Akim's own personal form of pleasure to invent such a thing. And if I myself got caught up in it, then his fun would be at my expense. I decided to be cautious, to avoid direct comment. "You said that your brother Ahmed disappeared?"

"Into that same tomb, Carter Pasha. I warned him. I told him what had happened to me. He must have known it was true, because after that day I refused to go back into any of the tombs, ever again. But Ahmed was curious and wanted to see for himself. He took our rope—this was months later— he took our rope and tied it to a huge rock and went down into the tomb. I watched him descend, begged him not to. But he laughed at me and called me a woman and descended into the shaft. And he never came out again. I waited for hours. Called to him repeatedly. There was never an answer. I went and got my father. He climbed down the rope himself. 'You wait here,' he told me. And an hour or so later he came back up and told me there was no sign of Ahmed. He looked in all of the rooms down there, and Ahmed was not in any of them.''

"So you never saw him again?" I did not believe it.

"Never."

"Perhaps he found an old tomb robber's tunnel."

"Why would he go in and not come out again?"

"Perhaps he could not find the way to open the door from the inside."

"Carter Pasha, we never saw him again. My father whipped me when I told him the story. He needed Ahmed to help on the farm."

This seemed to settle the matter in his mind. There was hardly any point trying to discuss it with him. "I need some sleep, Akim. Would you mind if I rested in the back of the cart with my friend? Later I can drive the donkeys and let you sleep for a while."

"I am quite awake. Please rest yourself, though, Carter Pasha."

"Thank you, I will. But first I want to bring my journal up to date."

"Of course. Your friend's hair is quite remarkably red. I had not realized in the darkness. What is his name again?"

"Larrimer. Hank Larrimer." I laughed to myself. "Of the Pittsburgh Larrimers."

"I beg your pardon?"

"Nothing. Just a private joke."

He has been watching me write this, smiling rather broadly. I do not believe Akim's story; I only wish I knew what to make of its teller.

"Carter Pasha."

"Yes, Akim?"

"Do not go to the old cemetery. I like you. I am warning you in a friendly way. You understand?"

I did not, and said so. I had told him several times I had no intention of going there. His pushing the point was making me irritable.

"I have told you what the tombs are like."

"You have told me your story, yes."

"Not just a story. Children still disappear like that. Many of them; dozens. So many that police from Cairo have come to investigate. They suspect the parents. Of murder. Or of . . . I know nothing of the minds of policemen."

Suddenly Akim had my interest again. "I've heard about this. They say children are disappearing all over the Delta."

"It is worst at el-Qatta and the towns nearby."

I put on my skeptical voice. "And you say the children are disappearing into the tombs."

"I like you, Carter Pasha, and I have warned you. Not all the Westerners who come to el-Qatta are warned."

He was obviously going to tell me no more about the missing children. I retreated to small talk. "There have been other archaeologists lately?"

"No. Not archaeologists. Priests. Nuns. Infidels subverting the word of the Prophet. They came a half a year ago to the old cemetery, to pry into its tombs."

"Were they Germans?" I tried to sound casual, but I had to know.

"I did not warn them. I thought, they are of little account. Let the mummies have them."

Rheinholdt and his people have been more active than I'd realized. "And what did they do to the tombs?"

"Nothing." He laughed. "They went down; they came back up. Took a few things. They found a great deal of old mummy-cloth and some papyri. They still come back now and then. We ignore them."

Thank heaven. I was afraid he'd tell me about still more destruction.

*   *   *

I fell into a deep sleep in the back of the cart. Woke to find Hank shaking me. "Howard, we're here. Or at least I think we are. All the signs are in Arabic."

I looked around groggily. It was late afternoon. We had stopped in front of the el-Qatta train station, which sits half a mile from the town. The ground was mud. The rains had hit here, too; the entire country north of Cairo must have been blanketed. Several people waited on the platform; stared at us with frank curiosity. There was no sign of Akim. "Your hair makes a sensation everywhere we go."

Hank laughed, held up a hand as if to hide it. "I don't know where Akim went. He said something in Arabic and walked off into the town."

"He'll be back, if only for the cart. How is your ankle feeling?"

He looked down at it in surprise. "A lot better, I think."

"Have you tried standing on it?"

"No."

"Then it's time you did."

He stood, tested it carefully. "It's still sore, but I think I'll be able to walk on it."

"Good. I'll go inside and get us fares to Khatatba. Can you unload some of our things?"

"Sure."

There was a train due within the hour. The stationmaster told me about the rain. "The station here sits on a rise. But the town was inundated, the streets were cataracts. A wall of the mosque fell down. There were snakes everywhere, driven out of their dens by the flood."

As I was settling the fares I heard a commotion outside; went to the door to see. There was a young man, obviously from the town, screaming almost hysterically at Hank. He wore a white galabea; brandished a knife. "Where is my daughter? Where is she?"

Hank scrambled atop the cart trying to get out of his reach.

"Where is she? What have you done with her?" He slashed at Hank with his dagger; missed.

I ran out; caught hold of his arm before he could realize I was there. Wrestled him to the ground. He held on to the knife, though. Struggled; looked at me with hatred. Hank climbed down from the cart, pulled the knife from his hand. This deflated him.

"I am Howard Carter, former Inspector of Monuments for Upper Egypt."

The man stared at me. Hearing a title with some authority seemed to sober him.

"What is the meaning of this attack?"

"He thought you were priests." Akim es-Sihri stood over us; had appeared out of nowhere. "His daughter is one of the vanished children. He blames the Western priests."

"Why?"

He shrugged. "Because he can think of no one else to blame." He repeated to the man who we were; that we were not priests.

The man relaxed; I loosed my hold on him.

Akim took the dagger from Hank; handed it back to its owner, who sheathed it. "I keep telling them that their children die in the tombs, prey to mummies. But they refuse to believe me. They call me a mad old man." Akim's dignity was obviously wounded by this. "Do you think me mad, Carter Pasha?"

We were spattered with mud. I tried to wipe it off my clothing but only managed to smear it further. I looked at him. "If Allah wills it, my friend, then you are mad."

Hank had understood none of this. I turned to him, explained it all. As I was speaking the train pulled in. We loaded our things quickly, thanked Akim for the ride and the peacemaking; boarded the train. Hank's attacker watched us sullenly. He had not said a word to either of us, not even to apologize.

The train ride north to Khatatba was brief, uneventful; the first we've had that was not plagued with delays. When we reached our destination in less than two hours Hank looked astonished; joked that it takes a natural catastrophe to make the trains regular.

The rain, the flood seems to have hit this part of the Delta even harder than it did Athribis. The villages we passed between el-Qatta and Khatatba are deserted; the people have fled someplace dry. Whole streets are submerged; inches of water fill the buildings. The railroad tracks are covered in places. We proceeded slowly, steadily. Hank leaned out the window time and again to see the odd spectacle of the train pushing forward through water. "It's like we're riding a line of barges."

I leaned out next to him. Grey sky, grey water. "In ancient times pyramids rose from the center of Lake Moeris. The causeways that led out to them were just at the waterline. Traffic on them must have looked like this."

"How magical it must have been."

It seems to delight him. I myself have been in Egypt long enough to know how disturbed nature is. There is no sign of the sun; only clouds. It will never dry out.

Khatatba sits on slightly higher ground than most of the neighboring villages. Except for puddles here and there the water has retreated; left in its wake a thick black mud. Children play in it with gleeful abandon, make themselves into Negroes. There are no adults in sight. They must be cleaning the mud out of their houses; I can't think where else they would be.

At the stationhouse we found no one on duty. The door

was open; lamps burned inside. We left our things there, took the stationmaster's keys from the hook where they hung, locked the door behind us. I asked a small boy to direct us to the Egyptian Salt & Soda Company. He laughed; splashed us with mud. We walked on. It was nearly nightfall.

Hank stooped to peer into one of the puddles. "Tadpoles. Look Howard, hundreds of them. I can't tell you how good it feels to see something alive come out of all this." He straightened up; walked on.

But I could not take my eyes off the tadpoles, swimming frenzied in their little universe. What was the word he had used to describe the rain? Biblical. I ran to catch up to him.

It was not hard to find the soda company. A large red-and-white sign crowned the building; it seemed the only colored thing in a landscape of grey sky, black mud. Behind the building sat the narrow-gauge railroad train that runs into the Wadi Natrun. We had still seen no adults. We knocked at the door; it was half open; went in.

The place was filled with oil lamps burning fiercely. Dozens of them; so many that the light dazzled our eyes. Sacks of salt, soda, sal ammoniac, other chemicals were stacked on every piece of open floor. We threaded among them. "Hello? Is anyone here?"

At the back of the room we found a desk. Seven lamps burned across it. Slumped over it was a grey-haired man, apparently asleep. On the desk next to him was a half-empty vodka bottle.

"Excuse us."

He snorted in his sleep.

"Excuse us, please." More loudly.

He snorted again, rocked his head back and forth.

I was about to shake him. Hank stopped me. "We should let him sleep."

"Rubbish." I shook the man's shoulder.

Groggily he looked up; dropped his head down again. I shook him more firmly. He looked up; propped his chin on his folded arms. "Who are you?" He has a thick Russian accent.

We introduced ourselves. "You are the Soda Company agent?"

"Yevgeny Zhitomiri, at your service." He belched. Started to stand up; thought better of it and fell back into his chair. "Carter of the Antiquities Service?" He has a deep, gentle voice, not at all like a drunkard's. It is filled with the gloom of his fatherland.

"Formerly, yes."

"Formerly?" He was trying to focus his eyes; was extremely drunk.

Hank was looking around the room. "All these lamps. Do you really need them? It's like sunlight."

Zhitomiri laughed. "A little bit of sorcery. It's all I can manage. I'm not in a league with whoever caused this rain."

"The rain has stopped."

This took a moment to penetrate. "Oh. Oh, that's too bad."

"You wanted a flood?" Hank seemed intrigued with the man.

"I never get what I want." Zhitomiri rubbed his eyes; yawned; looked morose.

"We need passage to the Wadi Natrun. Can you make the arrangements for us?"

"Why do you want to go there?" He was suddenly suspicious, cautious.

"Mr. Larrimer is conducting a photographic survey of the country. He wishes to see the old monasteries in the wadi."

Zhitomiri looked doubtful; was going to say something. But Hank cut him off. "Our friend, Father Rheinholdt, invited us to visit him at the monastery of Saint Pilate."

"You know Rheinholdt?" He looked back to me. "You should have made arrangements with the company in Cairo or Alexandria."

"Our plans changed unexpectedly." I improvised. "The rain—"

"Even so, without company permission there is not much I can do."

"We'd be extremely grateful." Hank reached for his wallet.

He stared hard at me. "Did you say you are Carter of the Antiquities Service?"

"Yes," I lied.

"I see. The train is here."

"Yes, we saw it. We will need donkeys or camels when we reach the wadi. Will someone be there who can furnish them?"

"I will drive you there myself. There are donkeys at the other end. I have to go every day to feed them. The regular driver is gone, so I have to do two jobs." He sighed, looked glumly down at the desk. "Your friend the priest is not popular here."

I tried to sound offhand. "Oh? Why not?"

"Children disappear. The people accuse him of spiriting them away. Him and his nuns."

"There seems to be no one in town but children."

"The adults fled the rain, some of them. The ones who didn't are in the mosque, cleaning. There are two feet of mud in it. They can work and pray at the same time, a rare opportunity for the pious."

We offered to pay Zhitomiri for a place to sleep but he refused to cooperate. "You should have made arrangements through the company." So we found our way back to the station, unpacked our sleeping bags, stretched out on the floor.

I could have gone to sleep at once but Hank was talkative.

"Everyone blames the weather on sorcery. Even Zhitomiri."

"A drunken Bolshevik."

"Still, we know that there is a sorceror at work here. At least an amateur one."

I propped myself up on an elbow, scowled at him. "You think Rheinholdt flooded the whole northern half of Egypt to cover his tracks?"

"He's a madman, isn't he? But it doesn't have to be that direct a thing. Sorcery involves a disruption of the natural order. Once that starts, things tend to keep unraveling."

I put on my best skeptic's voice. "I presume you are speaking as an amateur magician yourself?" Paused for effect. "What nonsense."

He grinned at me. "Everyone in Egypt seems aware of it but you."

On that exasperating note he went to sleep.

We woke at dawn, took our things to the soda company; hired two boys to help us with them. I was certain Zhitomiri would have forgotten all about us, but he was up and waiting for us, looking nothing like a man who had been so drunk the night before. "Carter! Larrimer! Good morning!" He is a more impressive man that I'd realized last night. Tall, muscular, deeply tanned; he wore nothing but khaki shorts and desert boots. Strode out and took two large packs from our boys. "Come on, let's get your things aboard the train." He must be in his late fifties; moves like a man thirty years younger. It must be the vodka.

Hank smiled his Larrimer smile. "I'm afraid we have a lot more things back at the station."

"Don't worry. We'll have them moved here in no time."

I peered into the company building; noticed that all the

lamps were still burning. "Do you have a telegraph, by the way?"

"Yes, of course."

"We've got to get an important message to the Antiquities Service in Cairo. Can you send it?"

"Certainly, if the floods didn't bring the lines down. Let's get the rest of your things and I'll check."

He tested the lines and they were jammed. "No news has gotten through for three days now. Everyone must be transmitting at once. But I'll send your message as soon as the lines open up."

Because Hank had told him we were friends of Rheinholdt I had to phrase it carefully, so as not to arouse his suspicion. "Athribis pyramid torn down. Repeat: torn down. Caïd of Benhir involved." Etc., etc. No direct mention of Rheinholdt. But I ended it by telling Maspero where we were going. "Come. Bring soldiers."

Zhitomiri read the text, looked doubtful. "The lines are still jammed. I'll send it as soon as I get back from the wadi. They should be clear by then."

I wish I were familiar with the Morse code. I would have transmitted it myself, from the train station.

"Well then, if you're ready, let us go." He stood up from the telegraph key.

"Father Rheinholdt is out at the monastery, isn't he?" It hadn't occurred to me before to check this.

"Oh yes. He came through a week ago, just as the rain was starting."

I was going to leave things there; no sense seeming too curious. But Hank pressed. "Did he have a young girl with him? A blonde?"

"No." Zhitomiri looked thoughtful. "No. A few of his nuns were with him, that's all. They were bringing back cases of things they'd found on a dig somewhere."

Hank glanced at me. Had Brigit been concealed in one of the crates? I decided to try to disarm any suspicion Zhitomiri might be feeling. "Father Rheinholdt is a first-class excavator. Painstakingly thorough."

"I wouldn't know. The only things I'm interested in taking out of the ground are chemicals."

We mounted the train. There was only an engine, a tender, and one flat car. Zhitomiri climbed into the engineer's compartment, looking like an eager child. We and our gear rode the flat car. Across the side of the engine, in large red Cyrillic letters, was written a word. Below it, in smaller letters in both Arabic and English, also in red, was the same word in translation: Alexandra.

The steam had been building for some time; with a quick lurch we began our journey into the Western Desert.

It was only a few moments before we left the cultivated ground behind; passed into the wasteland. The abruptness with which Egypt's black soil gives way to the red sand is almost breathtaking. One instant, lushness; the next, sterility. Nothing grows in the Western Desert, and only the fiercest of competitors live there. Jackals, lizards, snakes. There is life around the oases, of course; but these are widely spaced.

I settled back to write here in my journal; would have fallen asleep in time, but Hank and Zhitomiri kept up a lively conversation, shouting across the coal car.

"This isn't much of a train for a large company." Hank seemed to be enjoying the ride. We were slowly gathering speed.

"There are plenty more cars," Zhitomiri shouted. "We only use them during the season."

"The season?"

"Summer. That is when all the lakes and chemical pools in the wadi dry up. The only time we can extract the chemicals."

"I see."

Zhitomiri blew the train's whistle, a shrill, irritating noise. "By the way," he called, "have you heard any news from Russia?"

"News?"

"The war with Japan. The revolutionaries."

"Japan has the upper hand, the last I heard. That's all I know."

Zhitomiri lapsed into silence. I could hear him shoveling coal into the boiler.

Then suddenly we stopped. I looked up to see what had caused it. Sand. The desert sand drifts over the tracks, trying without rest to reclaim its own. We climbed down from our flat car, joined Zhitomiri. "We'll help you clear it away."

He stared at the sand as if its encroachment were a personal insult; handed us shovels. "I worked on the trains in Russia. There it was always snow. I should have become a sailor." He reached an arm into the cabin, groped around, pulled out a bottle of vodka. "You want a drink?"

"No thank you."

Hank watched him swallow. "I don't think I could drink it straight."

It took us an hour or so to clear the drift away. I wanted to sleep. "Why don't you ride with Zhitomiri? Keep him company for a while?"

He clambered to the front of the train, and I stretched out.

And awoke not much later. More sand, more work. This drift was not so large, and we were soon moving again. Hank decided to keep me company. "Zhitomiri is drunk, and reckless."

"Then perhaps one of us should ride with him, for safety's sake." I wanted him to go away and let me sleep.

"Would you know how to run the train?"

I was shamefaced. "No."

"Neither would I. We'll just have to trust him."

We sped far into the desert. The sand made mountains. Wisps of it curled and coiled on the wind, clouds of it rose in our wake. The sun's glare on it dazzled our eyes; our eyes watered, turned sore.

Then the landscape began to change. The Wadi Natrun is the corpse of a salt sea. The desert is dotted with pools of bitter water; they smoke and bubble, they seem alive. Around them are chemical deposits. Fantastic colors mottle the terrain; blues, purples, yellows, greens. The air has a harsh tang. One can smell the chemicals, taste them. Hank regarded it all with something like wonder. "It's like being on the moon, isn't it?"

"Yes. It is that barren, that sterile."

He leaned back, looked up at the sky.

"The ancients came here to mine the natron they used in mummification," I told him. "The salts dry out the flesh, turn it to leather." I turned to look at him. He was gazing up at the sky. "Don't stare at the sun, for God's sake. You'll blind yourself."

He had not been listening to me; had been lost in reverie. "Hm? I was watching the sky. Look at it, Howard. Clear and blue and transparent like nothing else. Nothing but the sun and the air."

"You think that healthy?" I did not want him to turn mystical. We were speeding through a mad landscape at the hands of a drunkard. That was enough.

"It's what I told you once before. The sky protects us from the void beyond; from the chaos. It is like a mother. The ancients knew that, Howard." He looked at me. "They made it into the mother of the gods. It protects us."

"Or shuts us in." I stared up into it. "Cuts us off from the gods who live beyond it." I looked at him self-consciously. This was not something I had wanted to say. But having started I could not stop. "There are ancient stories of a

Persian army that passed here, marched through this valley. They were on their way to capture the oracle of Siwa, far to the west. And one night the desert sands blew, swelled, engulfed them. An entire army vanished in a night. Where was their mother, their protecting goddess? The desert is death, Henry, and the sky is at best an indifferent witness. Look at the chemicals leaching out of the ground. Smell the corrosion on the air."

Henry looked away from me. My outburst, my uncharacteristic heat had nonplussed him. I watched him for a while; anything to keep my eyes off the salt deposits, the smoking waters. The train rocked rhythmically as it picked up speed. In a few minutes he had fallen asleep. I covered him with my jacket; did not want the ferocious sun to burn him. Then I slept myself.

There was another drift of sand, a huge one. The three of us stood on the tracks in front of the engine; regarded it glumly.

"It must be a quarter mile long." Zhitomiri sounded bitter. I think that he must hate Egypt. "It will take us hours to clear it. Maybe a day or more."

Hank leaned down, rubbed his ankle. "Does it usually get this bad?"

"No. Not like this." Zhitomiri took a handful of sand, scattered it in the wind. "Last week when I brought Rheinholdt there were no delays at all."

"Just our luck."

I took a shovel, began digging. Was in no mood to converse. In a moment the others joined me.

For a long time we worked in silence. Zhitomiri muttered under his breath from time to time, in Russian. At nightfall we stopped; broke out our provisions. When the moon rose we worked again for a while. Then slept.

* * *

More shoveling today. There were clouds from time to time, to block the sun. And wind. For a while it blew sand onto the tracks, faster than we could clear it. Then it shifted direction, began to help us in our work. By midday the tracks were clear. Then, abruptly, the wind stopped completely and everything was still.

Zhitomiri had been drinking all morning; was in a dark mood. "Have you ever been to Russia, Carter?"

"No, I haven't. I'm told it snows all the time."

"Russia is holy. It is the home of true religion."

Yes, I thought, just like every other place.

"The czar is God's agent on earth. And they are trying to pull him down." He swallowed some vodka. "Religion is dying, Carter."

He stared at me, leaning on my shovel. I could think of nothing to say.

"The Japanese, the Reds . . ." He shook his head, as if by this single gesture he could relieve the czar's woes. Climbed up into the engine, fired the boiler. "Let us go."

Hank had been somewhat bemused by what Zhitomiri had said; had been as silent as I. Turned to me. "Is this railroad the only way into the wadi?"

"Yes."

"So Rheinholdt must still be there."

"Yes. The only other place he could go is west, into the Sahara."

We climbed onto the train. Before we had a chance to brace ourselves it lurched forward violently. In a moment we were careening at breakneck speed. Zhitomiri sounded the whistle. Through the still air in the wadi it echoed, reflected from the towering dunes and from the distant cliffs that line the valley. Minutes later it was still coming back to us.

More delays; more work. It was sundown when we finally reached Bir Hooker, the small oasis that is the end of the line. Zhitomiri brought us in slowly; lurched into the office, rested his head on the desk, and fell asleep.

Out in the stable the donkeys were braying. They had not been fed for three days. We spread hay for them. Unpacked our sleeping bags and slept ourselves.

Morning. A brilliant sunrise. Henry—Hank and I were both awake early. Both fresh and feeling well for once. Hank tested his ankle. "I think I'm over it. It feels fine."

Zhitomiri was still asleep, snoring energetically, still slumped over the desk. "That seems to be his favorite position." There were provisions in the office. We breakfasted heartily on salt pork and beer. Hank kept staring out the door. "I've never seen an oasis. Can we go out and take a walk?"

"We should get an early start."

"We can't very well leave until Zhitomiri wakes up. Unless you want to get him up now . . . ?"

I stared at him, at the desk. He was snoring even more loudly, contentedly. I sighed. "Let's go."

Bir Hooker—"Hooker's Well"—has a large natural spring at its heart. The water is cool, almost icy, and clear as the finest crystal. Hank cupped his hands and drank. "This is wonderful. There is no taste at all, only wetness and refreshment." I drank too, deeply.

There were palms and acacias growing so thickly it was difficult to make way among them. Hank climbed a date palm, threw me the fruit. We were already full from breakfast but we ate, and they were delicious. There were birds among the trees, flapping, calling noisily. A small snake slithered between Hank's feet and he let out a yell. "Good God, Howard."

"Don't worry, it's harmless."

"I'm terrified of snakes. Haven't I ever told you that?"

"No. But I suppose there have been hints."

"Are there any poisonous ones here?"

"I don't know. If there are, they are probably shy. Don't worry about them."

We kept walking and after a moment or two he relaxed. We reached the edge of the oasis; stared out at the sand, the searing sunlight. The waste extended as far as the horizon; farther. We glanced at each other self-consciously. Our interlude had ended.

Zhitomiri was awake when we returned to the company station; nursed a ferocious hangover. He was anxious to rent us what we needed and see us gone. We took five donkeys, two for ourselves, three for provisions and equipment; a store of salt pork to supplement the food we had brought; a map of the wadi.

Zhitomiri rubbed his eyes. "You have a compass?"

"Yes. How reliable is this map?"

"Perfectly. Our prospecting teams prepared it."

"We'll be going then." We shook hands with him.

"Pray for the czar. Please."

From behind me Hank answered him. "Please pray for us." It embarrassed me.

We departed. Stopped at the spring to fill canteens. Spurred our donkeys to a moderate walk. Progressed into the Great Western Desert.

For a long time we were silent. The donkeys' hooves made crunching sounds in the sand; there was a light breeze, not really enough to cool us; everything else was silent. I tried to keep my mind blank; did not want to know what Hank was thinking.

It was nearly an hour before either of us said anything. Hank spurred his donkey up next to mine. "How do we navigate? I mean, there are no landmarks. At least, none that don't move with the wind." He looked at the barrenness around us; the desert was beginning to oppress him.

"There are oases every ten or fifteen miles along the wadi.

The map shows them. Guiding by the compass, we'll find them."

"How long is the wadi?"

"One hundred fifty miles."

"And the monastery . . . ?"

"Is at the far end. It will take us three days or so to reach it."

Hank stared at the sand, sighed. "Three days. And the priest already has a week's start on us. Can't we move any faster?"

"In this sun? The donkeys would drop dead under us."

"I could always reanimate them." He laughed, but it sounded hollow. We fell back into silence.

Nightfall. We reached a tiny oasis. There was enough grass and undergrowth for the donkeys; Hank found us more dates. Stripped off his clothes and dove in the water. I found the animals, tied them so they would not wander off in the night. Not that that was likely.

The sky is dark tonight. The stars are brilliant. Moonglow lights the western horizon. We lay beside the pool, waiting for sleep.

"Do you suppose they have sex?"

He could not have caught me more off-guard. "I beg your pardon?"

"Rheinholdt and his nuns. Do you suppose they sleep together?"

"Why would such a thing even occur to you?"

"Rheinholdt is young and handsome and all his nuns are fat. I can't picture it."

I thought I had caught his drift. "Oh. But you can picture it with Brigit."

"Yes." He stared at me.

"Has it occurred to you that we might be wasting our time? For all we know, Brigit took off on her own."

"She wouldn't do that."

"You don't know her that well. For all we know, it was she who left the baron, and not the reverse."

"Brigit is there, with the priest."

I know it. I know it. Why put it into words?

More of the same. The sun, the sand, the not-quite-cooling breezes, the crunch of donkeys' hooves. Hank is not taking it well; is showing signs of stress. He has never actually told me he is in love with Brigit; it isn't necessary for him to say it.

Around noon we stopped at another oasis, a rather large one. The water here breaks the ground in several places. The trees are more scattered, not so densely clustered. From the edge of the fertile ground Hank pointed out across the sand, to the rim of the wadi. "There's a building out there. What is it?"

He was pointing to a large black ruin on the horizon. I got field glasses out of one of the packs, looked at it more closely. A large, ramshackle black structure; high walls; the remains of a dome visible above them.

I let him look. "What is it?"

"One of the old monasteries."

"Not Saint Pilate?"

"No. This is one of the lesser ones. Saint Pilate is larger and older. And presumably blacker."

He turned, stared at me. "Don't be funny. Why doesn't the sand cover them up?"

"I don't know. Maybe it does, and then uncovers them again."

He looked through the glasses. "It's like a foul, black castle."

"Nonsense. It's only an old ruin."

*   *   *

We had planned to siesta at the next oasis during the hottest part of the afternoon; did not reach it in time. But it would be a mistake to travel more quickly. The donkeys could not take it.

So we got there early in the evening. Slept a few hours, let the animals rest. Had a brief dinner. The waning gibbous moon rose after ten. We loaded up the donkeys, mounted, rode. The moonlight was ghostly on the sand. A brisk breeze blew; we had to cover our faces to keep the sand out. The donkeys brayed their discomfort, snorted the sand out of their nostrils.

"The moon's face is like a death's-head."

"Stop it, Hank. You're letting the desert get the better of you."

He lapsed into silence, watched the back of his donkey's head.

Up out of the desert loomed another of the old monasteries, much nearer to us than the first one. Against the moonlit sand it looked black as sin.

"Look at it, Howard. It's haunted."

"Nonsense."

We were soon past it. And this, I thought, is the man who came to Egypt to find spirits. Perhaps he's had enough of them. Perhaps we both have. Christ, his mood is spreading to me.

We are sleeping next to the waters of another palm grove. The waters bubble up, trickle gently. After all the day's fierceness they seem . . . not enough; anticlimactic. The moon's white light is almost blinding.

Our third day heading west across the sand. We are not making good time. I had hoped to reach the end of the wadi, to reach Saint Pilate, by nightfall. We will not do it. But I am afraid to push the animals too hard.

Henry Larrimer is . . . Christ. He was frightening enough
to me in that tomb in the Valley of the Queens. Now he is
worse. What will he do if we do not find Brigit with the
priest?

Evening. We are resting. The moon will not be up till
nearly midnight, but he is pressing me to travel on.

Hours of crossing the desert by the moon's unfriendly
light. Its skeletal face staring down at us. The moon, the
sand, and we, foolish enough to challenge them both.

We reached the monastery just before dawn. It is enormous, massive; it is fifteen hundred years old and looks
prehistoric. The walls are massive; black stone, I don't know
where they got it. There is a huge double gate; heavy, ancient
beams of cedar. The chapel's dome towers above the walls.
Huge old palms grow around them; there is water. The
monastery sits on a crop of rock where the two sides of the
wadi finally converge; sits above the sand, where we are
camped, some fifty yards away.

A nun, fat like Sister Marcellinus, kept watch on the
eastern wall. Saw our approach; cried the alarm.

The sky was lightening. More people climbed to the top of
the walls. Priests, nuns, an Egyptian or two. Many of them
carried torches. They were too far away to be recognized, too
far away and too high up. I searched for the field glasses;
forgot which pack they were in.

"Hello!" Hank stared up at them. I hoped they could not
hear the desperation in his voice. I could hear it all too
clearly. Poor boy; he came to Egypt looking for one thing,
and found another instead, and then lost that.

"Hello!"

The people on the wall stared down at us, motionless,
silent.

"Hank." I tried to sound firm, confident.

He turned to me, looked at me uncertainly.

"We are here to photograph the monastery for your survey. Remember? If Brigit is here, we'll find her."

He looked up at our watchers; then back at me. "Of course. I think I'll let you do our talking." He was straining to hide his impatience. "They won't answer me, anyway."

"Then we'll just unpack our things for now. Later, when we've rested, we can climb up to the front doors and knock."

"Why is it so black?"

"Hank."

"Black, jagged place."

We unloaded our pack animals. There was water, grass for them. Pitched our tent, unrolled our sleeping bags. "There are clouds building up in the east. It should stay cool while we get a few hours' sleep."

Not long after we had crawled into our bags, there was a low creaking sound. I had just begun to nod off; looked up sleepily, lifted the tent's flap. The monastery gate had opened a foot or so. Someone had stepped out, an Arab; was walking toward our tent. Before he was halfway to us I recognized him. It was Ahmed Abd-er-Rasul.

He walked slowly across the sand, his galabea blowing in the breeze. Strode confidently up to the tent. Bent and looked in. Smiled. "Carter Pasha."

I stared at him. Ahmed, as I have written before, is an astonishingly handsome man. For a moment that was all I could think. His smile, his charm.

"And Mr. Larrimer of the Pittsburgh Larrimers."

I recovered my wits. "Good morning, Ahmed." I glanced at Hank; he was asleep. I was tempted to wake him but thought better of it. The desert ride had exhausted him. "And how is your son Azzi?"

"He is in Cairo with his mother, being protected from Germans. You always appear so unexpectedly, Carter Pasha."

"Mr. Larrimer is making a photographic survey of Egypt. I think you know that. He wants pictures of the monasteries."

Henry yawned, opened his eyes. Recognized Ahmed. Said nothing.

"May I join you in your tent?" Ahmed hitched up his galabea, sat on the floor. "I'm afraid we do not wish pictures to be taken here."

" 'We'?"

"Yes."

"The monasteries are public property."

"Not this one."

"And all we want are pictures."

"Father Rheinholdt does not believe that."

I sighed. "You can't legally deny us entry."

"You have a permit of entry from Monsieur Maspero?"

By this time Hank was wide awake; he sat up in his sleeping bag. "We're willing to pay if it's necessary. I'm a wealthy man."

"We have no need for material riches."

The incongruity of his presence here finally registered with me. Some things, at least, are beginning to make sense. "No," I prodded him, "no, I suppose not. The black market in mummies must be very lucrative."

He stared at me icily. This was getting us nowhere. "Go back to Luxor, Carter."

"I'd like to talk to Father Rheinholdt."

"Father Rheinholdt is unable to see you."

"We will wait."

"Face the facts, Carter, face the situation."

"We shall begin our photography tomorrow. The outer

walls. That should keep us busy until Father Rheinholdt can see us." I smiled. "Correct, Mr. Larrimer?"

Hank smiled back, agreed with me.

"Your presence here will do you no good." Ahmed was offhand. "Rest yourselves and your donkeys, Carter. Then go back."

Hank had been containing himself too long. "Is Fraülein Schmenkling here?"

Ahmed looked blank. "Who?"

"Brigit Schmenkling."

"The only women living here are the nuns."

"And if we don't believe you?"

Ahmed was astonished at his bluntness. "Doubt is an instrument of faith, Mr. Larrimer. Now, if you will excuse me."

There was no point to pressing him further; nothing more to say.

Ahmed stood to leave. "I pray you travel carefully. You know how treacherous the desert can be." In a few moments he was back inside the monastery. The gates closed heavily.

Hank was staring at me angrily. "What is he doing here? Why didn't you tell me he was mixed up in this?"

"Because, Henry," I explained patiently, "back in Cairo, when you met him, I didn't even know 'this' was going on. I was after him for something else." Carefully, from the beginning, I told Hank about the deformed mummies. The questions about them. Maspero's concern. And Ahmed's involvement in it all. "It never occurred to me that Rheinholdt might be behind it. But it is an efficient way to finance his researches, his excavations."

Hank is sleeping now. He clearly thinks there is something more going on here. I am relieved he did not bring up sorcery, the clay animals. It is bad enough he mentioned

Brigit. Oh well, Rheinholdt must have known we are after her.

I need some sleep myself.

We slept long and deep. Hank was snoring, muttering in his sleep when I awoke, just at sunset. I stretched, crawled out of the tent. The tops of the monastery walls were lined with blazing torches. People stood at intervals along them; watched us. I can't think why it should take so many of them. I built a small fire of my own.

"The sky is so black." Hank crawled out after me; had been awakened by my movements. "Even with the light from the monastery, the stars glow. Look at the Milky Way." A meteor tore across the southern sky. He followed it with his eyes. "My governess used to tell me that meteors were angels dying."

I offered him some water, some pork. "Shall we unpack the cameras?"

He sat down next to the fire. "It isn't very warm."

"Palm wood doesn't burn well."

"Oh."

We worked all night. Unpacking cameras, cleaning them, oiling shutters, polishing lenses. Finally assembling them. Hank plans to make some pictures at dawn, when the shadows are longest.

While we worked he was fine. When we were finished he became restless almost at once. "We're becoming nocturnal creatures, Howard."

"In the desert, that makes sense."

It was almost sunrise. There was a dull, metallic clicking sound coming from somewhere across the sand. "Listen. Do you hear that?"

Hank cocked his head. "What is it?"

"Cobras. That is how they sound when they sing."

His eyes widened a bit. I had forgotten his phobia.

"They sing when they are at peace. They won't bother us."

He wanted to rest; that was clear. But he kept glancing at the black walls. I wanted to keep his mind occupied. "Have you been following the calendar?"

"Hm?" He had been lost in thought.

"Tomorrow—or rather today, now—is Christmas Eve."

"Christmas." He ground his fingers into the sand. "Christmas, here."

"I can't remember the last time I celebrated. Not since before I came to Egypt. There's never been anyone much to celebrate with."

He switched on his smile. "Shall we decorate a palm tree?"

"Nothing to do it with."

After dawn we took pictures around the outer walls, from every angle. From the desert; from the rocks above the monastery. We had hoped to see inside but we could not get up high enough. By ten A.M. we were finished. And it was clear there was no way to get inside.

"Fifteen hundred years old." Hank packed his plates noisily. "You'd think there's be cracks."

"There are, but they're too small for us. They built to last."

"We can't get in."

"I know it. We'll have to go back."

It had never occurred to him. "Back?"

"To Cairo. To the authorities. These people are criminals, after all. We have no proof they took Brigit"—he was about to interrupt me but I cut him off—"but we know what they did at Athribis. We'll get Maspero and some soldiers and come back. We can get in then. The pictures we've just made will show people they're here."

We crawled into the cool shade of our tent, lay down to sleep. Hank reached up, scratched his fingernails along the canvas. "Christmas Eve."

"Howard, get up."

"Hm?"

"Get up. Something's wrong."

I rubbed my eyes, yawned. "It can wait."

"No. It can't."

I opened my eyes, gaped at him.

"Howard, something is wrong with the sky."

I crawled out of the tent, stood groggily up. And saw at once what he meant. The sun was hanging low in the western sky, in the direction of the great desert. It would set in another hour or so. And it was green. A foul brownish green. Its light was dim; I stared into it. "There is a sandstorm blowing up. This isn't the usual season for them."

I could see in Hank's face what he was thinking. But he simply asked me, "What do we do?"

"We'll have to cover the donkeys' faces with cloth. They won't be able to breathe if we don't. Then secure our tent, and hope it doesn't get too bad. Cover our own faces, just in case. And hope."

The wind was already picking up and the sky darkening. The monastery walls were lined with torches again; they flickered wildly. We set to work. I took care of the animals; they were clearly frightened, as much by having their faces covered as by the wind that was coming. Tethered them to stout palms. Hank worked at reinforcing the tent; doubled up the stay ropes, weighted the bottom with stones. The wind gusted erratically. Sand blew into one's face; burned. I went to join Hank at the tent.

"It stings. The wind actually stings."

"Grains of sand blown at forty, at sixty miles an hour or more. It could strip the skin off your body."

I checked the tent; he had worked well. We braced ourselves inside. Covered our eyes, mouths, nostrils with scarves. Outside the wind picked up even more; began to shriek. In its lulls we could hear the hysterical braying of the donkeys. The walls of the tent flapped, snapped against the wind. The storm was still growing; it could get much worse. Hank reached over and put his arm through mine; held it tightly.

"Carter Pasha."

There was someone with us. I loosened my scarf to see. It was Ahmed Abd-er-Rasul, grinning.

"Carter Pasha. This will be a bad storm."

"I know that."

Hank unwrapped his face. "What do you want here?"

Ahmed bowed slightly. "We cannot leave you to perish in the wind. You may come inside if you wish."

"Inside the monastery?" Hank was still clutching my arm.

"Yes."

A violent gust shook the tent. It would not last out the storm. "Thank you. Will you help us bring some of our things?"

Ahmed looked at our cameras. "There are conditions. Father Rheinholdt does not wish you to come. Some of us prevailed upon him."

"Conditions." I stared at him. We were plainly in no position to bargain.

"You are to take no photographs. None."

"We agree."

"And you are not to leave the cell we provide for you. Not at all, under any conditions."

"Yes, of course."

"Fine. Let us get your things and go."

"Our donkeys need shelter."

"We will take them in."

It was difficult to walk against the wind. Exposed places—one's hands, the back of one's neck—burned. We took our food, our clothing; left the equipment outside. With donkeys and provisions we could make it back to Bir Hooker. The equipment would be buried or carried away; but it could be replaced.

It was impossible to see more than a few feet. We linked hands, formed a chain, followed Ahmed, who knew the way. His galabea flapped in the wind like a sail. It took what seemed forever to reach the gates. Inside, in the courtyard, everyone was active. Securing things against the wind, rushing about. They knew how bad this storm would be. A young priest, blond like Rheinholdt, came in behind us, with our animals; led them across the court to an enclosure. They brayed constantly, balked at being led blind. A strong blast of wind knocked Ahmed off-balance; he fell backward into my arms.

Then we were inside. Long low corridors lit with hundreds of candles; black stone, like the outer walls. Ahmed unwrapped his face, shook the sand from his galabea. "Thank you for catching me."

"Thank you for bringing us inside."

"Come this way, please."

He loped off down a corridor, left us to follow. There were halls leading off in every direction; a labyrinth. Candles burned brightly in all of them, scarcely made a difference to the blackness. The walls were rough; undressed stone. There were crudely fashioned arches overhead. The ancient monks had slaved, suffered to build this place.

Ahmed led us into a small black room. There was a desk, a chair behind it, two more facing it. "Please sit here. Father Rheinholdt will join you. He wishes to see you."

We sat down. Ahmed vanished. Hank looked around wearily. "I don't like it in here."

"It is windproof. For the moment that is all that matters."

"If they don't want to let us go, how will we ever get out?"

"How indeed?" Rheinholdt had entered behind us; smiled his priest's smile. Walked to his desk and sat. "The storm is quite furious. I have never seen one quite like it. Did you notice the color of the sun?"

I was in no mood for obvious small talk. "Thank you for admitting us."

"Thank Ahmed and the nuns."

"We shall. I'm sorry you don't find our presence here agreeable."

Rheinholdt stared at me; I think he wanted to laugh in my face. "This monastery was built in the fourth century."

Hank smiled. "It looks it."

Conversation stopped. We sat uneasily, waiting for him to make whatever point he had.

Finally, "You have seen the animals. You know. You are not here to photograph the building."

I was going to bluff—of course that's what we're here for, you've seen our cameras—but there would have been no point. I said nothing.

Rheinholdt picked up a glass paperweight, tossed it idly from one hand to the other. "I don't know what to do with you now."

"A good magician would turn us into toads or flies."

"There are other things you could be made into. Don't provoke me. I don't see how I can let you go."

For the first time Hank spoke. "Give us the girl and we'll leave. No one would believe us about the animals, anyway."

"The girl. I have not seen her since that night in Benhir." He smiled. It was a lie.

"I want her," Hank barked. "Where is she?"

The priest was still smiling. "A lovesick boy. How touching."

Hank was turning red. I had never seen him angry before;

decided to get between them. In a soft, measured voice I said, "We believe you have her here."

Rheinholdt stopped smiling. The game was over; he held all the cards; we were mere annoyances. "Your beliefs are no concern of mine. Stay in the cell where we put you."

He stood to go. Thought better of it; sat down again. Stared directly at me. "You know what those clay figures mean. You know what they are. The girl is nothing." He chuckled; had made some private joke.

He believes in them. Hank believes in them. That leaves me the agnostic. I had no idea what I could say.

"I cannot let you go, Carter. You *know*." He made the verb sound obscene. He clapped his hands; a nun appeared. Sister Marcellinus. "Take them to their cell. You know where I mean." Turned to us. "We are putting you in the deepest part of the monastery. The corridors, as you have seen, make quite a maze. There are snakes in some of them; we try to keep them out but they get in somehow. And there are bats."

I stood, tried to look relaxed. "There are ways in and out, then."

Rheinholdt laughed. "Ones big enough for snakes and bats. Go find them if you want to." He laughed again. "But you would be wise to stay where I put you."

He was done with us. The nun led us back out into the network of corridors. Took up a torch, lit it from the nearest candle. The smoke billowed up to the ceiling; lost itself in the blackness there. "Follow me."

We walked behind her through the black maze, silent. I think we must have crossed back and forth, retracing our steps, doubling over our path; we were to be confused. I decided to make small talk; it was certain to annoy her. "Do you like living here?"

She said nothing, kept walking.

"I hope the dungeon isn't damp."

She ignored me. The corridor began to slope downwards. Within a few minutes we must have been deep underground. The halls here were narrow—so narrow our shoulders kept scraping against the walls. Sister Marcellinus had to walk sideways. The ceilings were so high we could not see them. Everything was black. The nun's torch made the only light. Finally she stopped in front of a low wooden door. Pulled it open; it creaked. "In here."

She thrust her torch into the room. There was an alarmed chittering; a pair of bats flew out, flapped madly about our heads, vanished. The nun had stood erect, unfrightened; this must be a usual thing here. "Go inside. Stay there."

I wanted to needle her just once more. "I take it your spell with the scarab never worked."

She stared at me; her face was ice.

"I don't blame you for trying it." I tried to sound hearty. "He is such a handsome man. And after all, if he can play at magician, you can too."

She did not move. There was hatred in her face.

"Why didn't you just seduce him? Oh well, I'm sure the other nuns will comfort you."

"Get inside!" Her voice was shrill. "Get in!"

We walked in and the door slammed violently behind us. The sound of her footsteps retreated. We were alone.

After a moment or two my eyes began to adjust. "We're underground but there is light in here. Look."

"And sound." Hank groped his way to the wall, pressed his hands against it. "I can hear the wind."

As we got used to the darkness we could see clearly the light coming in. Cracks; chinks in the wall; hundreds of them. Some of them no wider than pinholes; others large enough to get a finger into. One could feel drafts of air. When the wind gusted especially hard, there was a low whistling sound through them. By now I could see Hank clearly outlined in the dim light. "No wonder animals get in. We must be thirty feet below ground, but light and air filter down through the cracks."

Hank pressed an ear to a large crack, listened to the wind. "The storm must be getting worse." He looked around. "All these cracks. The building must be riddled with them."

"The wadi is geologically active. There are earthquakes."

"It's a wonder this place is standing at all. There must be so much structural damage."

I shrugged. "Why don't we go and see?"

Hank gaped at me. "We're locked in."

"No. There was no lock on the door, only a wooden bolt. And the wood looked rotten. We can get out any time we want to."

He walked over to the door, pressed his shoulder tentatively against it, pushed. "I think it's giving." It broke almost at once. Hank stared at the open doorway, as if he couldn't believe it was that easy.

"Well, what are we waiting for?" I sauntered casually out. "Isn't there someone here you'd like to look for?"

"We don't know where we are."

"We can learn."

He followed me uncertainly into the corridor. "What about the snakes?"

"What about them? You want to find Brigit, don't you? Think of her golden hair and her golden skin and her deep blue eyes and her smile. What are a few cobras?"

He swallowed. "I'm in love with her, Howard."

"I know it. I thought you'd never say it."

"Let's go."

I chose a direction randomly and we started off. The light was dim; enough to see by, no more. The sound of the wind followed us, preceded us, was everywhere. The air in the cracks piped, groaned. At every turn more tall corridors branched off ours. It occurred to me that the whole thing might collapse on top of us. I put the thought out of my mind. "There are other things to look for, too."

"What could be more important than Brigit?"

"Not more important, but worth finding. The mummies. There must be a store of them somewhere in the monastery. They and the things they were buried with could be worth a lot. Even the cloth they got rewrapped in is worth something." I looked back over my shoulder at him. "A bride-price for you. Not the most tasteful one, but it's real."

"Dead bodies for a wedding gift." He shuddered, walked on in silence.

We stopped now and then, looked inside the rooms we passed. Some of them had more light than others. Some were filled with bats. In one very dark one we heard hissing; moved away quickly.

"Howard."

"Yes?"

"Where would they find mummies out here?"

"The old monks. Egyptian Christians mummified their dead too, you know."

"Would there be many of them?"

"Hard to say."

"But . . ." He was thinking. "Howard, why would the mummies be children? The ones Rheinholdt's sold have all been children."

This had been at the back of my mind; I did not want to hear it.

A large rat scuttled down the corridor in front of us; squeezed under a wooden door. We followed it; found the door padlocked. The words KEEP OUT were painted across it in white. I pressed my ear against it, listened; there was nothing. "What could there be in there to attract a rat?"

Hank's eyes widened; he leaned close to it. Whispered.
"Brigit? Are you in there?"

There was silence.

Louder. "Brigit?"

Nothing. I gripped the padlock, pulled. It came off with
the wood around it. The door creaked open. There was
more light than in any room we had seen. There was a crack
in the wall, three inches wide, through which light filtered
dimly from above. Stacked up, dumped in heaps in the
corners, were mummies. Dozens of them, more than a
hundred. None of them were wrapped, they were all naked.
Children, adolescents. Twisted, mangled, faces contorted.
One could almost hear their screams, see their writhing.
Hank stared into the face of one at eye level. "Poor thing.
Poor things. What could have happened?"

"The old . . ." I looked around; could not find words.
Death, pain. Death, I tried to tell myself, must have been a
relief for them. But no; these were children; they wanted
life, they deserved life, got this instead. Seeing them all
together made me numb. There were rats, a dozen or more,
chewing busily on the bodies. As I watched, one of them
sank its teeth into the eyelid of a small girl. "We don't
know much, really, about the old monks. Why would they
have done this? Surely the Church . . ."

Hank was still staring into a dead boy's face. He reached
out, touched a finger to the mummified shoulder. The body
shifted, tumbled to the floor. Hank stooped, picked it up,
placed it carefully back on the pile. "What am I smelling?
Bitter, pungent. Do you smell it?"

"Natron. Embalming salts." A long-dead girl lay with
an arm extended to me; as if she were asking me for help.

"Why should it smell so strongly?"

"There are so many of them. I want to leave here."

We went back out into the black hallway. "So that's why

there were no objects on the bodies. That's why the confused wrappings. They were embalmed but never wrapped or buried.''

A short way down the same corridor was another padlocked door. KEEP OUT. We pulled off the lock. Went in.

There was only a table in the room. Two lanterns burned brightly at either end of it. Between them were the cages. Brass bird cages, very ornate. Within them the animals. Our Set animal in one; it seemed to recognize us, backed away, pressed against the bars at the rear of its cage. In the other cage was the hawk. It flapped about wildly, made shrill little noises. Hank leaned down for a closer look, pushed a finger between the bars. The bird flew at it, bit, drew blood.

I stared at them. They were real; I could not hedge anymore. Magic, Egyptian magic. I did not want them to be there, they had no place in my world. The Set animal brayed at me, laughed like a jackass.

Neither of us had spoken. Hank lifted his bitten finger to his lip, licked away the blood. ''We should take them with us.''

''We can come back for them.''

He stared at them uncertainly. ''I'd hate to lose them again.''

''We have more searching to do. Remember?''

He hesitated. ''All right. Will we be able to find this room again?''

''We found it once.''

''Howard.''

I was out in the hall, looked back at him.

''Perhaps we should stop looking. I'm beginning to be afraid. That animal . . .'' He held out his bloody finger. ''It's evil.''

''Come on. We have to find Brigit.''

The wind screamed through the chinks in the stone. We walked, passed more doors, looked into each of them. Came at last to an intersection of six corridors. One of them sloped downward, led still farther into the earth. There was light coming from the bottom, man-made light. Hank stared down it. "We have to go and see." I did not want to go; I had seen enough. I had never heard of anything like what the ancient monks had done to those poor children. Why should they have done it? It was not part of my Egypt, the Egypt I have always loved. My Egypt, or my vision of it, was vanishing in front of me, turning into something else, ugly, repellent. I did not want to see more. But Hank led the way and I followed. The sound of the wind began to drop off; whether it was because of our greater depth or because the storm was abating, I do not know.

Another wooden door, half-rotted away. Light poured through the cracks in it. Hank put his eye to one of them; peered in. "A huge room. I can't see the far end of it. Filled with vats, stone tables, pillars. Vaulted ceilings made of huge undressed stones. And there are lights everywhere, electric ones. This must underlie the whole monastery."

"Let me see." I looked. There was no one inside. Pulled the door slowly open. I had expected it to creak but it was silent. We stepped carefully into the vault. Looked around. There was no one. Yet even here the sound of the wind penetrated, more muted than above, a low steady hum.

Hank went ahead of me. Stopped next to a huge stone table. The top surface was concave with an indentation six inches or so deep. At one end was a slot leading to a stone spout. He pressed his hand into the table's hollow top, caressed the contour. Whispered. "What could a table like this be used for?"

I did not want to touch it. "It is an embalming table. This must be where the monks prepared their dead. The body lay in the hollow of the table. They slit it open along the left side of the chest and pulled out the organs. The brains they pulled out through the nose, with hooks. The blood and the other juices collected in the hollow and flowed out the spout at the end of the table.''

Hank made a face. ''I didn't want to know all that much. This place smells of death. Can you smell it?''

''Natron. There is a strong smell of natron here. It's probably inevitable.''

Hank bent over, looked under the embalming table. ''There are drains in the floor.''

''For the blood.''

There were dozens of tables stretching on down the vault. Hank looked down the row of them glumly. His eyes widened. ''What's that?''

Before I could respond, before I could even see what he meant, he broke into a run. Went to a table halfway down the line. ''Oh my God, Howard. Oh my Jesus.''

I moved to follow him. Knew what I would see. Did not want to see. My head buzzed; went numb. I could have fainted but I forced myself to keep awake. To see it.

The boy was young. Eight years old, nine years old. A beautiful Egyptian boy with olive skin and large dark eyes. Eyes wide open; a face mangled with fear. The embalming slit down the left side of his chest gaped open. His heart, his liver, all of his inner organs were lined up neatly beside him. He could not have been dead more than an hour. The tears in the corners of his eyes had not had time to dry and the blood stains on the table were still moist with life. They had cut him open while he was still alive.

Hank touched the boy. Cupped the palm of his hand along the boy's cheek. Then he turned to look at me. ''The smell of natron. Don't you see?''

''Yes.'' I did not want to see, but I saw. I looked around.

"There, farther down the chamber, along the wall. Those vats must be filled with it."

We went, looked. There were troughs of various sizes, all roughly oblong, all a foot or two deep. All filled to the rim with natron. Hank got down on his knees next to the first one we came to. Scooped, carefully, the salts out onto the floor. The face, the chest, the body lines emerged from the salt, more and more clearly. Another little boy, this one twelve, thirteen maybe. Twisted with fright. The natron had dried his tears but there must have been tears. I leaned close to his face and thought I could see their tracks.

Hank stopped his scooping, moved to the next vat, scooped again. A girl, this time. "They steal the children." He spoke without looking at me. Dug out the girl's corpse. "And they slaughter them. And they dry the bodies out here. And then . . ."

He turned to look at me. I was staring dumbly; I was made of stone. "And then they sell them. This is why the mummification seemed so perfect. It is not perfect, only new." I started to take a step toward him; could not move. "I . . . I have been a party to this. I have helped it. I have advised people to buy them. Told them they were real."

Hank lifted the girl out of the trough, carried her to the nearest table, laid her gently upon it. "They are real." Went back for the boy, placed him on a table of his own.

There were several dozen of the natron vats. "Hank, stop. You're not accomplishing anything." I wanted him to stop. The obvious horror had not occurred to him yet.

"I'm getting them away from the priest."

"But . . ." I sighed. I might as well do it; I did not want him to be the one. My eyes ran down the line of troughs. At the far end was the largest of them. I walked slowly down to it. Knelt. Began to dig. I should not have done it. I should have left her there. Should not have let Hank see her. I

knew she would be in it; I should have gotten Hank away.
But I dug.

Strands of fine blond hair. Then her face. Her eyes were
open wide; stared into my own. She was twisted like the
rest; like them had died in pain. Her skin was deathly pale;
there was no blood to give her color. She had been in the
natron a week or more; her skin already felt leathery. Poor
Brigit. I whispered a prayer, an ancient one, a verse from
the *Litany of the Sun God*. A prayer from before the age when
priests did things like this.

I did not want Hank to see her. Began to cover her up
again. But he was behind me. He saw. "Oh no, Howard. Oh
my God no." He fell to his knees, buried his face in her
chest.

"Hank, stop it. The natron will burn your eyes."

"I don't care." He was crying. His tears fell into the harsh
salts and were absorbed; his tears vanished. "Oh Brigit,
Brigit." He sobbed, he cried uncontrollably. The wind in the
monastery wall groaned, seemed to grieve with him. I tried
to pull him away from the vat. "Let me dig her out. I'll lay
her on a table."

But he fought me off, clutched the body. "No. No,
Howard, leave me alone." My heart wanted to break. For
both of them. I stood watching helplessly. There was nothing
I could do but let him mourn. Then something in the
atmosphere told me we were not alone. I turned to look
behind us. Father Rheinholdt had entered noiselessly. Stood
grinning at us. Held a revolver. At his shoulder were three
nuns; one of them held a long golden knife, a ceremonial
dagger, that glistened in the electric light.

I stared at Rheinholdt mutely. And he smiled more
broadly. Slowly Hank became aware of his presence. He
looked up, saw the priest; gradually took control of his tears.

Rheinholdt laughed. "Isn't that tender. Isn't that touching. Young Romeo weeping for his love. Well, take heart, Mr. Larrimer. You are going to rejoin your ladylove soon, in much the same way Romeo joined his."

We stared at him. I think Hank was too disoriented to know what he had said.

Rheinholdt handed his revolver to one of the nuns. Walked toward us. "And so you have found my experiments. The mummification techniques work quite well, don't you think?"

He took a handful of natron, let it trickle through his fingers. "Wonderful substance. I read years ago about that doctor in Edinburgh—what was his name?—who reproduced the old embalming methods. You see the results we get." He paused. "Poor Mr. Larrimer. I warned you to stay where I put you. You would have been happier not knowing about all this." He gestured expansively.

"Would I?" Hank was still on his knees beside Brigit. Got shakily up.

"Most certainly. The people are always happier ignorant. The truths, the inner secrets—those are for the priests."

My distaste for the man . . . I had to speak. "Did they have to die this way? Did you have to kill them like this?"

"I reasoned that a soul separated from its body by . . . abrupt and horrific means would be more anxious to rejoin it."

I did not follow him. "You make this all sound so clinical."

"Death is a clinical phenomenon. And so is life."

"And so, it would appear, is the priesthood. Surely the Roman Church has money. Enough to finance your . . . 'missionary work' here without resorting to this."

He laughed at me. "Is that what you think? That I did this for money?" He seemed to find the suggestion distasteful.

I watched him. He hopped up onto an embalming table, the one where Hank had placed the little girl; crossed his legs casually. "I came to Egypt just as I told you. To learn what Christ learned here, the secrets of eternal life. What He did to those little animals. What He did to Lazarus. What He did, finally, to Himself."

He smiled; was enjoying himself. "I used some ancient magical papyri to guide my researches. The prayers, the embalming rituals. I need bodies to reanimate, and so . . ." He waved a hand vaguely in the air. "The money I made selling the bodies was an unexpected compensation. It was Ahmed Abd-er-Rasul's idea."

"You could have bought mummies."

"Too costly."

"Dug them up, then."

"Too time-consuming. My early experiments had no results. It was dispiriting. Then on a visit to Benhir to sell mummies I found the clay bird at the pyramid, and I remembered the story of the young Christ. I knew I had found what I needed. Inscribed inside Khasekhemui's pyramid were the spells. Now I have what I want. I know what Christ knew.

"These bodies here"—his gesture took in the whole monastery—"I can make them do anything. I can replace them in the world of the living. These ones right here are not perfect subjects, you understand. The embalming hasn't been finished. But they will do for the moment."

He stood over the vat in which Brigit's corpse still lay. Extended his arms over her. Chanted. Then stopped. "You should like this, Larrimer." Went on with his chant.

I watched Hank. He watched, listened to the priest. His expression was somewhere between romance and terror. "I did it, Howard," he whispered. "He can do it too."

The jackal. The tomb. That night. No, I told myself, it had not happened. It had been a trick of the light. Rheinholdt chanted on. I found myself staring at Brigit. Watching, waiting. Her cheek twitched; her lips trembled.

A dozen different emotions showed themselves in Hank's face, warring with each other. Without, I think, even realizing it, he took a few steps toward the vat.

The nun with the revolver stepped forward, pointed it at his face. I put a hand on his shoulder, tried to calm him.

The sound of the storm above fell off; stopped. The electric lights flickered, went out, flashed on again. Rheinholdt intoned his chant.

There was a loud groan. The building shook. Bits of rock and dust fell from the walls, the ceiling, the arches. Hank looked up at the ceiling, then back at Brigit.

The door opened. Half a dozen nuns entered, calm on the surface but I think terrified. Ahmed followed them, walked over to the priest. Stared down at Brigit's naked body. "The outer wall is collapsing. Two of the mules were crushed by stones."

Rheinholdt tried to ignore him but his concentration was broken. He turned, stared at him.

"The whole building will fall."

"Nonsense. Do you know how many desert storms this place has withstood?"

"It is not just the storm. The earth is trembling."

The floor shook beneath us. With a grinding noise a crack opened down a wall of the vault. The wind blew in from above; sand blew in, whipped around the room. Then there was another lull.

"I can't stop," Rheinholdt said. "I have what I need now. All of you be still. Please," he added. He looked down at Brigit's body, lying still. Smiled tenderly at her. Got down on his knee and began to chant again, softly this time, as if he were whispering to her. He looked at Hank out of the corner of his eye; smiled. Chanted into Brigit's dead ear. At one point he seemed almost to kiss it.

Brigit's mouth opened. There was a dry sound as she

gasped for air. Hank fell against me, needed my support; I
steadied him as best I could.

Slowly, slowly she reached up a hand. Rheinholdt took
hold of it, stood up. Slowly, slowly, unsteadily, holding on
to the priest for leverage, Brigit stood up in the trough of
natron. The salts streamed off of her body; poured out of her
ears, her nose. The long embalming cut down the left side of
her torso was still open; natron poured out of it like water
over a cataract. Rheinholdt still held her hand in his. He
reached out his other hand, cupped it over her breast; slid it
slowly down the flat of her stomach to her groin. Smiled
triumphantly at us. "You see?"

The sound of the wind had stopped completely. Everything, everyone was still. The only moving thing in the vault
was Brigit.

Hank got hold of himself, moved away from me, took a
step toward her. The nun brandished her revolver. "Brigit."

The corpse stepped carefully out of its embalming vat,
eyes on Rheinholdt.

And the priest's eyes were on Brigit. "It is no use,
Larrimer. She is mine now." He said this softly.

There was a crash. More of the building above must have
collapsed. The floor, the walls vibrated.

"Rheinholdt!"

He ignored me.

"Rheinholdt! This is lunacy. There must be somewhere
safe we can go. Somewhere deeper or stronger."

His eyes were fixed on Brigit. He watched her every
movement, smiling gently. "This is the deepest part of the
building. We shall be safe here."

"Brigit!" Hank was near hysterical. I took him by the
arm, tried to hold him back.

The girl suddenly became still; for a long moment did not
move. Then slowly she turned her head toward us. Stared.

"Brigit. For God's sake, Brigit."

She stared. Turned her body slowly to face us. Her hand fell out of Rheinholdt's.

"Brigit. For God's sake, it's me, it's Hank."

She stared. Her lips parted slightly. Her dry throat rasped.

There was wind. The floor shook. There was a tearing sound, and a second later an enormous rock, part of the outer wall, crashed through the roof not ten yards from us. The nuns shrieked, ran into one another's arms.

But Rheinholdt did not flinch. He watched Brigit as she watched Hank. Smiled as she seemed to recognize him. "She knows you, Larrimer. You see, it is not just animation, it is life. Her soul, reinhabiting her body. She knows you." His tone was cool, detached.

The ceiling where the rock had crashed through was weakened. More and more stones fell to the floor. Cracks radiated. The whole thing would soon collapse. I kept looking to find a way out. Then it happened. The whole ceiling began to fall. Heavy stones. Some of the nuns were killed, others rushed off. Rheinholdt looked upward. "No!"

Hank had never looked away from Brigit. He held out a hand to her, called her name still again. And slowly she held out her own hand in return; very slowly, as if to do so gave her pain.

We were standing six feet or so from the nearest column. That would be the safest place. I took hold of his collar and pulled him back with me, just as the roof where we had been standing gave way. There was a roar, a cloud of dust. The electric lights failed. The storm blew in from above. In the distance I could hear the screams of the women. Hank cried, "No! No!" Rushed to where she had been.

I ran after him. "Hank, it's no use. We've got to find shelter."

There was a pile of stones, an enormous heap of them.

Brigit and Rheinholdt were under them. The only thing to be seen was her hand. It protruded from the stones, twitched faintly.

"We've got to dig her out."

"The stones are too heavy. We need to save ourselves from the storm." He clawed at the huge stones, could not move them; collapsed in tears. Then let me lead him away, weakly, like an injured child. At the side of the vault I found a small storeroom; barely enough space for the two of us, really. But there was a wooden door to keep out the wind, the sand. Hank curled up in my arms, crying so softly I could not hear him. He sobbed; I felt his body heave. We waited there for the storm to end.

Chapter Six

MORNING. THE SKY blue, clear. The air hot and still. It is Christmas Day.

The vault—what had been the vault—is open to the sky now. There is a yard or more of sand, and hundreds, thousands of stones piled up. The door to our little closet was blocked. I had to push out the boards that made the top of it; they were rotten, it was not hard.

Everything is covered in sand. Tables, vats, the stones from the ceiling. The bodies too. The sand has taken them. Most of the building is gone.

Hank did not want to come out of the little storeroom. "No. I want to stay here. I want to sleep."

"Come on, Hank. We have things to do."

"No. You do them."

"Hank." I took him by the hand, led him out. He looked around, seemed still to be terrified. "It will be all right now, Hank. The storm is gone."

"No."

I was afraid he'd break down completely. "Sit here and rest awhile, then. I want to look around."

There was no one else alive, at least not in the vault. I walked among columns that no longer had a roof to support, looking for others; but there was no one. Not even any bodies. They must be under the sand. In the corners the sand had drifted high. It was not hard to climb out of the vault into the courtyard.

There was not anyone there, either. Only two of the donkeys were there; dead. They had been chained to a heavy stone column. The sand had torn the flesh from their bodies. Only half of the outer wall was still standing. The wind was still; nothing moved as I surveyed this new ruin.

"Hello!"

I waited for my voice to echo. There was no response.

"Hello! Is anyone else alive?"

Nothing.

I went back to the vault. Hank was sleeping on a drift of sand.

The corridors—some of them far distant from any opening—are filled with sand too. Doors were thrown open, some of them were torn from their hinges, and there was sand. It is as if a whirlwind had actually passed through the building. I walked through the halls, looked into room after room. Mummies, rats, sand. The two brass cages that had held the animals were overturned, the animals gone. Finally there was a chamber with salt pork, wine. We will not starve here, at least not for a while.

But we cannot leave. The desert is impossible on foot and the animals are dead. We have food enough to wait. Someone—Zhitomiri, most likely—will come sooner or later. We will have to settle in.

All the wine here is Egyptian. For once it will taste good to me.

*   *   *

Our second day here. It seems impossible to me that none of the missionaries survived. But I have been through the whole place time and again. Called and called. There is no one.

Last evening, just before twilight, I found Hank in what had been the chapel. It is an eerie place. Half of the domed roof still stands intact, defying gravity, defying ruin. The light comes in, reaches the ground only dimly; the shadows at the bottom are so thick. He was in a corner, eyes closed, curled up like an infant. I could not tell whether he was sleeping or praying.

It is still possible to climb what is left of the outer wall. My first time up I went gingerly, uncertain whether it would collapse under me. But it is quite solid. I go up there several times a day, look east across the desert. No one comes.

Day three. I should write more here; it would help fill the time. But I am afraid of my mood, my thoughts. Hank's melancholy is affecting me. It is best not to dwell on it too much.

He does not sleep. At night he walks through the ruins, through the pitch-black corridors. I do not need to ask what—who—it is he is looking for. He woke me before sunrise, shook me hard. "Her hand was still moving. You saw it, didn't you? She is still alive."

Alive, alive.

This afternoon there came a howling through the ruins. I had no idea what it could be. Went to find it. It . . . Hank, in a room full of mummies. He sat in the middle of the floor; had arranged a half dozen of them in a circle around him. They stared. He wept hysterically, sobbed, moaned. I stood in the doorway watching him. "Hank." I whispered. "Hank, come away from here."

"There is no other place." He keened, he wailed.

I stepped over to him, tried to help him up off the floor. He swung his fist at me, flailed madly. "Leave me alone!" Then slumped down on the floor. Cried softly to himself.

Watching him, I began to cry.

Fourth day.

He has a mummy of his own, now, from one of the storerooms. He takes it around with him; pushes his hand into its mouth, drags it on the floor behind him. Even takes it to the chapel with him, to pray.

He will not eat. I fed him myself for a while, fed him like an infant. Now he will not even take food that way.

He does not sleep. At night he wanders everywhere, taking his mummy behind him, calling softly her name. I was afraid he would wander into the desert while I slept, but he never leaves the monastery. Just before sunrise I found him at the top of the wall, staring into the sky. "Brigit? Brigit?"

I have been eating too much. There is nothing else to do. I feel bloated.

This morning I climbed the wall to watch the dawn. Hank was off walking through the corridors. I sat, watched the eastern sky. Slowly the colors of the day pushed away the stars, the night.

There was a small noise, so faint I could barely hear it. I looked around; nothing. But it persisted. I began to wonder if the wall was not crumbling. Thought about going back down. Then I saw it. Ten, twelve yards away; watching me timidly, its movements betraying its anxiety. The Set animal.

I watched it in return; tried to keep calm, not to move. Did not want to alarm it. Sooner or later I will have to tell people what happened here. Part of it they will believe.

There are still all those child-mummies to prove the priest had manufactured them. But the rest of it, the sorcery— who could be expected to believe that? I watched the little clay animal as it inched closer to me, its caution giving way to its curiousity. Here was my proof.

I forced myself not even to look at it; faced the rising sun. Felt it as it came slowly closer to me. Stole glimpses from the corner of my eye. When the sun notched the horizon it was only six feet from me. I could restrain myself no longer; turned to face it.

It stared straight into my eyes. Slowly I held out a hand, beckoned it as one would a puppy; made gentle noises to reassure it. Shyly it took a step toward me, then another. It took what seemed an age, but finally it was only inches from my hand. My proof.

From out of nowhere rang a volley of gunshots. I jumped, startled. The creature bolted, ran to the far end of the wall, scrambled down the torn edge of it. Vanished amid the rubble in the courtyard.

Gunshots. From where? I stared into the desert. The new sun, just above the horizon, was blood red. Pieces of it detached themselves, fell to the sand, moved toward me. It was a long moment before I could resolve what I was seeing. Soldiers, a column of British soldiers, mounted on camels, their coats deep crimson against the yellow sand. Minute splotches of red, indistinct, the line of them snaking toward me. In a moment I was down off the wall, running to meet them. I paused for a moment in the courtyard. The Set animal. There was no use to it; I could never find it now. I went outside to wait for them.

It seemed forever before they finally arrived. And at the head of them, riding imperiously on his camel, was Gaston Maspero. "Howard. What on earth are you doing here? I thought you and your American were off chasing pyramids.''

"You never received my message? Zhitomiri never sent it?"

"Zhitomiri is drunk all the time. What happened here?"

"The earthquake." I was surprised he had to ask. "And the sandstorm. It was unbelievable, the worst I've ever seen."

"Earthquake?" His camel sat awkwardly down; he dismounted, slapped the dust off his clothing. "What earthquake?"

"There was an earthquake here. Nearly a week ago. And a ferocious desert storm. Between them, they brought the building down."

He stepped up onto a large stone, surveyed the ruin. "So I can see. But the seismographs at Cairo and Alexandria didn't record anything. I would have had reports. And there was no storm anywhere else."

"No . . . ? But Gaston, it was—"

"Never mind, Howard. We both know how capricious the desert and its storms can be."

I wanted to tell him about the magnitude of it. It seemed urgent to me. But I let it drop. Found myself thinking that Hank must have been correct about the cause of it all. Dismissed the thought. "There's something I don't understand."

"Yes?"

"If you never got my message, what brought you out here?"

Maspero put on a sour face, gestured vaguely behind himself. "He did."

I looked down the line of soldiers. At the rear, riding a donkey, managing nonetheless to look dignified, was Father Khalid. He stepped down off his animal, arranged his robes.

"He nagged and nagged about the Romans desecrating

Coptic ruins. Finally something had to be done. And so here I am.'' He looked around, suddenly puzzled. ''Where are the Romans, by the way?''

''Vanished. All of them. The morning after the storm they were gone.''

''Dead?''

''I thought so at first. But there are no bodies. Not theirs, anyway. It doesn't make sense to me that they should all have died. I mean, we survived. Surely some of them could, too.''

He stared at me. '' 'We'?''

''Larrimer.''

''Oh.''

''He's been through a lot. I'm afraid he's suffered a breakdown.''

Khalid joined us. ''Mr. Carter. So you see I was right about them destroying our heritage.''

''A storm did this.''

''Nonsense. Look at the vastness of the ruin. It would have taken an earthquake.''

I was in no mood for him. ''There was an earthquake too. Gaston, this is where those mummies came from.''

I told him the whole story; left out any reference to the supernatural. It was a device to make money. Children are an abundant resource in Egypt; Rheinholdt capitalized on it; it was as uncomplicated as that. I showed him the storerooms piled high with mummified children. Showed him the vault. ''There are vats of natron under the sand. Dig down through it, you will find natron.''

Maspero looked sadly at all the young bodies. ''We will have to bury them. The soldiers will dig a grave for them all.''

It has taken two days but they were all finally laid to rest.

We took Henry's mummy away from him, and he fought us
frantically, but it was finally buried with the others. Khalid
prayed over them.

We searched for the bodies of the Romans. Dug through
the sand, turned over stones. Found the corpses of two nuns
whose heads had been crushed. That was all. Dug at the
spot where Rheinholdt and Brigit had been buried. Moved
heavy stones one by one. Hank stood in the courtyard,
stared anxiously down to the vault. Hope, fear, horror,
anticipation all showed in his face. And love. But their
bodies were not there.

Hank refuses to speak, now. Does not move. Does
nothing. Lets himself be led, offers no resistance. He might
as well be one of the dead. When we closed the mass grave,
Hank got down on his knees, pressed his hands into the
sand. "The wind will uncover them again." Those were the
last words he spoke to anyone.

The Valley of the Kings. Have spent most of the last
month here. There are tourists; I have eaten well. Cross over
to Luxor every few days for provisions, maintain my room
at the guesthouse but do not use it. Sleep most nights in the
tombs.

I stopped writing in this journal a month ago. It was all
too terrible for me, and the things I have been feeling . . .
the things I have been feeling . . . Introspection would not
have been a healthy thing. Dwelling on what happened . . .
no. But the Valley is solid, timeless. Here, I know where I
am. I am ready to get on with it.

But this afternoon came a letter from Maspero, brought it
all back to me.

My dear Howard,
   *I hope everything is well with you, and that the Luxorite
tourists are making you fat.*

It is with sincere regret that I must inform you that I shall be unable to reinstate you as Inspector of Monuments. I should like nothing better than to do so. I told you how grateful I—and the Service—would be if you could clean up the mystery of those mummies. And we are grateful, truly.

But important influences have made it clear that your return to government service would be most unwelcome in their eyes. This saddens me. I tell you frankly that you are the best man for the job. I only hope that hearing the news in this personal way softens the blow somewhat.

Five days ago Father Rheinholdt and his colleagues were arrested, in Alexandria. He, four nuns, and two young priests. They were attempting to leave the country, to book passage on a steamer. They have refused to confess to their crimes; they will not even explain how they escaped from the Wadi Natrun, or where they have been. They will be tried and, I hope sincerely, hanged. You will be needed to testify at their trial. I shall notify you personally of the date and place.

I thought you would want to know that Henry Larrimer has disappeared from the Coptic hospital where we placed him. He was there for just under two weeks. He refused to speak to anyone in all that time, or to eat. Then one night he simply . . . left. A search was made in the Coptic quarter, but he was not there. So he must be somewhere in Moslem Cairo. The American embassy had only just sent word of him to his family. Now they will have to send this additional bad news. I promise to keep you informed of any future developments.

Your faithful friend,
Gaston Maspero

P.S. Why not move to Cairo? There are even more tourists than in Luxor.

And so I am not to have my job back. By "important influences" I presume he means the Coptic Church in the person of Khalid, whose dislike of me since Athribis has been no secret. But I find I do not miss being a public official as much as I once did. Egypt has changed, or I have changed; or the world has . . . And to be honest, I earn more money as a guide than I ever did with the Antiquities Service.

I would like to see Rheinholdt hanged. I would like to see that. I will testify. Then I will go and watch his execution. Then I will come back here, to my tombs.

But the priest, his death does not matter to me so much. It is Henry Larrimer that I feel for. And what I feel is release. He has found what he came here for, after all. He was frightened of Cairo before, and now he is not. The people there will nurture him, give him what he needs, let him take what he desires. For the rest of his life, he shall not want. He has melted into the world of the Moslems, who know what a blessing it is to be mad, and to understand nothing.